About the Author

Rosalee Brookes was born in Hamilton, New Zealand, and grew up during the Second World War in the small coalmining township of Pukemiro in the Waikato. Her working life revolved around reception and communication having spent three years as a telephone operator in the WRNZAF. A talented artist, she has been commissioned and exhibited extensively. This Same Flower is her second novel and fifth book including the set of four Waikato Coalmining history books.

*For my dear daughters Deborah, Melanie and Tracey,
who have always been so supportive of my writing.
For my late loving companion Barry Reid whose
encouragement gave me confidence.*

Rosalee Brookes

THIS SAME FLOWER

AUSTIN MACAULEY
PUBLISHERS LTD.

A CIP catalogue record for this title is available from the British Library.

ISBN 9781785542411 (Paperback)
ISBN 9781785542428 (Hardback)
ISBN 9781785542435 (eBook)

www.austinmacauley.com

First Published (2016)
Austin Macauley Publishers Ltd.
25 Canada Square
Canary Wharf
London
E14 5LQ

Cover photo Pukemiro Collieries 1940 copyright waived by Waikato Coalfields Museum Huntly NZ.

Image Rose Stretton copyright waived by theperformancenet Albany NZ.

On September 3, 1939, Britain declared war on Germany. Michael Joseph Savage was the first of the Commonwealth Prime Ministers to pledge troops to help defend Britain in their war. 'Where England stands we stand. Where England goes we go,' he vowed, when his announcement, advising that New Zealand too, was at war with Germany, crackled through the radio sets across the nation.

Gather ye rosebuds while ye may,
Old time is still a-flying:
And this same flower that smiles today,
Tomorrow will be dying.

Then be not coy, but use your time;
And while you may go marry:
For having lost but once your prime
You may forever tarry.

Robert Herrick

Prologue

Glen Afton had always been a special place. The generations before Meggie Morgan, and those who had come after, had all inevitably been touched by an inherent quality. A quality peculiar only to those who had grown up in the shallow coal-filled valley nestled between Pukemiro Junction and Township. Even those who had left the village, as Meggie herself had done, agreed that Glen Afton had been a special place. The closing of the underground coalmines in the 1960s had rung the death-knell for the miners and many had left the valley, but in Meggie's years of living 'out the back' the miners had still dug coal underground with pickaxe and banjo shovel. Men that knew little other than pit work, married local girls who, as their mothers had done, set their daily routine by the shrill blasts of the mine whistle. And their sons, when they came of age, also went to work 'down the pit'.

On a golden March day in 1984, Meggie Morgan, braked gently and steered her stylish Mazda off State Highway One and onto the bridge at Huntly that spanned the Waikato River. The low-sided concrete structure was new to her, despite being the main route crossing the river for the last twenty years. To the right something more familiar, and to her surprise still standing, was the long narrow railway bridge that had taken all the traffic back in the 1940s. Now its high wooden struts appeared darkly menacing against the new power station's tall silver chimneys glinting in the sun. The sight caused a warm flush. Yes, that was the bridge Meggie remembered. Stalwart and solid it had serviced road, rail and foot traffic, cattle drovers driving their herds with their footsore dogs. Back then the bridge had been the only access to and from the isolated settlements west of Huntly. Days when Glen Afton was alive with sounds of mining: the clatter of skips heaped with shiny black coal, from both the Glen Afton mine mouth and down the Mac track from the outlying MacKinnon mine, both spilling their loads into the rattling screens to be sifted; puffing steam engines hauling coal-laden wagons; sudden bursts of noisy shunting as wagons were marshalled late at night and the unearthly shriek of the mine whistle; the rhythmic clomp of the miners' boots as they trudged out of the mine mouth, teeth gleaming white in faces smeared black with coal dust. Meggie could hear all those sounds and more as she drove on. The creek that gurgled past the mine hurried along to join a myriad of other little streams pouring into that mighty Waikato River. Music blaring around the valley on Saturday nights dances in the local hall – the highlight of the week. She recalled the sound inside the hall of leather soles scraping the wooden floor as dancing feet stomped or skimmed across it, raising enough dust to choke the crowd of young men who stood apprehensively occupying a third of the floor space near the hall doorway. At suppertime the band laid down their instruments and filed outside to take liquid refreshments set up in someone's car boot. Outside the air would be sharp, the stars crisp and frail and the deckled outline of the bush clear-cut against the night sky. And on a dance night, if one listened carefully, they may hear the hushed whispers of lovers or snatched moments of deceivers. Then later the muffled sobs of those women and children who endured beatings from a drunken husband and sustained the evidence at the start of each new week. Oppressed women stayed with their abusers back then simply because there was nowhere else to go. Yes, there had been love and laughter, sorrow and pain, broken dreams and false hopes, but amongst it all there had been life. It had been a village where everyone knew everyone else, where Maori and Pakeha worked together, intermarried and drank each other's health. But that had been decades, nearly forty years ago. What would it be now, Meggie thought? Derelict, and forsaken, like most of the outback mining settlements had apparently become?

As Meggie drove on she noted the excellent road, wide and tar sealed, certainly a vast improvement from the dusty, metal track that had once served the miners and their families. That rutted surface wound across the farmlands, hugging the shore of Lake Waahi until reaching Weavers Crossing where the road crossed the railway tracks.

In the wet winters the floodwater would cover the rail tracks where they skirted the edge of the lake between Weavers and Rotowaro. The train would crawl; slow as a snail, as it hauled its cargo of wagons and passengers through the murky floodwater.

After Weavers Crossing the road climbed, twisted and plunged, until it reached the flat, drained swamplands of Rotowaro. Today the sleek black ribbon of macadam cut a swathe across the land, hardly linking with the path that the old road had taken. She remembered how parts of the old road past Rotowaro had never dried out. Even the hot summer sun had failed to penetrate a road surface that plunged down deep gorges and cut around the edges of steep, bush clad hills. And as Meggie's thoughts dwelt on the treacherous old road, time gathered her up taking her back to the winter of Nineteen-forty-two, days when a worldwide war raged on the planet. When in New Zealand every loyal Labour home hung a photo of the current Labour party Prime Minister, Mickey Savage, above their coal range mantelpiece and politics were taken with breakfast, dinner and tea. Days before the invention of teenagers, rock 'n' roll and before the Americanization of the world. 1942, was the year that the Morgan family had arrived to live in the little coal-mining village of Glen Afton, deep in the raw outback, west of the Waikato River.

CHAPTER ONE

GLEN AFTON. 1942

"Are you blind, woman? Can't ya see me windscreen's fogged up?" Dai Morgan snarled at his wife. "Jeez! How did a man get hitched up with such a useless cow as you?" he snarled. "Clear the bloody window will ya, eh, eh!"

Florrie Morgan reached across and cleared a circle on the steamed up windscreen of their tiny Austin Seven motorcar with her handkerchief. Emmie and Meggie huddled further down amongst the blankets and bric-a-brac strewn on the back seat. They were cold and hungry and even more scared now as their father shouted but knew better than to make a sound when he was angry. The trip had been hell so far but Florrie knew that Dai had the ability to make it even worse. His moods had become so much meaner since he had failed his medical to serve in the Air Force. Now he continued to curse as he maneuvered the tiny car through yet another cluster of mud-filled potholes, the car bouncing from side to side and splashing dirty brown water high up on the windows.

The Morgan family had set out that morning before the sun had risen above the jagged hills of Mapiu, and had been traveling all day. The rain had started, only a light drizzle at first, at the boundary that divided the craggy King Country from the lush and fertile pastures of the Waikato. Dai followed the furniture lorry for the first few miles, but with benzene stops and the heavy rain soon lost sight of the carrier's truck. Finding his way to the unheard of village of Glen Afton, somewhere west of Huntly, hadn't done a lot for his temper. Yet, with the exception of Dai's swearing, the trip had been uneventful. After leaving hilly bush country they had travelled long stretches of flat land between rain sodden towns. When the girls asked for a comfort stop, he exploded.

"I just want to get there," he shouted. "You'll have to wait 'til I fill up again."

After what seemed like an eternity Dai steered the car off the main road and onto a bridge with railway tracks running across it. He carefully positioned the right wheel of the car between the steel tracks, almost forcing the left tire against the wooden side rails, and then proceeded to drive slowly across. It had been raining for several days and the river was high, with brown water swirling only inches below the bridge. Halfway across Dai pulled the car to a halt on the raised passing bay to allow traffic from the west side to pass at the bridge centre. Finally the nightmare was over and they reached flat farmlands. Dai drove carefully around the shoreline of Lake Waahi before bumping over railway tracks at a place signposted Weavers Crossing. From there the road was tortuous, grinding uphill before plunging rapidly down to a narrow wooden bridge. Now the flat lands of Huntly were far behind.

"The bastards never told me the only way to get to this godforsaken hole was by bloody goat track," Dai growled.

The bitterness of his rejection from the Air Force, the reason for this trip today, was still with him. It was one thing to turn a man down for military service, quite another to manpower him into an essential industry. And a bloody dunny-making pottery at that! Makin' flash porcelain dunnies fer the military ta sit their backsides on, he mused. What's wrong with a good old long drop outside fer them. The authorities had told him there would be training on the job, there'd better be 'cause I know bugger all about potting. Why couldn't they have been sent me to a brewery? That would have made some sense with trainin' on the job. Dai smiled with silent amusement. Seriously though, he was an outdoor bloke. Stuck inside stokin' bloody furnaces all day. Christ! That's why I tried for the Air Force in the first place, he continued to muse. Flyin' around in a plane, havin' the freedom of the skies. Free from the missus and the kids.' Air force life had appealed to him so he'd volunteered when he suspected his call-up papers were due thinking that by volunteering he'd have a better choice of which service. Didn't want the bloody Army and didn't like the water so it was a real kick in the guts to be turned down by the Air Force as medically unfit. Up until then he'd been quite happy doing farm work and he made good money out of his sly grog business in the 'dry' King Country. But once the 'authorities got a sniff of things a man's had it, he thought sourly. Actually, he had got a bit excited about going away to serve King and Country. Not that he was a Royalist – nah, far from it. The Royals were nothing more than a pack of bludgers as far as he was concerned. Then to be turned down on medical grounds was a bloody affront – took away a bloke's manliness! Lungs not of sound constitution, the blasted military quack had written. Jeez, he thought, this bloody war is changing everything.

"Glen Afton!" he spat out. "The bloody place should be called Glen Hellhole!"

"Maybe we're on the wrong road," Florrie offered nervously.

"So yer a flamin' authority on roads now, are ya! Jeez, yer couldn't find yer way out of a brown paper bag. Unless you want to do the drivin' keep ya trap shut."

Anger crackled in the close confines of the car. By now they had emerged onto flat land again and were travelling around the edge of a swamp. The rain had stopped allowing thin rays from the sun streaking through the cold winter sky and glistening on the wet flax bushes that grew in abundance in the swamp. Rapidly moving clouds split the suns light into rays and splayed them out in several directions. The rays reminded Meggie of a coloured picture in her Sunday school book where Jesus, wearing a long robe rimmed with gold light, stood in the middle of the rays. Jesus frightened Meggie mainly because He lived in the sky. It had been a scary picture about dying and Meggie feared that if Jesus appeared in the rays now they would probably die.

The Austin Seven ground its way on up a small incline and before them, next to a Post Office, stood a wooden building with ROTOWARO MINERS HALL written in large black letters above the doorway.

"I'll ask at the Post Office if we're on the right track to this bloody no man's land," Dai emerged from the Post Office, spat on the ground, and leaned against the car door to make a roll-your-own before easing himself back behind the steering wheel. He drew long and hard on the cigarette as though his very life depended on it. The tobacco smoke started Emmie coughing again.

Through the window Meggie could see a whole street of shops with wide verandahs stretching right across the footpath. To the left there was a big grimy building with rusty railway wagons lined up beneath. Waikato Carbonization Works was painted across the dented corrugated iron.

Florrie frowned nervously and asked if they were going the right way. "Yep," he answered, flicking the thin slimy butt out of the window. "Postmistress says it's only a few miles on."

The Austin's motor purred into life and the car slid easily down the other side of the hill away from the township of Rotowaro. On they sped, past the clattering carbonette works and a row of mine houses running up a spur, oblivious that the Postmistress had failed to tell Dai that the worst of the road was still before them.

A profusion of ponga and ferns fringed the road as the car bounced from one pothole to another on a metal road carved from the side of a steep bush covered hill. Slush splashed up as far as the car windows while water from a swollen creek, running parallel to the road, touched the mounds of metal heaped on the roadsides.

Dai cursed loudly as the tyres skidded in loose gravel. Around the next bend a cluster of small, mean-looking houses encircled a railway station that seemed to cling with a sort of desperation to the side of a steep hill. Behind the houses bush and vines spiralled skywards. The little car laboured on up a steep ridge where reaching the summit Dai pulled the car to a halt. Sitting snugly in a valley, was a huddle of houses with wisps of smoke rising lazily from their chimneys. The pottery's tall brick chimney stood like a sentinel amid the rows of square colliery houses. Only the wet bricks and puddles that glistened in the sunshine suggested that the weather had been inclement at Glen Afton that day.

Dai pulled out his tin of makings for another roll-your-own. "Well, looks like we've made it, missus." His voice held a kindly note for the first time that day. "It's been a bloody arsehole of a trip but we made it."

Dai started the motor again and the little Austin gathered speed as it rolled down the hill and across a small bridge stopping outside the pottery building. A bald head, with strands of hair stretched across, taut as piano wires and stuck down with some sort of grease, poked out of a window.

"You Dai Morgan?" called the head.

Dai hopped out of the car and walked across to the window.

"Yep," he shouted expansively, "At yer service."

The man, wearing a big leather apron, came through the door and looked disapprovingly at the little car and the shabby-looking family inside.

"Bill Cowie." The man bit out the introduction. "Expected you earlier than this, Morgan. Got a lot on with these War Department orders. You can't hold the military up when there's a war on, you know."

That put Dai's back up straightaway. After a day of hard driving through bloody awful conditions to get here this bastard had a bloody cheek to tell him off. He fumbled in his pocket for his tobacco tin.

Bugger this old bastard, he thought. Don't reckon I'll last long here.

"Where's the nearest boozer, Cowie," Dai asked, with full intention of annoying his new boss. "Throat's as dry as a bone …"

Bill Cowie, furious at being addressed in such an insulting manner, cut across Dai's words.

"So you're a drinker are you, Morgan? Well you're out of luck here," he sneered. "There's no hotel." Cowie spoke with a vindictive note in his voice. "The nearest hotel is five mile on at Waingaro, or back to Huntly, the way you came. And mind this," he added. "There'll be no drinking on the job here."

The antagonism between the two men was crackling. As Meggie turned to look back in the direction they had come from, praying fervently that they wouldn't have to drive back, a straggling group of men carrying sugar sacks tied with rope, emerged from the mine bathhouse. They approached the bridge laughing just as a steam engine, hauling endless coal-laden wagons, rumbled along the tracks below. Steam and smoke swallowed the miners up and the buildings beyond disappeared behind the swirling cloud, which rose, as if by magic, from under the ground.

Bill Cowie directed Dai towards the two rusting corrugated iron houses that stood behind the pottery. Once inside Florrie bustled around lighting the coal range feeding the fire from the huge pile of coal dumped beside the back door while Dai busied himself connecting the valve radio. It squeaked and tweeped as he fiddled with the dial, and when satisfied with the wireless reception Dai turned his attention to hanging the picture of Mickey Savage above the mantelpiece. As Meggie helped him she wondered why Mickey Savage should still be so important after he was dead. She knew he was dead, clearly remembering her father and some of his friends, listening to the funeral on the wireless. The broadcasts announcing Mr. Savage's death had crackled through the radio day and night while Dai and his mates drank homebrew and shook their heads in disbelief. They sang along with the thin, reedy warbling of 'Abide With Me' and 'Nearer My God To Thee' that had trembled its way through the brocade hiding the wireless speakers. The commentator had announced gravely that thousands of people stood in silence on Auckland streets awaiting the cortege. Meggie knew that a lot of Kings and Queens pictures were still hung after they had died so she supposed Mickey Savage must have been like the New Zealand king. One thing she knew was that she felt a whole lot safer in this funny tin house with Mr. Savage's kindly face looking down from above the mantelpiece. That night, as Meggie waited for sleep to come, her mind relived the events of the day. The thought of the river water rushing under the bridge brought her out in a cold sweat. Then she remembered the grumpy bald man her father would be working for. But the best memory was the magic moment when the mining men had vanished in a puff of smoke. In the next room Dai fiddled with the knobs on the wireless set in an attempt to tune in to the war news on the BBC. Big Ben striking nine o'clock tolled above the crackling short wave reception and these were familiar and comforting sounds. The clipped accent of the English radio announcer was the last sound that Meggie heard before drifting off into an exhausted sleep.

CHAPTER TWO

Next morning Emmie was coughing too badly to go to school so ten-year-old Meggie, feeling very alone, was sent to find her way to the nearest school at Pukemiro. "Just keep walking until you see a school," her mother had told her. A group of school kids ahead of her rounded the corner by Ed Hubbard's General Store, which was tucked in between the Glen Afton railway station and the cattle yards, but she felt too shy to catch up with them and instead followed at a short distance behind.

Further on was a yellow-painted sign pointing to a rough gravel road running beneath another overhead rail bridge. The black letters on the sign read, GULLY ROAD. Beyond there were more squat colliery houses with chimneys pouring forth smoke into the bright morning sky. It was scary leaving the Gully houses behind; the road curved sharply and ran between a creek, swollen with rainwater, and a clay bank cut into the side of a hill. A stand of tall pines growing on the bank further chilled the narrow, dark pass and Meggie shivered with both cold and fear. As she hurried along to keep the school children in view a loud rumbling sound, accompanied by the mournful bellow of cattle, began to echo through the gorge. The noise became louder and Meggie sensed danger so she stopped to determine where the noise was coming from but establishing a direction was impossible in the narrow gorge where sounds bounced off the hills on either side.

Suddenly, a huge herd of cattle rounded the corner. Knowing nothing of the cattle drives from the out-lying Te Akau and Waingaro farms to the railway cattle yards at Glen Afton, or that there were safety shelters built at intervals against the bank for pedestrians' safety Meggie could only stand there terrified, as a huge horde of galloping animals came bearing down on her and getting closer by the minute. With the sound of her own heartbeat pounding in her ears she stood paralyzed at the roadside. In that instant a pair of strong young arms encircled her, steering her roughly between a high wooden fence and the dank smelling clay bank. She stood gasping from panic as the cattle thundered past the shelter, spurred on by the crack of a whip and the loud, and fortunately unintelligible, shouts from the drover.

Once the cattle had gone, to Meggie's amazement, the kids now lining the embankment returned to walk along the road as though nothing unusual had happened. The girls formed a group that walked ahead of the boys, who stayed just far enough behind to hurl flirting insults at the 'jam tarts'. Meggie began to feel accepted when some of the girls asked her where she came from. She fell into step with Sarry Adams, somehow knowing instinctively that she and Sarry would become lifelong friends.

Meggie kept glancing back, trying to get a better look at the boy who had pulled her into the shelter out of the way of the stampeding cattle. She'd noticed he had fair hair but in her fear had not taken notice of anything else. Finally, as they climbed to a school perched on the very top of a hill, Meggie found the courage to question Sarry.

"Sarry," she squeaked, quite puffed from the long climb. "Who was the boy that saved me?"

Sarry opened her mouth wide and let out a loud cackle. "Hey, Si," she bellowed at the boys kicking stones and straggling along in the rear. "This new kid thinks you saved her. Ha ha ha," she carried on in a rowdy laugh.

The boys took the cue straight away shouting things like, "Jeez! Where's your halo, Si? We didn't know we had a holy man among us."

Mick Galloway slapped Simon on the back as he jeered, "Christ, mate. You'll be taking the service at the Gospel Hall next and doing old Fleming out of a job."

Everyone hooted with laughter and Meggie's face burned painfully. She scanned the golden-headed boy from beneath her lowered lids. His face was pink with embarrassment and his bright blue eyes widened as he lashed at his mates with his schoolbag.

Once they reached the schoolyard the Glen kids joined in the hopscotch and skipping with their Pukemiro mates and forgot about the new girl. Meggie stood self-consciously alone by the main door. Simon, being bell monitor that week, came up onto the porch and picked up the heavy cast iron hand bell.

"You okay now?" he asked, looking straight at her with his china blue eyes.

"Yeees," was all she could stammer.

"Well, if ya don't want to go deaf you'd better skedaddle," he advised, before swinging the heavy bell to and fro, its loud donging sending the kids scattering away from their games.

Mr. Short, the Headmaster, wrote her name in his spidery handwriting into a long ledger on his desk, dipping the nib of his pen in the inkwell many times to form the letters.

"Where is your mother?" he asked, not looking up from his task of writing in the register. Meggie transferred her weight from one foot to the other. She didn't know what to answer. Mr. Short asked the question again, this time looking into the new girl's frightened face.

"Why didn't your mother come to enroll you at this school?" he asked again.

It was all too much for her. First the cattle nearly ran over her, then Simon telling her to scram, and now the Headmaster growling at her. She burst into tears. Mr. Short looked down at his register again as Meggie sniffed and rubbed her eyes with her fists. After an interval of silence he took a snowy white handkerchief from his top pocket and handed to her.

"Come now, child. This will never do on your first day here." Under his breath he muttered about parents who cared little about their children's education. Meggie explained about Emmie and told him she would be starting school when she was better.

Mr. Short nodded and then stood up. Towering over Meggie he led her along a corridor of oiled boards and into Room 3 where Miss Strang taught Standards Three and Four. Immediately the teacher set about supplying her new pupil with pencils and stationery from a big cupboard behind her desk.

"Did you practice Air Raid drill at Mapiu School?" she asked Meggie in a high voice.

Meggie shook her head to indicate 'no'.

"You'll have to speak up if you want to be heard above this lot of ruffians," she shrilled, shushing the class at the same time.

"Class. This is Megan Morgan. She's come to us from the King Country. Does anyone know where the King Country is?" she asked, looking over the class expectantly for an answer.

"Yes Brian," Miss Strang asked hesitantly, very aware that Brian Harmon considered himself the class wit.

"It's the country where the King lives," he answered pertly, looking around at his mates for approval, and being rewarded with hissed giggling.

"If you were to take your education more seriously, Brian Harmon," Miss Strang snapped, "you might find yourself working in an office, rather than down a mine shaft, in the years to come."

Brian lifted his desktop and sniggered behind the lid. Miss Strang ignored him and carried on.

"Megan. You will sit with Sarry Adams." Meggie was pleased. "Now, Sarry. Show Megan your Air Raid bag."

Sarry removed a cloth bag from a hook on her side of the desk.

"Now class. What should we have in our Air Raid bag?"

"Scissors, sticking plaster, ointment, cotton wool, a cork and an I.D. tag," the class droned in unison as Sarry displayed the items.

"What do we do when we hear the Air Raid siren?" Miss Strang continued, encouraged by the good response from her class so far this morning with the exception of the Harmon boy.

"Take our Air Raid bags off the hooks and run to the trench under the macrocarpa trees," they droned again.

"Very good. Very good. Now, Megan. Please stand and look out the window at the trees across the top of that hill."

Meggie stood and looked.

"That is where the trenches are, and you will run and jump in if the Air Raid siren sounds. Do you understand?"

Meggie squeaked out a "yes".

"Good. I'll give you an instruction sheet to take to your mother and try to have your Air Raid bag complete with all items to school by the end of the week. We can't be too prepared in these days of uncertainty," she finished with a long sigh.

Meggie was astounded. This was a much bigger school than the one she had left at Mapiu. There had been only one room and one teacher for all the classes there. But this school sounded far more dangerous with Air Raid drills. She began to wish they'd never come to such an unsafe place. Meggie was aware that there was a war on somewhere. She knew it was a bad thing and was also the reason her father had been sent to Glen Afton to work in the pottery. And he always listened to the war news on the wireless at night. Now Meggie wondered why the kids here had to do war drill. Was it because the war was coming here but not to Mapiu? She remembered again her Nana Bowen crying and saying that Dai had no right to take the girls to such a vulnerable place to live when there was a war on. Meggie hadn't understood what her Nana had meant then but now she felt sure it was to do with the war drill they had to do at school. A new fear filled her as Miss Strang addressed the class with another question

"Now class!" her shrill voice penetrated above the hum of children whispering. "Why is it so important that we do war drill?"

The kids all squirmed around on their seats, obviously not really understanding why it was done either.

"Come now. One of you must know. Davy Howard! Why do we do war drill at this school?"

"Umm. Cause ... the Japs are comin' to drop bombs on us." With that he grabbed his ruler and striking the pose of a gunman he rat-tat-tatted around the classroom, dribble sliding down his chin.

"That's enough," Miss Strang shouted. "Sit down at once, Davy. Now, does anyone else know the reason we do war drill?"

Marion Holmes, whose mother was also a teacher at the school, waved her arm high.

"Yes Marion?"

"Mum said it's because we live above huge areas of coal which is essential to keep industry in the country going. If the coal fields were destroyed by bombs our coal fired industries would not be able to operate and that would bring the country to a standstill and the Japanese could easily conquer us." She paused to take a breath, giving Jack White, sitting behind her, time to make a soft "yah yah yah ... Miss Know-all" at the same time poking her in the back with his ruler. Marion squealed loudly.

"It's all right, Marion. I saw that, Jack," Miss Strang said over her shoulder as she wrote the name

Jack White in the right-hand corner of the blackboard, a space specially reserved for listing the names of those wrongdoers who warranted the strap on arrival at school next morning.

"You're first on the list for the strap tomorrow. And Davy Howard," she shouted over the noise. "If you don't stop playing guns with your ruler your name will be next!"

Davy, looking dejected, put the ruler down, at the same time wiping the river of dribble from his chin onto the sleeve of his jumper. Miss Strang put her chalk down on the blackboard shelf and after dusting her hands resumed with the lesson as though nothing untoward had happened.

"A very good answer, Marion. Now whose turn for morning talk today?"

Bigfoot Rayner jumped up and began a tirade about the Hopalong Cassidy film he'd seen at the picture hall the night before. Miss Strang was finally able to halt his outpouring and Bigfoot sat down looking somewhat crushed. She then asked Meggie, as the new pupil, to bring an item of interest for tomorrow's morning talk.

Before morning playtime Simon and Riki Whetu, the other school monitor, carried in a crate of milk and a box of apples. The rest of the day was a blur for Meggie because her thoughts seemed to dwell entirely on the war and the war drill. When she left to walk home after school she was surprised to see Sarry Adams, Simon Griffith and Riki Whetu waiting for her at the school gate. They dawdled around the metal road and through the clay cutting talking about the war. Simon seemed to know everything about it.

"Why is there a cork in the air raid bag?" Meggie asked him.

"That's to put between your teeth so you don't bite your tongue off when a bomb lands."

Meggie wasn't sure she believed him but didn't say so. Sarry laughed and said he was bullshittin'.

"Well, don't put it in yer mouth then when the Japs bomb us and see what happens. You talk too much anyway so it wouldn't hurt for you to bite ya tongue off," he responded.

Sarry left them just past Ed Hubbard's Store and Meggie, Simon and Riki walked on in silence. She desperately wanted to thank Simon for saving her from the cattle but became too tongue-tied to say anything. Riki left them when they reached the rise where Griffith's Boarding house stood overlooking the mine. Meggie stood gaping at the rattling screens and the big concrete hole where the miners went in under the ground to work. Across to the right was the miners' bathhouse that she had seen the men come out from last night.

"That's where Riki lives," Simon told her as they watched Riki run past the bathhouse to some long baches beyond. "D'ya want to come in for a while?" he asked, scraping the side of his scuffed shoes in the metal. Meggie couldn't believe her luck. She followed him trying to keep up with his long strides. Inside his house there seemed to be people everywhere scurrying back and forth carrying big black enamel pots of food between the two large coal ranges. Simon's mother, Rose Griffith, was stout and soft of flesh. Wiping the perspiration from her brow, she stopped for a moment to look at the little raggle taggle girl Simon had brought home. Good 'eavens, she thought to herself, he's picked up another stray.

"And 'ho's this then?" she asked, in a heavy Welsh accent. "Where'd you come from?"

"Meggie Morgan," she whispered, "Dad's working for Mr. Cowie at the pottery."

"Oh, yes. Your Mam was 'ere today looking for work."

Meggie didn't answer, as she hadn't known her mother was looking for work.

"She'll be starting next week," Mrs Griffith continued. "Just mornin's for now. And you are Megan but they call you Meggie then?" She raised her brows. "Such a pity to shorten Megan."

"Yes." Meggie spoke louder as her confidence grew. "My sister's named Emily but we call her Emmie. She's sick and has to stay at home by the warm stove."

"Oh dear. That's no good then." Mrs Griffith patted her on the head.

"Emmie's older than me but because she's littler everyone thinks I'm the eldest. So I have to do all the jobs."

Mrs. Griffith smiled at the serious little girl. "Well that's keeping you busy isn't it? Now if you're going to stay 'ere you can help Simon with the tables. The men'll be in soon and they'll be wanting their dinner." With that she disappeared into the pantry off the huge kitchen.

That night Meggie forced herself to stay awake to hear about the war on the BBC News from London. She listened hard to hear what the broadcaster was saying, above the constant crackling, on the short wave band that drifted through the half open door. Somewhere there was a war going on, with bombs and guns, and getting closer to here every day. The Japanese had invaded the Coral Sea, the newscaster announced in his posh voice, and in doing so had cut off New Zealand and Australia from America. She heard her mother gasp loudly and her father switched off the set with a loud click. "Not much bloody use sendin' the Yanks here to defend us when we're cut orf from their bloody country," Dai growled. "And all our own jokers fightin' on the other side of the world. Might as well kiss our arses goodbye once those slit-eyed little bastards git here."

Florrie began to sob. "Oh, Dai. What will we do? Mum was right. We should never have come here. I want to go back to Mapiu. Please Dai. Can we go back?"

"Yer won't be any safer there. Once the nips get here they'll jest overrun the whole country. Look what they've done already. Bombed the shit out of

Malaya and Singapore. Ta hell with this bloody war anyway," he finished, with a loud hoick and spit into the firebox. "It's no good whingin' now, womun. This is where the bloody authorities have sent me and that's that."

A cold shiver slithered through Meggie as she listened to her father's words. She didn't really understand what it was all about so she deliberately steered her mind away from the war and back onto her new friends, Sarry Adams, Simon Griffith and Riki Whetu. When sleep finally came her dreams were of the golden haired Simon Griffith, who had saved her, and his fair good looks.

Next morning Meggie checked her bag to make sure the precious book she had chosen for her morning talk was still there. The book, a pocket sized *Men Only*, belonged to her father and was full of bright colourful cartoons. Meggie had selected a particular drawing that appealed to her and turned down the corner of the page.

Miss Strang's face paled when Meggie opened the book at the pre-marked page and held it high so that all the children could see a drawing of a naked lady with voluptuous breasts sitting in a bathtub enjoying the butler scrubbing her back with a long loofah. Before Meggie could read out the caption beneath the cartoon, Miss Strang had lunged forward from her stance at the back of the room and snatched the book from her, locking it in the top drawer of her teacher's table. Meggie, not knowing what she had done wrong, was totally humiliated.

The boys were all sniggering and Brian Harmon said in an Irish whisper that was 'the best morning talk he'd ever seen'. Miss Strang ordered everyone to get out their arithmetic books for an extra period of sums. A groan echoed around the room and Meggie knew that her morning talk, which she thought would be a success, was the reason for the extra arithmetic. At playtime the boys flocked around her in the playground in an attempt to get a loan of the *Men Only* book. She knew now it had been a terrible mistake to bring the book to school but it was, at the same time, the catalyst for her acceptance with the kids at the new school.

* * *

Summer came early that year. The crisp frosts and wet winter merged into warmer evenings and longer days. Gardens and paddocks in the little coal mining valley glowed with buttery yellow and cream spring flowers. Florrie had scratched out patches around the sides of the rusty corrugated iron house and rich coloured pelargonium and geranium blazed brightly when the hot summer sun arrived.

Dai had found a watering hole at the back of Ed Hubbard's shop, which was much closer than the hotel at Waingaro. The room was locally known as the 'Hogs Head', but the village women called it the 'Pigs Pen'. Dai was actually on the lookout for somewhere to start making his homebrew again and behind the warm pottery bricks would have been ideal for a still. But there was no show of making anything there as that old wowser, Cowie, wouldn't allow drink on the premises. Dai was a clever bloke and had picked up the trade of potting quickly. Even Bill Cowie had to admit he was a damn good worker despite him having a drink problem. Dai might have enjoyed the work if Cowie's pay wasn't so miserable. Compared to the money the miners were earning it was a pittance and Dai began seeking out the prospect of being transferred into one of the mines, since mining too, was an essential industry. They'd have to move again but so what! Dai's heart was a wanderer's heart inherited, most likely, from his Romany ancestor.

Flo working at Griffith's boarding house suited Meggie well. It gave her a good reason to call there and see Simon. Emmie's health improved with the dry summer weather and she was attending school regularly. Being older she was one class ahead of Meggie. Despite her frail health, Emmie was a quick learner and excellent with figures. Meggie had lost her fear of the war drill, as it had become a game, with the boys and girls deliberately tumbling on top of each other and wrestling, in the earthy clay trenches. Sarry Adams, being such a mischievous child, was the instigator of most of the devilment and pranks carried out during air raid drill.

Meggie had learned plenty from her new friends. In the winter they had broken ice from muddy clay puddles and sucked it until it numbed their lips. They peeled the prickles from the outside of scotch thistles that grew along the roadside and ate the delicious nutty kernel inside. The boys would save their milk straws from school and blow up the frogs they caught from the creek until the poor things burst. On the long summer evenings the girls would run onto the high footbridge at the sound of an approaching train and let the hot steam from the engine's smokestack lift their skirts high in the air while the boys lay in hiding beneath the bridge to get an eyeful.

Sometimes Meggie was allowed to stay overnight at Sarry's house. They had a gramophone and were allowed to play records on it and the two girls would dress up in Mrs. Adams long frocks and practice dancing. Whenever staying on a Tuesday night the girls would force themselves to stay awake so they could watch the night cart collection. As the night man passed their window they would BOO loudly, hoping to scare him into dropping the can. It never happened.

As the summer wore on the corrugated iron house behind the pottery became hot and airless. At night all the doors and windows were left open. The BBC news that crackled forth at nine o'clock now had to compete with crickets chirping loudly in the undergrowth outside.

Since the fall of Singapore the Japanese had marched on to victory after victory, moving ever nearer to New Zealand shores. Japanese reconnaissance planes had been sighted over Auckland and Wellington. There was even rumour of Jap submarines being seen around the Australian Coast. Conversations were invariably about the evil Japanese. Stories of their inhuman treatment to our soldiers in the Japanese Prisoner Of War camps spread like wildfire throughout the country. The threat of an invasion became so mighty that, regardless of the fact there were only 4 anti-aircraft guns in the whole of the country, New Zealand coast patrols were readied for action. Home Guards began forming in the towns and privately owned vehicles were commandeered for that service. The catchphrase of the day changed from 'Thank God the Yanks are here' to 'what the hell is the Government doing leaving our divisions overseas when our own country is in danger'. Mother England offered little other than sympathy.

US Marines invaded Auckland and Wellington cities and the country looked to these young American lads to protect New Zealand shores. Never in its history had New Zealand been threatened with such peril.

CHAPTER THREE

THE GLEN 1943

XMAS GREETINGS
from
N·Z AMMUNITION C[OY]
MIDDLE EAST

N.Z.A.S.C.

XMAS 1942
NEW YEAR 1943

It seemed no time before their first Christmas in Glen Afton was upon them. Florrie received a Xmas Greeting from her youngest brother John, who was fighting in the Middle East, and she cried wondering if she would ever see him again.

The shortages of almost everything imported had been strongly felt by 1942. It was a treat for Meggie and Emmie to find an orange in the stockings hung on their bedposts on Christmas morning. They amused themselves cutting false teeth from orange peel as they waited for Florrie and Dai to get up. Later that morning they met up with Sarry, Simon, and Gerry Dunstan, at the bridge over the railway line and made their way up the track to the blackberry bushes that grew behind the Maori baches. Riki Whetu came hurtling out of the baches when he saw them climbing the hill towards the footie field.

"Where you jokers going?" he shouted loudly.

"Blackberrying," they yelled back to him. "Ya comin'?"

The six of them made for the footie field, teasing and giggling, as they trekked up the rough clay track. The place was a mass of blackberries and the fruit was big and glintingly ripe. In no time they'd all filled their billies made from cut down kerosene tins with No 8 wire handles with the fat juicy berries that grew everywhere in these parts. Meggie and Emmie had eaten as many berries as had gone into their billy.

After filling her billy Meggie threw herself down on the grassy edge of the paddock and stared up at the brilliant sky. She was filled with certain warmth, not just from the hot summer sun, but also from the wonder of her life since moving to this little mining village. She hoped now that they could stay here forever. A shadow crossed her mind as she remembered the wet, cold day they had driven into the Glen and she looked, with eyes half shut against the morning sun, at Emmie and remembered how sick her sister had been back then. The too cold in the winter and too hot in the summer corrugated iron house had not been an ideal place for a fragile child to recuperate in. But recoup Emmie had. Simon broke across her daydreaming by attempting to rub the blackberry stains from around her mouth.

"Get out," she yelled in mock annoyance, and pushed him. This was just the cue he needed to start to wrestle with her. "Ya look like a golliwog," he laughed, as he rolled her down the slope at the edge of the footie field. When she stopped rolling and lay still on the warm, sweet smelling grass, she licked her lips and began rubbing them hard. Simon rolled down after her and grabbing her he made a clumsy attempt at a kiss. Her heart gave an uncomfortable lurch, but even so, his nearness was thrilling.

Sarry and Gerry Dunstan had disappeared into the manuka to smoke the loose tobacco Sarry had brought with her in a Riverhead Gold tin. She reckoned it was in her Christmas stocking but no one believed her. It was more likely she had taken it from her father and brother's tobacco rations. She had offered them all a roll-your-own, but only Gerry wanted to smoke. Meggie had considered trying some, as she was sure that smoking gave Sarry that wonderful husky croak when she talked and laughed. She waited to see what Simon would do, and when he refused, Meggie refused also.

Riki sat pulling stalks of long grass and chewing the soft sweet ends while talking to Emmie. He was a good-looking boy, quiet and clever, excelling at most things. That he could run like the wind kept him in demand for local sports, and Andy Neismith, the Rugby League coach, thought Riki was shaping up so well he'd go places. Suddenly Emmie let out a loud squeal when she noticed Meggie in Simon's embrace. "I'm gonna tell Mum on you, Meggie," she shouted.

Simon raised himself up. "You better not," he said. "I can't stand pimps."

Emmie began to cry at being called a pimp and the commotion brought Sarry and Gerry scrambling out of the bush to find out what was happening. Sarry let out a loud throaty laugh.

"See I told ya, Megs. Si's got a crush on you. That's why Hazel Hutchins is snitchy with you. She's got tickets on Si herself." She chortled again, enjoying the beginnings of what may soon become a romantic dilemma, like in the films.

Simon's sunburnt face went even redder. "Shut up, Sarry. Ya don't know nothin'. Anyway, I'm going," he said, jumping to his feet. "Mum wants these blackberries to make a pie for Christmas dinner."

Emmie was still sniveling and Sarry told her to shut up or she wouldn't be coming out with them again. The kids trailed back down the track and parted company at the railway bridge.

"Come up this arvo," Si shouted to Meggie, as she hurried towards the corrugated iron house with the billy of blackberries. Florrie made the pie in the sweltering kitchen but there was only she and the girls for Christmas dinner. Dai had left earlier driving his drinking cronies out to the Waingaro Hotel. It hadn't taken Dai long to mate up with Bill Ingman, Chook Anderson and Snowy Antrill, the local drunks in the area. It suited them all round as they had been banned from the Hog's Head and Dai had the transport. Snowy wasn't so bad; Florrie tolerated him but the other two she despised. All three were, not surprisingly, bachelors and Chook and Bill were untidy looking individuals. Florrie often felt sick when she looked at Bill with his large fleshy lips that were always wet with dribble and the yellow stain at the fly of the only pair of trousers he possessed. The word was that Bill had syphilis and as a result was becoming incontinent. Florrie wouldn't let him inside the house. Chook, a small wiry man, wasn't much better, and always wore an oversized houndstooth overcoat that was filthy to say the least. No doubt they would all get pickled out at Waingaro and vomit and make a mess of themselves. What a charming way to celebrate

Christmas, Florrie thought, as she set a cloth on the scrubby grass behind the house.

"Come and get it," she called, and the girls filled their plates with salad and dressing made from an egg yolk. That was followed by blackberry tart with pink blancmange and the real cream that Florrie had fetched from Arch Hill's dairy farm on the hill behind the pottery.

Later in the afternoon Florrie put on the green frock that was her best and mustard coloured suede sandals with ankle straps and wedgie heels. The girls loved those shoes because they were just like the ones Betty Grable wore in the films. Then she dabbed her lips with the cork from the cochineal bottle, making them look like a dark red bow, before they walked up the short piece of dusty metal road to Griffith's boarding house. The kids were given a piece of cake each and sent outside to play rounders' on the back lawn. Some of the single men who were on backshift joined in the game with the kids.

Inside, in the cool, dark sitting room, Mrs Griffith poured sherry into tiny glasses for Florrie and a couple of other women whose husbands had also abandoned them in preference for the Hog's Head. When Florrie emerged to take the girls home her eyes were bright and red patches stained her nose and cheeks. She was happy and expansive. Emmie clasped her mother's hand and Meggie fell into step behind them.

"Do ya want to see the caves up on the Mac track tomorrow?" Simon called after Meggie, as she walked away from him.

"Can I, Mum? Please!"

"Course you can," Florrie replied absently, not really comprehending what she had agreed to.

Dai didn't come home that night so Florrie fiddled with the wireless knobs to catch the BBC news from London. Europe was in flames, the staccato voice announced, and the war raged on in North Africa. And closer to home there was news of the war in the Pacific.

But war took second place in Meggie's thoughts that Christmas night as she waited for sleep to come. Her head was full of the events of the day. She ran her fingers slowly over her mouth as if to feel again Simon's kiss. She could hardly wait for tomorrow when she could go to the caves with him. With her father away all day, her mother red-faced and happy surely this had to be the best Christmas ever.

Boxing Day dawned the usual glorious clear mornings of the valley's summer and Meggie packed a lunch for her outing with Simon to the caves.

"I want to go, too," wailed Emmie. "It's not fair."

"Well you can't," answered Florrie, much to Meggie's surprise. "And I'm not so sure you should go either, my girl."

"Oh, Mum. You promised. You know you did." Meggie moaned, as her heart sank.

"Well. All right this time. If I didn't know Rose Griffith I wouldn't let you go. But I think her boys would be trustworthy. Anyway, off you go and remember," she shouted after Meggie. "No monkey business, you hear."

Emmie was crying and Florrie hugged her. "Come on, lovie. We'll have a party lunch with ginger beer. I'll make some pikelets and we can whip up the cream to put on them."

That satisfied Emmie, not knowing the real reason her mother had kept her at home was her fear of being alone when Dai finally came home.

The caves seemed far away once Simon and Meggie left the village, walking on the bed of slack beside the mine's skip ropeway for a mile or so, and then veering right through the scrubby grass and manuka. Finally, when the sun was directly overhead, they reached a row of odd shaped holes between outcrops of rock in the side of the hill.

"Are these them?" Meggie asked excitedly.

"Yip. There's seashells inside. Millions of years ago all this would have been sea." Simon raised his arms expansively to illustrate his statement. Meggie's eyes widened as she looked around and tried to imagine water lapping up against the edge of these rocks and into the caves. It was like nothing she'd heard or seen before.

"Gee!" she exclaimed, full of admiration for Simon's knowledge.

They sat on the hot rocks and ate their lunch before venturing into the caves. Fossilized shells were embedded into the rock on the sides of the caves. The air was cool and musty. Their sandals crunched on the shells and pebbles that lay amongst stones on the cave floors. They gathered a few shells and stones and Meggie thought Simon looked so handsome with his creamy hair glowing in the half-light. Simon noticed her staring at him and asked why.

"Well." Meggie's face glowed red with embarrassment. "You're really clever to know about the sea and the war and everything ..." she finished lamely, her voice resounding around the cave.

Simon laughed loudly. "Ya want ta know why I brought ya up here, really?" he asked.

Meggie nodded indicating 'yes'. She wondered whether he wanted to kiss her again because so far he'd made no attempt to. Perhaps he hadn't liked it yesterday.

"Well, Brian and Gerry reckon they like ya." She didn't know that, but wasn't going to let on.

"Well," he started again, looking sheepishly out of his pink face. "Well, I wanted yer to be my sheilah."

Even though Meggie was delighted at the idea she ran out of the cave giggling uncontrollably. Simon chased her and catching her threw her onto the grass where they rolled around giggling together.

It was late when they walked back down the Mac track to the village. The sultry heat of the afternoon sun had slipped into a splendid summer evening, that fleeting time between day and dusk that feels like magic. For Meggie they really were magic moments and she glanced coyly at Simon as he made her cross her heart and promise not to tell their secret to anyone else. And already Meggie was feeling the stirrings of hero worship.

* * *

"Hear you're moving," Stan Fleming addressed Florrie Morgan, as he unpacked a small cardboard box of groceries onto her kitchen table. Then, with scissors taken from the pocket of his large white grocer's apron, he carefully cut the appropriate coupons from the ration books she offered.

"Yes. We're moving into Cooper's old place up behind the Post Office." Florrie sounded pleased. "Dai got himself transferred to the mine, you know."

"Be better than this place," Stan commented, scanning the ramshackle corrugated iron house, which was already like an oven at ten in the morning. "When do you move in?"

"End of the week," Florrie replied, stuffing the precious ration books back into the safety of her handbag.

"Well. Good luck to you then." Stan lifted his hand in a mock salute as he climbed back into the cab of his van.

"How did that wily Dai Morgan swing that," Stan muttered, as he drove off to finish his morning deliveries? "That man's got the cheek of the devil and the luck of Lucifer."

He liked Florrie Morgan and the girls, and thought, along with most of the district, that they could all have done a whole lot better than a good-for-nothing, wheeler-dealing, cove like Dai Morgan. He'd been nothing but trouble since he'd arrived, especially since exchanging his Austin Seven car for an old Buick truck. He used the truck to run a service out to Waingaro for the drinkers who had fallen out of favour with Ed Hubbard and were no longer welcome in the Hog's Head. Evenings and weekends his cronies piled onto the tray of his Buick to negotiate the perilous metal road that ran parallel to the creek all the way to the Waingaro Hotel, General Store and hot springs. Most times, by the grace of God, Dai got home okay. But there had been a few narrow squeaks when he had put the truck into the creek on the return journey. It was the general opinion in the Glen and thereabouts that sooner or later there would be an accident and lives would be lost.

Stan knew that Florrie was too embarrassed to deal from Ed Hubbard's Grocery Store since Dai had been banned from the Hogs Head so had put her weekly order in with him at Pukemiro. Not that he minded the extra business. Far from it, in fact. And as Stan reflected on Florrie and the children he decided to invite them to the meetings at the Gospel Hall. Some religion would change her life, he mused, with all the zeal of a true Christian. Yes. He'd ask Florrie to the Gospel Hall service when he next delivered her groceries. And her girls could go to Sunday school.

At the end of the week, Dai, Snowy, Chook and Bill, with some other drinking cronies, loaded up the Buick with his precious wireless set and other sticks of furniture and moved it into the colliery house behind the Post Office. Meggie wasn't at all upset by yet another move of house as this time it meant she would be living closer to Sarry Adams and just across the road from Simon Griffith. She watched happily as her father hammered in a picture hook and carefully re-hung Mickey Savage above the mantelpiece over the coal range.

Dai, for all his drinking faults, was a worker. In no time he had built a chook run at the back of the section and had also converted half of the large outside washhouse into a home brewery. When the day old chickens arrived at the Railway Station, Meggie and Emmie were sent to pick them up from the Goods Shed. Out of the octagon shaped cardboard box came a dozen little cheeps from the fluffy yellow chicks inside. They were kept in the hot water cupboard at first and the girls loved to feed and cuddle them at mealtimes. In no time they had grown enough to be put out into the coop to join the older birds Dai had got from Archie Bell. Meggie loved the chooks and liked her job of feeding them morning and night.

* * *

As the last golden days of the summer holidays wore on, a tanned Meggie and Emmie in the coloured shorts and blouses Florrie had cut and sewed from old garments, roamed the countryside exploring every corner of the Glen and its environs. Simon and Riki, both knowing the valley like the back of their hands, roamed with them.

One Sunday morning the usual crowd of Gerry, Sarry, Riki, Simon, and the Morgan girls were joined by some of the Gully kids. Hazel Hutchins had heard that Simon Griffith had been going everywhere with Meggie over the holidays, so she decided to leave nothing to chance and go with them. Hazel ordered Ruthie Smith and Jan White to come with her. Brian Harmon, the class wit, had seen the gaggle of kids from his house and hurried after them, managing to catch up as they climbed high onto the ridge above the Mac mine. Once over the other side they stopped to catch their breath in a bush clearing. It was very quiet. The ridge between silenced the continuous rattle of the mine machinery. The only sounds were the calls of the native birds as they twittered and soared in and out of the large expanse of beautiful native bush.

Simon and Gerry lay flat on the ground with their hands beneath their heads pretending to sleep and deliberately not answering the girls so Sarry Adams picked up a dried cowpat and flung it at the two boys. It skimmed past their heads and they were up in a flash. The chase was on. It was no contest with the girls too weak from giggling to run. Simon grabbed Meggie and threw her to the ground. He pinned her beneath him as he lunged over her threatening all kinds of punishment. She squirmed beneath him trying to get away. Suddenly all the play fighting stopped as each of the kids turned their heads and looked in the direction that a strange new sound came from. The high-pitched, mosquito noise grew into a louder drone as the lone aircraft drew nearer to them. It circled almost directly above their heads and then swooped low over the mining village.

"Shit! It's a bloody Jap spotter," whispered Gerry. Having a full set of 'Sergeant Dan the Creamota Man' aircraft cards from the porridge packets; Gerry was the local expert when it came to identifying warplanes. Sarry squealed, a harsh rasping sound.

"We're going to be bombed. Help! The Japs are going to blow us up."

As they all watched, white-faced, the plane turned, revved, and once more flew low across the little valley.

"Don't be so bloody stupid," Gerry growled at Sarry. "Spotters don't carry bombs. They're not big enough."

He scanned the sky again. Simon said nothing. With his hand across his forehead, shielding the glaring sun from his eyes, he followed the path of the craft across the cloudless sky. The buzzing plane distanced itself, turned again, and made another mighty swoop over the valley, turning and climbing, until it seemed to be above the Pukemiro mine and township. It circled again over that area, and then rose, rapier-fast, moving away until it was no more than a dazzling speck in the great blue bowl of afternoon sky.

"Hey Gerry, do ya reckon it was photographing the mines," Si asked.

"Reckon so," Gerry answered, again with his knowing attitude. "It's only a matter of time now before the bastards get here."

They'd seen films of the Japs on picture nights at the hall. The newsreels portrayed the level of barbarism in the treatment of 'our boys' who had been captured and imprisoned in the Japanese P O W camps. Although they contained old war news by the time they arrived at the outback picture halls, the local picture goers had already seen flickering images on the screen of the Japanese victory in the Java Sea and the Philippines. It seemed that Hitler's prediction that the war would last only one more year would prove to be right as the Japanese Fleet advanced down the Pacific heading south.

"Jeez," Gerry snarled, breaking the hushed silence that now pervaded the little mining village. "I'd like to get loose on those little slit-eyed bastards." He surged forth, snatching up a couple of dry cowpats and firing them, as one would a hand grenade, at the innocent stand of native trees. "Take that!" he bellowed. "And that, and that!"

A new battle started. Soon all manner of missiles were being flung at the girls who, now in the boys' minds, had become the unscrupulous Japanese soldiers pouring down the Pacific. They ran into the bush for cover and the boys chased them yelling and hooting. Hazel Hutchins wasn't impressed with the war game and called them all childish and silly.

"I would have expected better from you, Simon Griffith," she snorted, as she turned and began stalking her way over the ridge towards home. Brian Harmon yelled after her that she was a snooty jam tart. After that they all straggled over the ridge, slipping and sliding on the toe toe stalks they rode, in lieu of horses, down the hill. At the crossroads where all the kids went their separate ways home, Simon asked if anyone was going to the flicks that night. Meggie prayed she'd be allowed to go because she was afraid Hazel would sit with Simon if she wasn't there. However, in view of the visit of the Japanese reconnaissance plane, picture screening was cancelled until further notice. Blackout curtains were required on all the windows at night.

The following week a local Home Guard was formed and Dai Morgan's Buick truck was fitted with a gas producer and seconded as the official Home Guard vehicle. Parades were organized to be held weekly at night in the hall. Every able-bodied cow cockie and miner was required to join The Emergency Precautions Scheme. A few men had pig-shooting rifles but in the main the men whittled their own guns out of pieces of old mine timber. Harry Bloomfield, a farmer from way out past Waingaro, became the envy of the Home Guard men when he arrived with his Grandfather's 1892 rifle. It was a full 303 in lovely condition, just a spot of rust halfway down the barrel, and while it threw slightly to the right it was otherwise dead accurate.

Dai Morgan was delighted at this turn of events. It gave him the importance of being in the military and he did, of course, hold the notable position of driver of the Home Guard vehicle.

On the first parade night the local kids gathered around the hall and tried to peer through the cracks in the wooden building. Davy Howard gave them away by bursting into the hall and rat-tat tatting with a piece of old rusty pipe at the serious Home Guard members. They got chased away by Bob Cochrane, the newly appointed Corporal, and they scattered out eventually trailing off to their own homes.

That night the BBC Newscaster told of a turning point in the Pacific war. The U.S. Marines had taken control of Guadacanal and Jap losses were 20 to every one American. The Yellow Peril paranoia in New Zealand waned a little and life returned to almost normal in the little mining villages west of the Waikato River.

CHAPTER FOUR

The Japanese reconnaissance plane that had caused the stir in the valleys, west of Huntly, was all too soon forgotten. For the mining families, life settled back to what it had been before the unusual event had taken place.

Since the fall of Singapore, the previous year, the Japanese had spread across the Coral Sea and into the Pacific as swiftly as an oil slick spread across water. Then the HMNZS ACHILLES, complimented by New Zealand navy personal, had been bombed near the Solomon Islands and that news sent the next shock wave through the country. This was countered by the news that the U.S. Marines had Guadacanal under control and that lulled New Zealanders into a false sense of security again. Or perhaps it was just easier to cope with the war by believing it was still a long way away.

School resumed after the long summer break. The days were still hot, with not a whisper of wind or a cloud to mar the golden weather. Meggie and Sarry, now inseparable friends, had a new teacher, Miss Kalman. She was tall and attractive and wore clothes that were neat and softly flowing. The girls adored her thus beginning a new phase of femininity amongst them. They lost all interest in the former tomboyish games thought up by the boys and instead spent most of their playing time dressing up. Bracken fern fronds were held above their head for lacy umbrellas and delicate pink foxglove flowers were carefully picked to slip onto their fingers as fancy gloves. Sarry continued to smoke and from somewhere she had acquired a jeweled cigarette holder, which in her mind gave her the status of a Betty Grable or some other film star. Each week, under Sarry's instructions, they acted out the Tuesday night movie, Sarry always claiming the principal role whether it be Yvonne De Carlo, Kathryn Grayson or Jane Powell – whoever was the star of the latest film.

Miss Kalman taught the girls to knit. Due to rationing wool was unobtainable, except to knit for the Red Cross parcels for the troops overseas, so they used raffia. The boys hated the sissy job of tying the lengths of raffia together and then rolling into balls. The girls also made cushions covers and potholders with frayed edges from cut down sugar sacks. The boys were not impressed at such a dramatic change in the girls who now refused to join in the war games, or blow up frogs and catch crawlies. Brian Harmon reckoned that dropping rocks down the tomos between the boulders up the Mac track, then counting, sometimes well past twenty, before hearing the hollow plop when the missiles finally hit the water in the underground rivers below, was much more fun than knitting or acting out the talkie films.

Meggie saw less of Simon. He seemed to be ignoring her and she wondered if he had forgotten the secret they had made together that day over in the caves.

One Friday night, when summer had melted into autumn, Meggie walked into the picture hall early and stood looking around for Sarry. Emmie had already slid into a seat next to her friend, Biddy Stoutman. Simon saw her standing alone in the foyer and hissed at her from his seat. "Megs… over here."

The lights went out and the whining sound track that accompanied the silent 'Rin Tin Tin' serial began to wail. The jerky pictures of a dog saving a person from dire circumstances twitched on and off the screen. Under the cover of darkness Si slipped his arm around Meggie's shoulders. Suddenly, though not an unusual occurrence on picture nights in the hall, the wailing soundtrack stopped and the film reel broke down. Mr. Raine, the ticket collector, switched on the hall lights. Simon quickly removed his arm from around Meggie's shoulders and, thrusting two fingers into his mouth, he joined in the whistling and foot stamping at the breakdown of the serial.

"Where's the tin that Rin Tin Tin shat in," the young jokers chanted over and over, until the lights went out and the plaintive moan of the soundtrack began again.

Meggie was disappointed that Simon didn't put his arm around her again before the lights came on for half time. The men lit their cigarettes and the kids all scrambled up to the open hatch at the far end of the hall where they could buy ice cream or a limited selection of sweets. Si rose from his seat asking Meggie if she wanted anything from the hatch. When she shook her head indicating no he left her and went out the side door. Meggie knew he was too young to drink beer outside but sure enough when he returned for the main picture he smelt of alcohol. With added Dutch courage he soon slipped his arm around her again and drew her against his shoulder. She loved being so close to him even though his beery breath reminded her strongly of her father. She didn't like the sour smell but was prepared to put up with it just to be near him.

On the screen a clap of thunder brought her attention back to the flickering black and white film. Fred Astaire and Ginger Rogers were caught outside in the rain in a park. As if by magic, in the deserted park, the strains of a full orchestra accompanied Fred as he sang, 'Isn't It A Lovely Day To Be Caught In The Rain'. Fred and Ginger, despite having only just met in the park, launched into a complicated dance routine and never missed a step.

"Aren't they gorgeous," squealed Sarry Adams, only to be loudly shushed from all sides of the hall and the click of knitting needles resumed once more.

It was a sure bet that next day they would be acting out 'TOP HAT' and Sarry would be Ginger Rogers and Meggie would probably have to play Fred Astaire.

Ginger and Fred whirled and tapped and spun on the screen while Simon became more amorous towards Meggie. He was becoming bored with the film and after more cuddling on the uncomfortable theatre seats, that were old throw-outs from the Huntly picture hall, he whispered to her, "Let's get outta here."

They waited until another particularly complicated dance routine held the audience spellbound then slipped out the side door hoping no wagging tongues had noticed them. Simon walked her to the hawthorn hedge behind the old Post Office. For a while they stood saying nothing. Then Simon gently lifted her face with his hand and expertly placed his lips on hers. It was a soft kiss, slow and tender, and Meggie felt her legs go weak as she responded. With calculated deliberation he opened her mouth slightly with his tongue. It flashed through her mind that this kiss was very different from the immature attempt he had made when they were gathering blackberries from the footie field last Christmas. She wondered how he'd acquired such knowledge in such a short time.

The chatter of the picture crowd coming out of the hall, clomping away from each other along the various metal roads, broke the spell. They stayed out of sight until the entire crowd had dispersed.

Meggie squirmed in his arms. "I'll have to go or Mum'll give it to me."

Simon held on. His hormones were racing out of control and he liked the feeling. He felt an urgent need to lay this soft girl down and caress the buds that, he'd noticed more than once lately, were developing very nicely on her chest.

"Let me go," she squealed.

Simon wasn't pleased, but he released her.

"What about Sunday?" He looked at her with questioning eyes. "How about we go up the Mac track? What do ya reckon?"

Meggie had liked the feelings, too, but was more afraid of her mother than to stay and indulge him further.

"Anyone else going?"

He shook his head. "Meet me down at the White Bridge."

Meggie was quiet for a long time. The picture crowd was well indoors and the silence of the crispy night was broken only by the gentle whine of the pines up on the hill.

She nodded. "Okay. I'll be there about one. See ya."

Meggie ran home to make up time. She felt jubilant, overjoyed – just her and Simon. She decided to lie to Emmie and say she was going to Sarry Adam's place. Emmie didn't like Sarry so wouldn't want to come with her. That night she lay awake hugging her pillow, pretending it was Si kissing her.

Sunday took an age to come. Simon was already standing on the bridge, whistling softly, his hands pressed deeply into his trouser pockets, when Meggie stopped before him.

"Hi, Megs," was all he said. They fell into step on the dusty metal road then leaving the road they crossed the footie field kicking a few lumps of dirt into touch on their way. In no time they'd climbed the Mac track and from there decided to go on over the ridge to where they had been the day the reconnaissance plane had flown over the valley. They lay on the cool grass at the shaded edge of the bush clearing and listened to the gentle breeze mingling with the bird calls.

Si pretended to be asleep for a while so Meggie lay back and watched the ever-changing shapes in the cloud formations. One moment she could make out a face or an animal. Within minutes the pattern would he broken as the clouds scattered like woolly sheep outpacing a dog. Her attention focused on the intensely blue sky that was making the clouds look extra white by contrast.

"Persil white, Persil bright, happy little washday song," she sang and hummed the radio jingle as she stared at the snowy puffs and streaks in order to memorize their shapes and draw them later at home.

Simon disturbed her thoughts by combing his fingers through her wind-tangled hair. The movement of his fingers across her scalp sent soft warmth flowing through her entire body. Suddenly he pulled her head back roughly and brought his mouth down on hers. Even before she was aware of what was happening to her she was responding to him. Her own mouth opened slowly beneath his and their tongues explored soft lips and strong young teeth. The sensation was glorious, like nothing Meggie had ever known. He ran his hands over the new fullness of her breasts, then running his mouth the length of her throat he seized the newly formed bud between his teeth and suckled her like a babe would its mother. Warning bells rang in her head but she didn't want to move away from such delicious sensations. She had suspected he had brought her here today to kiss her but this was more than she had ever imagined in her fantasizing. A trickle of fear ran through her.

"Si. Don't," she whispered.

He didn't answer. She cried out again, pushing him away with strength she hadn't known she possessed. He lowered himself and rolled slightly to one side, relieving her of his weight.

"Jeezus, I'm sorry. I didn't mean … I got carried away."

Meggie looked up at the clear blue sky above. It seemed to waver as her eyes filled with tears. Simon pushed himself up on his elbows and looked at her with concern.

"What's the matter, Megs?" he asked as he cupped his hand under her chin forcing her to look at him. His blue eyes were soft with caring. "I'm so sorry, honey. I didn't mean to frighten ya."

"I'll get a baby now, won't I?"

He looked at her in amazement. "For Christ's sake, I only kissed ya, Megs." He couldn't believe she was so dumb. "Struth! Jeezus!" He hit his forehead hard with the heel of his hand. "Jeez, I'm so sorry, Megsy. Yer a big girl and I forget how young you are."

The concern in his voice only served to make her cry more. He pulled her to him and brushed the tears from her face with his lips. She noticed his lashes lay long and curling against his cheek. They were a honey gold, nearly black at the tips but pale blond at the roots. Drawing her even closer he rocked her gently whispering sorry over and over, until she stopped crying.

"Don't worry, honey. It won't happen. I didn't go all the way."

They stayed in the clearing for some time and Simon explained a few facts to her.

"It's not easy for us jokers when we get to hold a curvy little tart like you are," he joked. "It's harder for a man to stop than a woman," he further imparted, knowledgeably.

"I didn't want to stop. But I'm really scared of what Mum would do to me if she knew."

"I know, honey. I should never have come on so strong to ya."

They remained silent listening to the liquid notes of the birds.

"Well, don't tell anyone, will ya? Especially Sarry. She's got a big mouth and would likely land me in jail."

"What for?" Meggie looked puzzled.

"Never mind. Jest don't tell her anything about today. Come on." He jumped up and pulled her with him. "Time we got back."

It was late when they ventured back over the hill. The wind had dropped and the evening air was cooling quickly. Meggie would always associate the feel of that Sunday with Simon. In the days that followed it seemed to her that now her childhood had gone, was over. The fun of dressing up as ladies, roaming the hills, swimming naked in the creek on the way home from school, had all lost appeal. She felt eager now to explore the new stirrings Simon had unleashed within her.

* * *

The visit from Mrs Stafford, the mine manager's wife, took Florrie by surprise. She'd only slipped home from the boarding house to do a few of her own chores and was listening to the radio when the knock came. The wireless had masked the clomping of Mrs Stafford's cuban-heeled brogues on the rough brick path outside. Florrie straightened her apron and patted down her hair when she opened the door to the important visitor.

"You will have tea with me, Mrs Stafford?" She asked in her posh voice, reserved for the manager's wife and the doctor.

Iris Stafford didn't usually fraternize with the miner's wives but she nodded, thus giving Florrie the chance to lay out her best cloth with old fashioned ladies embroidered in each corner. From the cabinet she took the teaset of fine bone china decorated with blue forget-me-nots.

"Are you a knitter?" Mrs Stafford asked, as she sipped her tea and reached for another slice of thin bread and butter arranged on a forget-me-not plate.

"Well, yes. But I don't do anything fancy."

"What about socks and balaclavas?"

"No. I've never mastered the art of turning a sock heel," Florrie replied, dreading the thought of having to knit balaclavas for the Red Cross parcels.

"I'll leave you some wool and a pattern for the balaclavas then. Pity about the socks. I've only got two good sock knitters."

She took a last swallow of tea, which ran visibly down her long stringy neck and disappeared beneath her pearl necklace. Placing the forget-me-not cup back on its saucer she rose to leave.

"Thanks for the tea, Mrs Morgan. Have to dash now. I still have a lot of wool to deliver."

Florrie saw her to the door and as Mrs Stafford took the last step she turned and addressed Florrie again.

"By the way, Mrs Morgan. Was that your Megan we saw yesterday? Quite late in the afternoon too. Walking down the Mac track with that fair haired Griffith boy." She narrowed her eyes to gauge Florrie's reaction before she spoke again. "I must say Mr. Stafford and myself thought it unwise of you to let her go off on her own with an older boy."

"You must have mistaken her for someone else, Mrs. Stafford. Meggie spent yesterday afternoon with Sarry Adams."

"I think not," replied Mrs Stafford, as she clomped up the path to the gate. "Mr. Stafford commented Griffith is a big lad for his age."

The visit from the manager's wife left Florrie agitated for the rest of the morning. She couldn't concentrate on her work at the boarding house. Wait till that lying little cat gets home from school. I'll give her Mac track with Simon Griffith and Florrie contemplated mentioning the incident to Mrs Griffith. She had confided in Rose Griffith many times since they'd become friends but never anything that involved Mrs Griffith's own kin, something Rose was obsessively protective about.

No, she thought; better to leave it until she had all the facts. She didn't want to lose her job at the boarding house and if that little cat has done anything to put her job at risk she'd be in for a damn good hiding. She might even tell Dai and he'd give the jumped up madam what for. Then again, perhaps she would not. Dai was hardly ever home nowadays anyway. The Home Guard had come at just the right time for him. With benzene rationed the gas producer was a godsend on his Buick and the Home Guard gave him good reason to drive out Waingaro way on military exercises.

But Florrie reasoned that even in his state of almost permanent drunkenness these days, he still must have noticed how Meggie was developing far beyond other girls her age. Emmie was still small and not as tall as Meggie, which was understandable considering her poor start in life.

The morning dragged on, as Florrie went over and over this new threat with the Griffith boy, until after the midday lunches that some of the miners working on top came home for. Finally the dishes were done and she put on her cardigan in readiness to finish for the day.

"'Ere, Florrie," Mrs. Griffith called. "Would you hand in this order to Ed Hubbard's on your way 'ome."

"Yes," Florrie answered despondently.

"Ere. What is the matter? You look awful." Mrs Griffith was concerned. "It's Dai again, isn't it?"

Florrie shook her head.

"It's all right. We all know about his piece out at Waingaro."

Rose Griffith patted Florrie's hand. That was another shock for Florrie. She had suspected Dai was on with someone but didn't know for sure and was probably the only person in the valley who didn't. She started to cry.

"Oo, dear, dear, now," Rose Griffith exclaimed. "Sit down and I'll make you an 'ot drink."

Rose Griffith filled the teapot from one of the steaming kettles on top of the coal range, and then sat opposite Florrie as she waited for the tea to draw. They talked while they sipped the hot tea. Florrie said nothing of what Mrs Stafford had told her about Simon and Meggie. After the second cup Florrie got up to go.

"I'll be okay now," she said, picking up her handbag and the grocery list. "I'll drop this off. Thank you for the tea and sympathy."

Rose nodded and watched Florrie as she walked towards the road. How on earth did she get tied up with that no good blaggard, she thought? She was a good-looking woman and Rose knew she'd come from quite a well-to-do family back in the King Country. Florrie had told her that her folks were very much against her marriage to Dai Morgan.

Florrie had to pluck up courage as she approached Ed Hubbard's Store. She'd been too embarrassed to go to his shop since Dai had been banned from the Hogs Head. Ed was behind the counter. He smiled widely at Florrie.

"Hello Mrs Morgan. It's a long time since I've seen you in here."

Florrie's face burned as she gave Ed a trembley smile.

"Here's Mrs Griffith's order. She needs it this afternoon."

Ed scanned the piece of paper, and then lifted his gaze to look Florrie straight in the eye.

"You should know that you're welcome to shop here, Mrs Morgan. What's between Dai and the Hogs Head doesn't affect you, you know."

"Thanks Mr. Hubbard. But I'm quite satisfied with Mr. Fleming."

With the mention of Stan Fleming an idea came to her. Why hadn't she thought of it before? That's how she'd put a stop to Meggie's escapades. Send her to the Gospel Hall on Sundays. That would keep her out of mischief with Simon Griffith. Stan had asked her several times to go to his church on Sundays and the girls to the Sunday school.

"That's it," she said out loud, smiling broadly at Ed Hubbard.

And with that she dashed out of his shop leaving Ed looking quite bewildered. He shook his head and murmured 'Women' under his breath as he began packing Mrs Griffith's order.

Things did not stay secret for long in the Glen. Rose Griffith found out soon enough that Florrie was concerned about Meggie and her Simon. Beads of perspiration stood out on her brow as she black leaded the top of the kitchen range and waited for Simon to come in from school. Simon suspected his mother had something on her mind as soon as he entered the kitchen and that it concerned him. He walked in and dumped his books on the well-scrubbed tabletop.

"'Ello luvey," she puffed at him. "Get that bag off the table now."

She waved a blackened hand to indicate out. Simon dragged the bag away but before he could get out of the door Rose pounced on him.

"What you been up to with the Morgan girl, Simon?" she asked.

Simon's heart gave a lurch. "Nothing. Why?"

"That's not what I hear. Florrie Morgan is worried. She thinks you were up to no good with her Megan last Sunday. Stafford the manager and 'is wife saw you two together."

"Oh Jeezus. Where did those nosy old buggers see us?"

"Comin' down the Mac track. Quite late it was they said. Meggie Morgan has lied to her mam. Said she spent the afternoon with Sarry Adams. And don't swear in here, mind."

Simon suspected that his mother had guessed his feelings for Meggie long ago. Rose Griffith was what the Welsh referred to as 'fey' and Simon always felt she could see right inside him.

"We just went for a walk, that's all," he lied. "Nothing happened."

"Well you just mind what you're doin', boyo. You'll not be workin' a while yet so don't you go

65

bringin' shame on this doorstep 'til you're bringin' in a wage, my boy."

Her voice held a veiled warning that scared Simon. Guilt made him protest. "Fer Chris sake! Why don't the bloody Stafford's mind their own business? They don't own us, do they?"

"You'll be sayin' different when you're lookin' to Stafford for a job in the mine. And don't be usin' that language with me, you cocky young haerllug, you."

Her sing song voice followed him as he stormed out of the door. He wanted to talk to Meggie but common sense told him he wouldn't be welcome at her place now. He'd have to work out some way to see her after school, since now he traveled by train into Secondary School in Huntly each day. It was going to be difficult with both their mothers watching them like hawks from now on.

Riki Whetu knocked on Morgan's back door. Simon had cooked up a reason for him to say he needed help with his arithmetic and Emmie Morgan was a whizz at sums. If he could get inside he could slip Simon's note to Meggie. Florrie answered the door and invited Riki in. Riki and Emmie scanned over the arithmetic book, while Meggie, looking perfectly miserable, sat in the overheated kitchen knitting the horrible khaki wool into balaclavas for Mrs. Stafford's Red Cross parcels. Florrie had made the Red Cross knitting part of Meggie's punishment for lying to her. When Mrs Morgan went back into the scullery Riki leaned close to Meggie, and spoke out of the side of his mouth like a gangster in an American film.

"Si sent this," he hissed, slipping Simon's note into Meggie's hand.

Her face went scarlet as she hurriedly pushed the folded scrap into her dress pocket.

"Get away from the fireplace, you silly little cat," her mother called when she caught a glimpse of Meggie's bright red face. "Are you so stupid you'll still sit there when it's far too hot for you," she growled.

Meggie started to cry, partly because her mother had been picking on her endlessly ever since that horrible Mrs Stafford had told her she'd seen her and Simon coming down the Mac track, and partly because she felt so guilty over what had happened between her and Simon.

"Oh for God's sake! Take the knitting to the bedroom, Meggie. You'll embarrass Riki bawling like that."

Meggie gathered up the wool and shut the bedroom door behind her. She unfolded the note and read, MEET ME TOMORROW AFTER DINNER BEHIND THE BATHHOUSE.

Meggie would need Sarry's help to pull this off even if Simon didn't approve of Sarry knowing anything. Sarry was only too happy to assist in an intrigue and called for Meggie to go to the pictures next evening. Riki led Meggie up the track to the back of the bathhouse, and then took off for the pictures himself. He was becoming very fond of Emmie and planned to sit with her at the pictures so didn't want to be late getting there. Simon was leaning against the back wall when she got there.

"We can't stay here," Simon said.

He'd brought a torch but on this cold, clear night they didn't need it. Holding onto each other, they took the narrow track that ran off into the bush just at the back the Maori baches. At first they scrambled through prickly gorse and manuka, and then the path led into deeper native bush. They made their way slowly until their eyes became accustomed to the darkness. Looking up through the bush canopy, stars twinkled in the frosty night sky. Somewhere a morepork called and bush moths flew around them. Meggie pretended to be scared and Simon pulled her to him, just as she hoped he would.

"You know I'm not allowed to see you again," she said.

"I guessed as much. I've had a bawling out from the old lady, too."

"They don't know what we did though, do they? What are we going to do, Si?"

"We haven't done anything wrong, Megs. Get that through ya head." Simon sounded annoyed with her.

"I'm sorry. What are we going to do now?"

"I reckon we'd better cool it for a while … at least 'til I start working. And that won't be long now. We'll jest have to wait, and believe me, honey, it'll be a bloody sight harder on me than it will be on you."

"Mum says Emmie and me have got to go to the Sunday school at the Gospel Hall every Sunday afternoon now. We used to go to Sunday school before we came here but that was in the morning." Meggie looked miserable again.

"Didn't you like it? Hey," laughed Simon. "Gerry and me might come too. That'll give old Fleming a kick if he thinks he's reformed us jokers."

Meggie brightened up. "Oh beaut. That would be great."

The future didn't seem so bleak now with the possibility of seeing Simon on Sundays at least. She didn't see him at school now that he went to High School in Huntly.

They were about to go back down the track when crackling twigs and muffled voices rendered them silent. They strained their ears to listen. Locating the noises from behind a clump of bracken fern they crept slowly towards it. Their eyes now well accustomed to the night light they could clearly see Ces Howard lying on top of Girlie Whetu, Riki's older sister. They were wriggling around and Ces was making loud grunting noises. Simon shushed Meggie and drew her quietly away.

"Don't say nothin' about what ya saw to anyone," he warned. "If Ces's missus finds out there'll be all hell let loose. And poor bloody Davie will bear the brunt of it. When Meggie got home Dai was listening to the BBC nine o'clock war news, which had broadcast details of an R.A.F. air raid on Hamburg in Germany. 40,000 people had been killed and as many injured. Dai was pleased and felt sure that this was a sign that the war was turning in Britain's favour.

"Bloody Huns," he snarled, as he knocked the top off another bottle of his homebrew.

"To celebrate the victory," he told Florrie when she gave him an icy glare.

CHAPTER FIVE

Bess Hamilton was from the Scottish Highlands and easily the best sock knitter in this coalmining district. She accepted the wool that Mrs. Stafford offered her to knit more socks for the Red Cross parcels. Then, carrying a box of matches, she followed Mrs. Stafford down the path. When they reached the Pukemiro main street Mrs. Hamilton piled the skeins of precious wool into a heap in the middle of the street and using several matches she set fire to it.

"What on earth are you doing?" Iris Stafford shouted, alarmed. She ran over to the burning pile and stamped at it with her shoes. It was too late as the skeins of wool were already badly singed.

"Are you out of your mind, Mrs. Hamilton? What on earth did you do that for?"

"Because your man is wearing the socks tha' I knitted for the troops. I dinna mind knitting for those in need but I'll no be knitting for your man's feet."

"That's absolute rubbish," said Iris Stafford, as calmly as she could. "How could Bill get your socks?" But Iris was worried. How could Mrs. Hamilton possibly know that Bill Stafford had been wearing the socks she had knitted for the Red Cross parcels? Only her and Bill knew that.

"Because you gave them to him," was Bess Hamilton's reply. "I saw him putting his feet into those socks after running in a race at the sports field last Saturday."

"That doesn't prove a thing." Mrs. Stafford poofed loudly.

"Aye, but it does," Bess replied triumphantly. "There's no another knitter in these parts who turns a heel like I do. Nay, I would swear on the bible, those socks were my knittin'."

Mrs. Stafford was stumped. Attack was all she had left to do. "You're mad," she shouted. "Burning good wool meant for garments for those poor soldiers in the trenches. Only a mad woman would do that." She turned and strode down the road.

"And dinna ya be bringin,' any more of your wool here or the same thing will happen," Bess shouted after her, walking back up her path that was embedded with stones that read out THE ROAD TO THE LORD. Bess glanced irritably next door at the sign their neighbour, Wally Brown, had erected just to annoy her. Wally had nailed bottletops onto a board to read out, THE ROAD TO THE DUNNY and an arrow pointed to the wooden outhouse at the back of the section. The sign had incensed her but moreso today because of the run in with the Mine Manager's wife.

"Nay, I'll no let the English get away with their stealin' and pokin' fun at the Lord," she muttered as she legged it over the fence with the matches and set fire to Wally's outhouse.

Stan Fleming's eyes, directed at the Morgan girls, were deep-set and gleaming under his crepey lids. He was really pleased that Florrie had kept her word and sent them to Sunday school at the Gospel Hall. To his way of thinking it would follow now that Florrie would come to the morning services and it warmed his heart to know that he had brought more souls to redemption. To get her away from the sin and damnation brought on her by Dai's behaviour would be, for him, a coup indeed.

The opening prayer had just started when it was rudely interrupted by a commotion at the door. Simon Griffith, Riki Whetu, Gerry Dunstan and Brian Harmon tramped noisily into the Gospel Hall and sat down. Stan's tongue darted in and out as he wetted his lips.

"What do you lads want?" he asked a trifle too sharply for a man of the cloth. "You're a bit old for Sunday school, aren't you?"

The boys shuffled their feet on the wooden floor until Brian Harmon finally spoke up.

"We're here to seek the Lord," he half-pie sniggered, with a silly grin on his face. The Sunday school kids began to giggle. Old Fleming was furious. He beetled his brow. These boys were ruining his plans to impress the Morgan girls and therefore their mother.

"Well," he said, quite uncharitably. "I think you are only here to disrupt the Sunday school class. I'd like you to go quietly now. Without any fuss, if you please."

The boys scraped their chairs rowdily across the bare wooden floor as they rose and filed out of the little church hall.

"Meecha later," Simon hissed as he passed Meggie.

Stan composed himself and with the assistance Paulie Davidson and Bess Hamilton he brought the children to order and divided them into three separate groups. Emmie was in Mr. Fleming's group and they were led into an area that had been partitioned off by a large sheet to make it private. On the wall hung a very big piece of brown cardboard that had been brightly painted into four sections. The pictures conveyed what would happen to anyone who sinned. The last picture, painted with bright orange, red and yellow flames licking burnt black figures was meant to depict hell. It was too scary for Emmie and she decided that she wouldn't come back here, no matter what her mother said. In the far corner of the hall Meggie's group was being shown a tank full of water that had been hidden beneath the stage and were being instructed in baptism.

The smell of cigarette smoke was faint at first, but persistent. Eventually, when the smell became quite strong, Paulie Davidson informed Mr. Fleming. After satisfying himself the smoke was not coming from inside the hall Stan ventured outside and found the boys he had evicted were underneath the hall puffing away on roll-your-owns. All hell let loose as Stan Fleming bellowed at them to get out, using some words that didn't really fit in with Christianity. While this was happening Emmie found Meggie and dragged her out of the hall.

"I'm not going back in there," she whined. "Mr. Fleming reckons we're all going to burn up in hell."

Meggie wasn't over enthusiastic about the Sunday school either. There had been no lessons about Jesus or God and she didn't fancy getting her head dunked in the tank of water. They hurriedly made their way to the main road but before they'd gone far the boys caught up with them and they all began fooling around and giggling about old Fleming and imitating Mrs. Hamilton singing 'Shall We Gather At The Rrrrriverrrrr', in her broad Scottish accent.

"Where did you jokers get the tobacco from?" asked the girls. "Dad's always moaning that he doesn't get enough in his weekly ration."

Brian Harmon tapped his nose. They dawdled on along the rough metal road towards Glen Afton.

"I know where we'll go," shouted Brian. "The Home Guard is having a rifle practice up at the mine horse paddock this arvo. If we go up into the bush behind Riki's place we can get a good view from there."

The idea was a hit and they turned off the road and took a shortcut through the pines that bordered the native bush on the hill. Simon took Meggie's hand and guided her along the tracks through the pine plantation. When they reached the bush a secret glance passed between them as they remembered this was where they had seen Ces Howard and Riki's sister a few nights ago.

They settled at the edge of the bush where there was a perfect view over the horse paddock. Meggie and Emmie could see their father and he seemed important as he ordered the other men around. When the Home Guard rifle practice had finished the men began throwing hand grenades made from old tins, black powder and off-cuts from the mine's metal stamper, into the swamp next to the horse paddock. The noise of each explosion was deafening, echoing around the valley hills. When they stopped several of the men went over to the swamp to pick up the huge juicy eels that had been blown out of the water. The kids all knew that would be dinner tonight.

"Well. How was Sunday school?" Florrie asked, as she removed Emmie's coat.

"It was too scary," said Emmie. "I'm not going back again."

"Come on now. It can't have been that bad. Meggie. What happened at the Sunday school?" she asked accusingly.

Before Meggie could answer Emmie had launched in. "Old Fleming reckons we're all going to burn in the hell fires. I'm not going back. I don't care what you say, Mum," she ended determinedly. A healthy Emmie was developing quite a mind of her own.

"It was awful, Mum," Meggie put in. "Not a bit like the Sunday school at Mapiu. There was nothing about God or anything."

Maybe this isn't going to work, thought Florrie. She didn't want to force Emmie to go and, after all, it was Meggie's fault that she'd had to resort to such ends.

"Well, Emmie doesn't have to go again but until I'm sure you'll stay away from that Simon Griffith, Meggie, you'll still have to go. And Emmie, how did you get all these pine needles on your coat?"

They both went red and eventually had to tell Florrie where they had been, carefully leaving out the bit about the boys going to Sunday school.

"We just wanted to see what Dad does at the Home Guard, that's all," Emmie wheedled.

Florrie seemed satisfied and the excuse was more successful coming from Emmie as she had much more sway with their mother.

Dai arrived home in time for the BBC news that night, bringing with him a huge muddy eel for Florrie to fry up for his supper. "Here, slap this in the pan, missus," he ordered her, as he poured himself a glass of home brew. With the pong of hot lard and frying eel permeating the house Dai tuned into London for the war news.

In the Battle of the Atlantic German submarines had now been ordered to withdraw from the North Atlantic marking the end of the U-boat wolf packs. This meant that Britain would now receive more of the much-needed supplies essential for her survival. When the Atlantic battle had reached its climax earlier in '43 the German U Boats had sunk 120 Allied Merchant ships and attacked a further convoy of 42 ships thus sending 13 more ships to the ocean bottom. Nearer to home the news was not good. A Japanese submarine had been captured in Sydney Harbour. The Yellow Peril seemed not so far away at all.

Since Singapore had fallen in 1942 the Japanese Army had swept through the Philippines, Java, Dutch East Indies, Sumatra and Burma. In the Battle of the Java Sea the Allies lost 12 warships, this being yet another victory to Japan. Thousands of captured New Zealanders and Australians were now experiencing the barbarism in the Japanese POW camps. In those camps they died a slow despairing death and later Navy pictures, beyond the power of words, would show the total lack of humanity in how the Japanese had treated these prisoners.

With the capture of the Japanese submarine in the Sydney Harbour the threat of a Japanese invasion was now on everyone's lips. A rumour that the Japs were going to land at Raglan sped through the little townships. The New Zealand Army directed the Glen Afton Home Guard to set up blocks on the roads and bridges coming in from the Raglan coast. Huge logs were transported out to Waingaro and Mill Roads and the Home Guard men worked nightly setting them into place across the metal roads. It was clear that the roadblocks would only slow Japanese vehicles as their foot soldiers could easily walk around the sides of the logs. A large pine log and a timber jack with a crank handle were delivered to the site of the Waingaro Bridge and on Sundays the Home Guard men, who were not working shifts in the mines, practiced the swinging of the log across the entry to the bridge and back again. That was followed with the continuation of the war drill done out at Matera Beach near the Raglan coast. An American base was set up on the site of the old brickworks at Glen Massey which had formally been The China Clay and Porcelain Company Limited and had closed somewhere in the 1920s. The local girls were warned not to associate with the randy Yanks living on the base. This camp was formed as an effort to prevent the Japanese from reaching the Hopuhopu Army Camp and the Te Rapa Air Force Base near Hamilton. Further north military camps had been formed at beaches that were thought to be potential landing places for the Japanese.

At school the teachers seemed uneasy and distracted and war drill for the kids was stepped up to several times daily. Meggie continued to attend Sunday school alone and Simon came to walk her home but only as far as Snake Gully afterwards. Meggie would take the pictures and caricatures she'd drawn of local people to show Simon. At that time he seemed to be the only person interested in her artistic talent.

One morning Miss Kalman called the roll and then beckoned Brian Harmon to the front of the classroom to give his morning talk. New Zealand birds were the subject of the talks this week. The class was exceptionally quiet as they waited for Brian to unfold the dirty scrap of paper that he had retrieved from his trouser pocket. With a perfectly straight face he began to speak.

"The bird I have chosen to talk about is the New Zealand jail bird." He looked around eagerly to see what affect his opening sentence had on the class. There were a few sniggers and a nasty frown crossed Miss Kalman's pretty face but she allowed Brian to continue. "The New Zealand jail bird is white with black arrows all over him and he spends his time breaking up rocks."

"That yer old man?" shouted Bigfoot Rayner, above the loud giggling in the classroom. "He was away fer safebreaking, wasn't he?"

Brian's father had indeed served time for that crime but was now appreciated when at the mine office the safe jammed the office staff knew they could depend on Ron Harmon to do the job. He was often called away from his mine shift to help in this way.

"Enough! Enough!" squealed Miss Kalman, as she jumped up from her chair. Her usually soft voice resembled a raucous birdcall. "Sit down, you stupid, stupid boy," she squawked at Brian Harmon. "I should have known better than to expect a sensible morning talk from you."

Most of the kids felt sorry for Miss Kalman, as they knew she was really worried about a Japanese invasion. It was rumoured that when the Japs got here they would castrate all the men and rape all the women, then bayonet them as they had done in Singapore.

For the last six months Wilma Kalman had been walking out with Bluey Knowles, a handsome young farmer from out on the Waingaro Road. That rumour had worried Bluey immensely and with such a real concern he had been successful in persuading Wilma to taste the fruits of their love before the wily sons of Tojo arrived and took away his manhood. Wilma Kalman had not only the imminent arrival of the Japanese to worry about at this time but also the stirrings of a new life within her.

Miss Kalman drew herself up to full height and took control again. "I'll have Mr. Short deal with you after playtime, Brian," she said in a softer, less tearful, tone. "I am heartily sick and tired of you disrupting this class."

Brian received 6 of the best from Mr. Short but he reckoned the strap hadn't hurt much at all.

The Colliery tip-truck backed up to Florrie's gate and discharged the remaining coal into a pointed heap on the ground. Florrie coughed with dust caught in the back of her throat as she shoveled the shiny black lumps into the coalscuttle. She was out of coal and had been waiting for this load all day. Suddenly her eye caught pieces of dirty screwed up newspaper spread all through the heap. Immediately her thoughts went to Bill Ingman remembering Dai telling her that Bill, because of his social disease, was always being taken short underground. "This must be paper used by that filthy pig," she muttered. "I'm not using this coal."

Dai came in and washed his face under the sink tap. "What's happened to the fire, missus," he asked, noting that the room was cold and there was no dinner cooking on the stove. "The coal's here. Are ya too bloody lazy to get a bucketful?"

"I'm not using that dirty coal," Florrie said, pursing her lips into a crumpled line. "It's full of that filthy Bill Ingman's mess. Get the colliery to come and take it away."

Dai was at a loss for words. He had told Florrie about Bill's activities down the mine and went to inspect the coalpile himself. He came back with some of the paper and, chuckling to himself, informed Florrie that the offending scraps of paper were the dummies, rolled up newspaper filled with damp clay that was tamped in behind the plugs of dynamite and detonators. Florrie took some convincing but finally the dinner was boiling on the stove.

The next news to come was what the country had been waiting for. The Prime Minister, having twice postponed an election because of the war, announced there would be a general election in October. This was followed by the news that the Government would bring home New Zealand soldiers for 3 months' furlough. It was not a popular decision with the Army who were worried about losing too many battle experienced men and would have preferred the furlough be taken in the Mediterranean. But with an election looming the Prime Minister could see an opportunity to win public favour and brought 6000 men home to vote in the October election.

American Marines were still hard in training for island hopping on the New Zealand beaches and hills. As the battle weary Kiwi soldiers returned they were appalled at how much their Godzone country had changed in the three years they had been away. The city streets were full of American Marines, in their glamorous uniforms and with pockets full of money, paying too much attention to their girlfriends and wives. The joy of their homecoming soon soured and resentment between the New Zealand soldiers and the American Marines began to fester. Inevitably fights broke out in Auckland and there followed in Wellington the infamous Manners Street Battle, which lasted for four long hours.

CHAPTER SIX

There was a telegram amongst the mail that Meggie collected from the Post Office. Florrie immediately decided it must contain bad news and hesitated to open the brown envelope. She felt sure it would be about her young brother, John, who was fighting overseas in the Middle East. John had never been one for writing letters and her only news of him was from their mother, Nana Bowen, and the military Xmas card.

"It'll be from Mum," she muttered, as she turned the envelope over again and again. "God. What's happened to him?" she wailed. "He can't be dead. He just can't be!" And tears sprang into her eyes.

"Do you want me to open it, Mum?" Meggie asked.

Florrie didn't answer. A happier thought had come into her mind. "Maybe he's coming home with the big contingent Mr. Fraser's bringing home for three months furlough. I suppose Mum wants us to come down to the farm to see him."

Florrie smoothed down her pinny and became her put-upon self again. "Well, he'll have to come here if he wants to see me. Mum must know we can't get rail passes."

With that she tore open the brown envelope and extracted the yellow telegram from inside, then smiled,

"It's not bad news, Meggie," she said quite kindly. "Your Granddad Morgan is coming to stay for a few days. He'll be here on tomorrow afternoon's train."

"Oh, beaut." Meggie jumped around excitedly. "I'll meet the train tomorrow."

***

TROEDYRHIW SOUTH WALES 1884

If old Jack Morgan, Meggie's paternal grandfather, was to be remembered for anything it would he for his tenacity. For never letting go of any injustice once he'd sunk his teeth into it. He had been then, and still was now despite his age, like a dog with a bone once he'd taken up a cause. Rarely did he ever let go until he was satisfied that justice had been done. He had been still classed as a new immigrant to New Zealand when the miner's Go-Slow, during the First World War, took place and in the trial that followed, Jack, then President of the New Zealand Miners' Union, and five other miners from Huntly, had been arrested and jailed for their part in that

Go-Slow. Jack Morgan was very much the product of his environment. He'd been born into a world of poverty and disillusionment, backbreaking work, pittance wages, long hours that were a miner's life, all to make huge profits for English mine owners. In South Wales the rapacious English had laid waste to valley after valley in their search for coal.

That Jack had been forced into pit work as a small boy was something that would be etched on his mind forever. He remembered with chilling shivers that miserable day he had accompanied his ailing Mam underground, a day that marked the beginning of his working life and the end of his Mam's. That cold, grey morning his Mam had been so ill she could barely stand, let alone lead a pit pony. She'd taken him, Jack, her eight-year-old son, down the pit to help her.

Further and further they'd stumbled into the airless bowels of the earth and with each step the panic within him grew, until finally, when the mine mouth was nothing more than a pinprick of light, his thin body shuddered and he let out a frightened wail.

"Come now, bachgen!" The effort of speaking in the foul underground air sent Marghed Morgan into another paroxysm of coughing. A resounding chorus of coughs and spits from the coalface joined his Mam. Silicosis sang its sad song beneath the Welsh ground again that morning. "There'll be no wage if we don't keep going, cariad," Marghed gasped between coughs. "We must keep going, bachgen. We must!"

He'd screamed when she collapsed and the men carried her from the mine. He'd wanted to stay with her, go with the men, anything to escape from the death-hole that threatened to close in and crush the life from his own thin body too. But the men had urged him to stay and keep the pony going.

"You'll do better to keep the earnin's comin' in, boyo," Daffydd Jones had told him. "You must he brave for your Mam now, bachgen."

And Jack had replied by retching his miserly breakfast crust onto the pit floor.

"What's this then?" Taff the Rail, who had slipped home for a quick pipe just as the blackened miners carried his unconscious sister into the house, had asked.

"She's no good no more," one of the men sighed, shaking his head. "We'll leave the boyo with the pony for now."

Taffy laid his sister out on the wooden settle in the front room of their stone cottage. Cold it was, stone. So thin and frail she looks, he thought, gently tucking a woollen shawl around the limp frame, skin darkened by a fine layer of coal dust. She'd been unconscious for a long time now and that worried Taff. He walked over to the window and looked out at the grimy monochrome scene before him. Row upon row of grey terraced houses, crouched together, each opening directly on to the street, climbed every steep rise, and beyond the houses, the ugly scar of another pit. The land, as far as his sad eyes could see, was grey and disfigured by the workings of more ugly pits. There were no gardens, no colours to relieve the grey. Just the huddled houses, slagheaps and the collieries dominating and overpowering the poverty-stricken villages in the valleys.

Taff the Rail had considered himself a cut above the miners in Troedyrhiw. He was a bit of a snob, he supposed, but after all he had earned the better job at the railway because he had the skills to read and write. That was thanks to his wonderful Mam, passed on now she had. Taff was one of the few people in Troedyrhiw who could read and write. In fact, he was one of the few in the whole of the valley who had such skills. But now, as he scanned the dismal landscape, waiting for his beloved sister to regain consciousness, he had to accept that he was no different. We are all in the same boat 'ere. Slaves to the bloody English, he thought bitterly. We're all trapped like bloody rats in a sewer. Anger at his sister's condition and the unfairness of their lot, licked through him like a flame melting lard, causing the vile tasting gall – an ailment that seemed to be with him daily now – to rise again in his throat. Like acid it was.

Is there never goin' to be a way out? Are we destined to be born 'ere, generation after generation, just to toil and die before our time? Die – from what? Well, it was choice they had. It could be the miners' lung disease, or they could die of the cold, or of hunger, or of just plain bloody despair. Indeed it was some reward after spending lifetimes extracting wealth from the ground to keep the bloody English rich.

"Englishmen!" Taff spat the name out loud. Englishmen, all soft hands and clean nails they were, with their fashionable clothes and carriages and condemning the Welsh people to wretched lives of beggary. And just whose wealth was it anyway? Not the bloody English, that was certain. They were thieves. Just bloody thieves purloining from the poor.

It could not be right for a man to spend his life in darkness, digging in the bowels of the earth, a miners lamp his only source of light, and then receive no more than the merest fraction of the wealth, hardly even enough to keep body and soul together. There's where the real sin lies; Taff mused, not in the rubbish the preachers concocted on Chapel Sundays. Taff turned and looked again at the face of his sister. And most certainly it was not right for a woman to be sentenced, like a criminal, to a life underground.

Marghed's mouth had taken on a bluish look and the cheek hollows looked even more cavernous.

"Duw," he whispered. "Duw! She's gone. To join our darlin' Mam." He bent forward to close her eyes, remembering at that moment how beautiful she had been. "Ie, cariad," he murmured. "Gone somewhere where there is no dust to fill your lungs and throat and guts. No gas to rot your innards. No wet that keeps your bones chilled day and night.

And who among the ruling classes," he asked out loud. "Who of the unstained hand brigade, would know, let alone care, that they had in essence, murdered another human bein' today."

Wickedly it had been done too. Wickedly, by depriving her of sunlight, of fresh air, working her too long and too hard when there was nothing in her belly to sustain her. Yes, murder it was to his mind as surely as the mine owner had taken a gun in his delicate white hands and shot his sister. Tears gathered in Taffy's eyes, but did nothing to melt the hard lump that pressed against his ribs. Nor did they take away the sour bile that filled his mouth. That's what poverty did to the human soul. Hardened and numbed the spirit until nothing meant anything anymore. Duw, but she was surely better off gone, he thought, as he draped the shawl up over Marghed's bloodless face. God knows it wasn't much of a life she'd had. And some of it had been down to him. Oh, yes. Guilt still lived with him. For hadn't it been himself who had invited that rascal Gypo into this house. Shouldn't he, being the older, have had sense enough to know that the handsome Didikai Morgan would do no more than seduce his beautiful guileless young sister. Didikai had at least spared Marghed the added shame of illegitimacy by giving the child a name. The irony was Marghed, at fifteen, had been little more than a child herself.

"Protect her I will," he remembered his promise to their Mam on her deathbed.

Oh, so beautiful she was then. Like a rosebud about to open into full bloom when Didikai had plucked her. Mind you, Didikai Morgan hadn't been the only man interested in his beautiful sister. If it had been known what the other young lad's thoughts were, well, respectable they were not.

Didikai wasn't a bad person. Deep down Taff knew that. It was just that the wanderlust in his Romany blood was too strong to hold him to a woman in a miserable coal-mining village. For him there were still green meadows to roam, woods to be hunted, brooks to be fished, and songs still to be sung by the roving Gypsies. Passing through he'd only been when he came to Troedyrhiw, when he'd sowed the seed that had condemned Marghed, and the child, to a life of toil. Taff had learned at Chapel that was how the devil worked but he'd learned since, from life, that God did not do a whole lot better. Didikai, for all his fickle ways, at least was no slave to any wealthy English mine owner. Taff walked to the window again with tears flowing. Even the sky was grey in this dismal valley. By way of death Marghed had escaped, but Taff knew it was too late for him. Much good his reading had done him. All the fine books on socialism, workers' parties, and a government of workers for workers. Hummph. He having sat by with the fine words and theories in his mind and watched his sister die perhaps made him as guilty as the mine owners that he accused. Maybe he could make amends by seeing that the boyo didn't fall into the same trap. "I'll educate him," he resolved. "I'll educate him myself and see that he doesn't rot in the valleys as you and I have done," he whispered softly to the form of his dead sister.

CHAPTER SEVEN

There was a raw feel to the September wind that funneled through the Railway Station and Jack Morgan pulled his coat collar higher. The clatter of heavy boots reminded him why he too was at the Auckland Railway Station today. Khaki clad men, kitted out for war, spewed out of the troop train even before the sooty carriages came to a standstill. The big Ka engine panted and squealed, finally coming to a halt beside Platform A.

The sight of the soldiers had Jack call to mind again his telephone conversation with Langtry two nights ago. There was unrest brewing amongst these furlough men. From what Langtry had told him it was clear that Fraser was nothing other than a damned fool. Calling the soldiers deserters was absurd, especially coming from Fraser, himself with his anti-conscription history during the First World War.

Jack understood and sympathized with the protests of these men. They were battle weary. They'd done enough, seen enough. Even Freyberg had said of his soldiers, 'they've fought well –

they've done their stuff.' Why should they go back and risk their lives for a second time, and for what – a miserable seven shillings a day. They'd come home on leave to discover there were 38,000 fit men that had never been conscripted and this was the basis of their quarrel. Thirty-eight thousand were working in essential industries and not for a miserable seven shillings either. Oh no. They were drawing a good fifteen and sixteen pound a week. No wonder the boyos had their backs up. Of course Langtry was totally against conscription and he and Fraser had already quarreled over the issue.

Frank Langtry and Jack Morgan had a lot in common. They'd both known the taste of poverty. Both came from backgrounds of want and destitution. Langtry was right as far as Jack could see. Fraser, by introducing the 'furlough scheme', had introduced trouble. Why hadn't he heeded the Army's recommendation and let the tired fighting men recuperate in the Mediterranean? It seemed logical that from there the soldiers would surely have returned to continue to fight the war.

Coinciding with tens of thousands of US troops in New Zealand to train for island hopping, the furlough could not have been more badly timed. City streets bulged with Yanks with a girl on each arm and too much money in their pockets. Could you blame our poorly paid lads for feeling cheated? At the protest meeting Jack had attended yesterday the soldiers' words rang loudly around the smoke filled Town Hall, "We'll go back to fight when the rest of the yellow bellied bastards have been and done their bit."

Disenchantment was rife among these returned men. They felt cheated, deceived. And when they had protested, Fraser called them deserters! Duw. It had been a sad day for the country when Mickey Savage had passed away.

After the meeting Jack had immediately acquired himself a train pass, on Federation business, to Glen Afton to see just what was happening at the coalface. According to some sources the outback valleys were full of shirkers hiding behind a protected industry. Well, Jack thought, I'll kill two birds with the one stone. I'll pay Dai and Florrie a visit, time I saw the granddaughters again, and at the same time ascertain what truth there was in the allegations amongst the essential industry mine workers.

A glance at the station clock told him it was time to board the hissing train at the platform. Showing his rail pass he strode on through the ornate doors and walked beside the huffing train until he found his carriage. Once settled he flicked through the latest Free Lance. The train chuffed out of the station gathering speed. Clickety clack ta took ta took. Clickety clack ta took ta took. The rhythm distracted him. He placed the journal on his lap and looked out the carriage window. His mind sped back to his childhood in Troedyrhiw. That bleak place where he'd grown up on slag heaps. The dark cold villages that had no green, a stark contrast to the lush pastures and trees that flashed past his window today. Heaven forbid this lush land should ever be turned into grey slag heaps and rusting iron as the mine owners had done in South Wales…

They'd lived beside the railway tracks back there in Troedyrhiw. Jack, his Mam and Uncle Taff the Rail. So young his Mam had died. Just twenty-three she'd been and he a lad of only eight when she'd passed. And already down the pit himself. Now here he was marching on towards a grand sixty-seven years himself. Uncle Taffy had looked after him then, taught him to read and write. Been hard on him, mind, he had as far as his learnin' was concerned. But Taff had known that without those skills Jack would have joined the rest of the village folks in living and dying right there.

Uncle Taff had acted like a man with a mission back in the days following his Mam's dying. Guilty, he was, Jack knew now. Jack had stayed in the pit albeit the deputy foreman had transferred him into operating the ventilating shafts because he was of small stature. So his youth had been spent in pitch black, opening and closing the heavy doors to let the horses hauling their cargoes of coal through, and each evening Taff had the lessons ready, never letting Jack have a night off, sickness or no. And tired though he always was after a full day beneath the ground, Jack soon found he had an aptitude for book learning.

The memories of the first days of Socialism began to live again in Jack's mind. The excitement of those early socialist meetings held in drafty, cold halls. The forming of the Trade Unions and the bitter fights for decent wages and better conditions that followed. Those were the days when royalty and the capitalists held the sway in the Empire and the new colonies. Oh, yes, he'd had fire in his belly back then. Moving up fast in the ranks of the Trade Unions and the I.L.P. he eventually became involved in the campaign that saw Kier Hardie, the Father of the Labour Movement, win the Merthyr Tydfil seat in 1900. The following year he'd led the hostile miners down the Rhondda marching for better wages and conditions. He could hear the tramp, tramp, tramp of hundreds of pairs of boots in his head right now. After the Rhondda Valley riots leaders, like Jack, had been singled out by the mine owners and heavily leaned upon. They had their ways like arranging to send the rebels to the furthest edge of the working face, therefore making it a less productive day, or to a face where the coal was so hard, again, less was produced in a day.

Jack was still musing on the memories when the train braking brought him back to the present. At the Mercer Refreshment Station he fought his way through the throng of travellers, successfully making his way back to his carriage gripping a thick railway cup of tea with a soggy slice of fruitcake on the saucer. This'll have to do for lunch, he thought. He would need to change trains at Huntly in order to take the branch line to Glen Afton. He emptied the slopped tea from the saucer back into the cup and smiled again as he thought of the days when he was lucky if he could take underground for his crib two sandwiches and a bottle of cold tea

Duw, that was going back some, wasn't it now. Over thirty years since he'd left the Rhondda Valley and arrived at the West Coast mines looking for work. Conditions in New Zealand hadn't been that different from the old country; except that was a hell of a lot more crib than he'd ever taken down the pit in Troedyrhiw. His arrival at Blackball had coincided with a dispute over crib time and it wasn't long before his past caught up with him. Socialists Webb and Hickey discovered his Wales involvement with the Unions and the I.L.P. and began pressuring him to become active in their newly formed Socialist Party.

"Fer Godzake, man," Bob Semple had urged in raw Australian intonations. "With yer background yer surely not siding with the bloody parasites who own the companies, are yer?"

The suggestion had stung Jack to the quick. It would be so easy to get involved. The fire was still in his belly. But he had to think of Medwyn, the wife he'd left in Wales, and their six young ones. She'd instructed him the day he had set sail from England, "Work hard, cariad, and save the money to bring us to New Zealand."

So he'd answered Bob in his musical Welsh accent, "Now look you, mun, I left the valleys to be free of agitation …"

But Semple cut across Jack's soft Welsh lilt with a loud poooff sound, "Jeezes, man. Agitation! That's all these bloody ruling classes understand."

Da de da took took. Da de da took took. The clacking of the train wheels crawling over the swamplands that sloped away to the Waikato River cut across Jack's thoughts. He knocked his pipe noisily on the cast iron arm of the carriage seat. A passenger across the aisle glared disapprovingly at him. He nodded apologetically and slipped the warm pipe into his jacket pocket. The train began gathering speed again only to squeal to a shuddering halt at the next station. Nearly there, he thought. Only three more stops before Huntly.

Huntly. He knew Huntly well. It had been to Huntly that Medwyn and the children had come, when they finally arrived from Wales, some ten years after himself.

It had taken him that long to save enough money for their fares. He hadn't recognized his children. And Medwyn, she had grown old and drawn and who would wonder why. How hard she'd worked to raise their children. He coloured with shame when he thought of his faithful Medwyn, taken two years ago with the cancer. She'd had more courage in her little finger than he possessed in his whole body. Fighter for justice he might have been, but would he have the mettle to do as she had done, to cross an ocean of battlefields on the other side of the world, with their six children, to join him. No, he would not have had such courage.

Nor could he have told her he'd been a faithful husband in those years apart. There had been more reason than Unions and politics as to why he had left Blackball. There'd also been his indiscretion with Molly Black, the hotelier's wife. He could hear her squeals now …

"EEEEK! Stop!" she'd shrieked, as Jack had pressed his muscled leg hard against her soft thigh, whirling her dizzily around the Blackball Miners Hall, swinging her off her feet. He inhaled a whiff of scent, mingled with her woman's glow, and the smell had stirred arousal in him, reminding him he'd been without a woman far too long.

He walked her home that night after the dance. Outside the night was fresh and somewhat cooling to his ardour. But not so with Molly! They'd walked slowly arm in arm towards Black's Hotel, a timber slab building on the main street of Blackball. Jack felt comfortable with her. If he was to have been truthful he had admired Molly Black for some time, but had never dreamt he'd be walking her home from a dance. Molly maneuvered him into the dark recess of the hotel doorway and murmured huskily, "Darling Jack."

Then she kissed him, long and sweet, her lips as luscious as any juicy berry. He'd walked back to his boarding house slowly with Molly's throaty invitation still fresh in his ears.

"Be on the bush track tomorrow at two," she'd breathed.

Jack enjoyed the walk up into the bush that hugged the rugged hills around the tiny mining settlement of Blackball. The well-worn track twisted and turned through dark tunnels formed by dense bush canopies where only a little afternoon sun could penetrate. In the sun-dappled stretches where ponga and ferns fringed the track, cheeky fantails flittered and twittered. My God, he thought. What a contrast to the grey Welsh mining towns. God forbid this beauty ever be reduced to that of the scarred valleys of Wales.

Jack didn't see Molly at first. She could have been observing him from the carpet of leaves for some time. The green frock, that flattered her bright red hair, lost her in the thick green of the bush behind. He lowered himself to the ground beside her.

"Duw, and I thought that last night was only a dream," he began, liltingly.

She slithered towards him. "This is no dream," she murmured, as her lips found his.

His firm full mouth was as delicious as she'd remembered from the night before. After being subjected to Harry's wet beery slopping's, kissing Jack was like drinking nectar from the Gods. Jack placed his hands either side of her face closing her eyes with his fingertips. He eased his mouth around hers gently kissing the outline of her lips. He felt her shiver as he parted her mouth with his tongue.

Molly responded in a way she had no control over. Jack ran his hands from her face down along her spine to the hem of her dress. She gasped as he lifted it.

"Jack," she moaned.

He silenced her with his mouth and slipped his fingers inside her underwear. The leaves felt damp on her exposed skin. Jack had unfastened himself. Very gently he eased himself onto her and cupping his hands around her hips he ever so slowly entered. She cried out, the intense pleasure of him taking her breath away. She gripped his body with her thighs, arching her spine, and slowly Jack began to move inside her.

"Darling Jack," escaped from her in a throaty whisper. Desperate for him not to stop she held his waist, scraping her nails down his muscled flesh. When she began to move with him she closed her eyes, the eyelids flickering as the pace increased. He felt her shudder and as her whole body became tense he finally allowed the life to flow out of him …

Jack shook himself as the memory faded. Duw, what an affair that had been, that was until Harry Black got wind of them. So he'd left Blackball with a black eye and under a bit of a cloud. Arriving in Huntly he'd thrown himself headlong into Unions and politics. Then had come the Waihi strike. Duw, there they'd conscripted scab labour from the pubs, the jails, and even the doss houses. It was there his countryman, Evans, had been killed. What year was that now, Jack mused. Nineteen-twelve, if his memory served him right. Yes, that was it, for the next year, nineteen-thirteen, unexpected and unwanted came the wharf strike. September the following year, World War One, described as the war to end all wars had begun. And here we all are thirty years on and involved in another World War to end all wars!!

The go-slow in 1917 had earned him a stretch in Mt Eden prison. The coalmines had also been essential industry back then but not with the high wage the miners earned now. They were a new generation of workers today. The old timers had gone, along with the sugar bag and sandshoe days. Now the workers had a decent wage and security with Labour Government in office. So why was Fraser so hell-bent on buggering things up, pitting soldier against worker. In Jack's opinion if Fraser's brains were made of gunpowder there wouldn't be enough to lift off his hat.

The steel wheels squealed as the steam engine jerked to a halt at Huntly. Carriages clanged and groaned from the guardsvan down, as each carriage became responsible for stopping the one behind. The mighty engine, now motionless, breathed a hollow chuff, chuff, as though the journey so far had exhausted the huge iron horse. Jack crossed the railway lines and settled himself in the Glen Afton branch line shelter. Soon the 3.30pm snorted its way past the branch line station and after what seemed like miles of empty coal wagons the train finally halted two passenger carriages and a guardsvan most accurately beside the concrete platform. Jack stopped the Guard as he jumped out of the van.

"Jack Morgan, from the Federation," he introduced himself.

Jack knew it was a pretty safe bet to acquaint the Guard with his political leanings with Huntly being almost totally red. Ernie Laurence held out his hand. He'd heard of Jack Morgan from the Federation. "Howja do," he bellowed, being used to talking above railway noises. "Pleased ta meetcha."

The two men shook hands with firm strong grips. "Jump inta the guardsvan if yer like. We'll have a cuppa tea when we get under way."

This was great, exactly what Jack had hoped for. He made himself comfortable and waited for Ernie to reappear. A long, shrill whistle from Ernie was answered with two resounding whoops from the engine standing stationary halfway across the high wooden road/rail bridge. Inside the firebox swung open spilling red dancing light as the fireman fed the flames. The whistle blew once more and the engine jerked its contingent into motion. Within minutes they were clattering across the huge wooden structure that bridged the darkly menacing Waikato River. Once off the bridge the long train puffed and tooted through the flat farmlands, skirted the edge of Lake Waahi on towards the raw outback mining townships.

Ernie poured the tea from a thermos. "This rationing's a bastard," he muttered, as he laced the tea heavily with sugar substitute.

"Here ya are." Ernie handed Jack a stained bakelite cup full of steaming tea. "Well, what do yer think, Jack? About the election next month? Reckon Labour will pull it off again? Should do with that galoot Fraser bringing the boys back to vote."

He'd answered his own question. Instinct told Jack to be careful. Yes, he was in Labour territory but Ernie's tone wasn't endearing towards the Prime Minister. He obviously thought him a bloody fool, too.

"Don't know, mun. Don't know. Might be best to stay with the War Cabinet until the whole business is over."

"Come on, Jack. Yer must know something. Yer ain't bin sent down here for nothin'." Ernie cast a suspicious look at Jack.

"No. No. Mun. I'm 'ere to see my family, you see."

"No kiddin'!" Ernie wasn't convinced. "I didn't know ya had relations out the back."

"Oh yes. Got a son and his family at Glen Afton. Didikai Morgan."

"Di ... D'yer mean Dai Morgan?" Ernie stuttered.

He could hardly believe his ears. Jack Morgan, big in the Federation, father of that boozing Dai Morgan. He took a large swig of the sweet tea to hide his surprise. "Yip," he said after a swallow. "Everyone knows Dai Morgan."

So Dai had already made a name for himself. Everywhere he went he seemed to attract trouble like a magnet. Jack had surely been accurate when he had named him after the father he had never known. The raggle taggle Gypsy who had breezed through Troedyrhiw and left behind him a child, himself Jack Morgan. For sure the same restless blood ran through his Dai's veins.

The men remained silent for a while, Jack sensing he had struck a wrong chord in the mentioning of his son Didikai Morgan. They passed dark piles of sleepers and rails and the maintenance men waved from their jiggers as they ceased to work while the train went through. Leaving Pukemiro Junction the engine whooped loudly as they left behind the flatter land to cut through the side of a hill. At Glen Afton Jack swung down from the guardsvan to find Meggie waiting for him on the platform.

"Granddad," she squealed.

Jack scooped her to him in a bear hug. "My word, cariad. I didn't recognize you. Indeed and you are almost all grown up now."

Meggie blushed. "Emmie didn't come," she said. "She's got a cold but she's waiting for you at home."

"And have you picked enough blackberries for my pie?"

Meggie giggled. "It's not blackberry season, Granddad."

"Duw, now. Silly me. Where's Da?"

"He's still at work," she answered, struggling with his big suitcase.

Jack stopped her. "Ere. You take my portmanteau, cariad. I'll carry this one."

The pair walked slowly across the overhead bridge with Meggie chattering continuously. "That's the Hogs Head down there."

Jack followed her finger with his eyes.

"It looks like the General Store to me."

"That's what makes it so spooky. The door to get in is at the back and only men are allowed in there. Mum calls it the Pigs Pen. She reckons she wouldn't go in there even if she was invited."

Jack smiled. He could just hear Florrie saying that.

"I suppose Dad goes there a lot, does he?" Jack asked.

"He does now. But before he couldn't because Mr. Hubbard banned him. He lets him in now, though. And guess what else, Granddad? You're giving a speech in the Hogs Head tonight. And Mum said she hopes you've brought your ration book with you."

Jack smiled again. That sounded like Florrie worrying about making the food go around. He had brought his ration book and two tins of nut butter additive that made the butter go twice as far so that should please her. He'd even managed to acquire a bag full of frosted caramels for the girls. They walked on past the colliery houses with truckloads of coal dumped at every back door. Duw, what luxury, Jack thought. Damn Dai arranging a speech tonight. He hadn't had time to evaluate the situation. He'd have to be mighty careful he didn't put his foot in it.

Dai decided to drive his father the short distance to the Hogs Head. He was anxious to promote his position with the Home Guard vehicle. Word soon spread that an important Union Official was visiting the district and that brought a large crowd of neighbouring Pukemiro Colliery workers to the hostelry that was already bulging at the seams. As they walked into the dingy back room the rowdy buzz of voices silenced. Dai thrust a ten bob note onto the bar.

"Knock that out," he ordered Skeety Hill, the barman, in a voice full of authority.

Jack tamped down and lit his pipe, at the same scanning the room from under lowered lids. He noted Mickey Savage's photograph, like that of a saint, dominating the wall above the open fireplace. Rhys Evans sidled up to Dai.

"This yer Da then?" he crooned. He had a lovely Welsh voice; everything he said was music

"Yep. Da meet Rhys," he introduced the pair. "He's from the Rhondda too."

"Where abouts in the valleys do you come from?" Jack asked.

"Treorchy I was born."

The two men settled down at a table and became engaged in memories of the bad old days in Wales. Others joined their table and soon Jack was regaling them with talk. Dai downed his beer in one long swallow and thumped the glass on the bar. Wiping the back of his hand across his mouth he gazed intently at his empty glass. "C'mon. Fill this bastard again," he shouted to Skeety Hill.

Then, with certain envy, he looked across at his father, yarning and smoking with the locals. That's how it had always been with Jack. He just settled in anywhere and before long had everyone hanging on his every word. Dai, desperate to regain the attention held his hand up for silence. "Quiet," he bellowed.

The loud buzzing lessened as Dai captured the drinkers' attention. Chook Anderson staggered about with two jugs of homebrew and was ordered to sit down and shut up. When at last he commanded silence Dai continued. "Comrades and friends," he bawled. "I give you the past President of the New Zealand Miners' Union, Dominion Executive of the Labour Party," ... he paused looking around his fellow miners' for effect ... "and Secretary to the Federation of Labour ... I give you ... me old man, Jack Morgan."

He ended with a bow and an expansive wave of his hand and the miners responded with loud clapping and whistling. Jack had had enough time to assess his audience well, noting first that the crowd comprised almost entirely older men, immigrants from the old country, so he felt safe to fault the young miners who seemingly had little interest in the harsh conditions of the old days in mining. Conditions that all these present would remember only too well.

"Friends and fellow mine workers," Jack began keeping a careful eye on the crowd as he launched into his speech, quickly earning their silence as he shared his views for some 20 minutes … "and the young ones, born here in far better conditions than we their fathers, and grandfathers from the old country ever knew. They have grown up in good times, and now a war, demanding ever larger amounts of coal than the miners of New Zealand can satisfy. They have had a decent wage and security with a Labour Government."

Jack paused, tapping his teeth with his pipe as he scanned the room through narrowed eyes for the effect of his speech. It looked good so he continued. "Generous overtime after the forty-hour week, sweat time for moist conditions, wet time for working in ankle deep water, dust time for the dust filled atmosphere. Compo, higher wages, and extra time for smoko and lunch breaks. Do they acknowledge that they only have them because we, their forefathers, fought for them? Or have they taken them for granted?"

Jack finished with the questions in his musical Welsh. A roar of applause exploded, followed by a rumble of boots on the floor, catcalls and cheers, in the backroom of Ed Hubbard's Store.

"'Ear, 'ear! Bloody Oath, the young ones are goin' soft on it. Only interested in horseracing and beer."

"And the sheilahs," someone else called.

Laughter snorted through the room followed by some rather unsavoury comments about women. Dai leaned heavier on the bar. He was proud of his father, but he was also very jealous. He'd never had that tongue, that intensity that could hold crowds silent, receptive, and spellbound. Skeety Hill filled his glass again and he downed it in a swallow.

"Whatcha really here for, Jack?" demanded a voice from the back of the room. A silence fell as the crowd waited for his answer.

"Well. Indeed to goodness, that's a poser now, isn't it." Jack smiled at his audience as he jabbed his finger in the bowl of his pipe. He would have to be careful here, and then again, he couldn't treat them like idiots either or he'd have a bloody riot on his hands.

"Well, you see, it's one of two things. Is it to visit with my family or it is to find out if you are a pack of no good boyos. And you'll never know which now, will you, mun."

The majorities seemed amused by his reply and settled down to enjoy a good evening on the booze.

Dai parked the truck and dropped Jack off outside the mine house, then returned to the Hogs Head. He'd arranged with Chook and Bill to take some booze out to Waingaro. Florrie didn't seem

112

surprised that Dai had returned to the club and Jack wondered just what sort of a life she and the girls had in this outback valley with his son. Meggie and Emmie were still making newspaper spills for him to light his pipe from. They'd filled a large cardboard box, which he'd never use up if he stayed the week, but bless them for making them.

Florrie switched on the radio to catch the local and BBC news. The allies had landed in Italy. America's First Lady, Eleanor Roosevelt was visiting New Zealand and at Rotorua she had rubbed noses with Guide Rangi. Her recorded speech was broadcast.

"Many of the women at home would like, I think, to send a message to the women of New Zealand," she said in American twang, "because so many of our boys have been stationed here that they know already how hospitable and kind the women of this country have been to the sons and husbands and brothers of the women in the United States."

Jack smiled wryly. He'd witnessed the hospitality in Auckland's darkened shop doorways and in his opinion the sons, husbands and brothers of the United States were doing a fine job of educating the women of New Zealand's straight-laced society. He thanked goodness that his granddaughters were too young to be ruined by some randy Yank.

Florrie switched off the wireless and made a cup of tea. Miners and the elderly were granted extra tea rations so a supper pot didn't cut into the rations too much. It was after eleven before Jack and Florrie said goodnight and still no sign of Dai coming home. Tomorrow Jack would have a word with his son.

CHAPTER EIGHT

Dai woke in his dishevelled bed with a pounding head, bleary eyes and a parched mouth. He screwed his eyes up against the blinding daylight. It took some little while for him to realize what a mess he had been last night at the Hogs Head. He couldn't remember where he had gone after that or how he'd come home. What was becoming abundantly clear was that Florrie had abandoned the marital bed as the realization of what was sticky on his face and person was vomit smelling of sour meths and distilled whiskey.

He lifted his head slightly to listen. The house was quiet. Focusing his eyes on the alarm clock told him the time was midday. He reached for his tin of makings and with unsteady hands managed to roll a cigarette. Slowly painfully he eased himself out of the bed and staggered towards the kitchen. The heat that greeted him from the banked up stove almost knocked him over. He picked up a spill from the pile the girls had folded and with trembling hands he poked it into the firebox embers until it caught then lit his smoke. Mopsy, sleeping on the mat in front of the coalrange, opened one eye and peered at Dai.

"Git out, ya mangy fleabag," he snarled, at the same time giving the cat a feeble kick. Mopsy hissed at him and fled out the nearest window.

After a long harsh draw on the thin roll, memories began returning to him. Guilt-filled, he remembered that his father was staying and he had disgraced himself when he'd gone back to the Hog's Head last night. Florrie would be at work at the boarding-house, the girls at school, but he couldn't fathom where Jack would be. Maybe he'd caught the early train out, left in disgust! Dai went to the kitchen sink and washed himself noisily. Just then the back door opened as he splashed water around his head and face and Florrie, with a face like thunder, walked into the stifling kitchen.

"Why didn't you wake me, womun," he accused. "I've missed half a day's yakka now."

Dai knew it was best to attack first in this sort of situation and that then put the missus in the wrong. Florrie didn't answer. She went straight to the bedroom and began pulling the soiled sheets from the bed. Dai followed her ready to attack again. In one deft movement Florrie pushed his alcohol-weakened body onto the bed and rammed the foul stained sheets in his face, grinding them down with every bit of strength she possessed. Then, stopping only to retrieve her purse, she left the house and not knowing where to go or what to do she began to walk rapidly along the road to Pukemiro. When she reached the township she went into Fleming's General Store. She didn't know where else to go. Stan Fleming lifted his beetling eyebrows in surprise when he saw her. She looked troubled and he already knew why.

"Good heavens, Mrs. Morgan. You do look upset," he said kindly.

The story of Dai's escapade last night with that old metho, Missy Thompson, had raced like wildfire through the township barely before daybreak. Missy lived in a shack deep in the bush where she often entertained men, especially if they would buy meths for her. Most of the men were scared of her violent temper. It was reputed that in a drunken rage she had bitten off her husband's ear so he had left her. Stan could believe that when remembered the time Ed Hubbard had been brave enough to refuse to sell her any meths. That very same night, as Ed sat in the picture hall, Missy had come up behind him and whacked him over the head with an empty bottle knocking him out. And then there was the time when she was so crazed with meths, she held up the pay train carrying hundreds of pounds in wages for the miners. Ernie Laurence, the Guard, had thought it a great joke and told the story often.

"Well the engine had slowed ter take the last sharp bend before Jacko would open her up along the straight ta the Glen." Ernie would recount. "Yer shoulda seen her." Ernie would stop to guffaw. "There wus Missy standin' in the middle of the railway line with one of them wooden rifles the Home Guard uses fer trainin".

Ernie would have to stop again to control his gales of laughter before he could continue the story. "She raises tha' gun as the engine comes round the corner. Jacko couldn't slow down and she loses her nerve and she jumps out of the train's way. Ha Ha Ha." Ernie would wipe his eyes. "Well, Jacko pulled ta a halt when he saw Missy standin' there and by the time the old girl had stopped Missy wus right opposite me in the guardsvan."

"'Hand over the wages, Ernie,'" she yelled, pointin' the wooden gun at me. Well, I jumped down from the guardsvan. "What the hell are ya playing at, Missy," I said. "Don't yer know it's a serious offence ta hold up a train?"

"Jacko and the pay clerks were all hangin' out the windows watchin' and der ya know what she said?" Ha, Ha, Ha. Again Ernie would wipe the tears from his eyes. "She said, 'I only want the pay, that's all.'

"Well, I helped her up inta the guardsvan. 'Here I'll givya a lift back ta the Glen,' I said, and I signalled to Jacko to continue on down the line. Jacko and me laid her out in the waiting room at the station ta sleep it orf."

Stan had asked the Lord again on that occasion, as he had done on many times before, for some spiritual intervention to come into Missy's life. But it never had so he had accepted that she was beyond redemption. So is Dai Morgan, he thought now. They deserve each other.

Florrie could hear her heart beating a fast, incessant, thumping. She tried hard to answer calmly but instead burst into tears. Stan looked furtively around the shop and thankfully it was empty. He walked around the thick wooden counter and placing his arm around her shoulder, ushered her through to the back of the store and into his living quarters. When he had her safely out of sight he called to young Paul Brown, who was bagging up produce in the storeroom, to take over the counter for him.

Stan's wife had died long before the Morgan's had arrived in the Glen, leaving him alone with the shop. There had been no children to the marriage. Florrie noticed that there were several photos of the late Mrs. Fleming placed on the dust free surfaces in Stan's spotless sitting room. Stan returned to the room and sitting in a deep padded chair opposite her he listened as Florrie sobbed out the story of what she had been told had taken place last night after Dai, Chook and Snowy had been thrown out of the Hogs Head. "Why can't he behave himself," she whimpered. "Why does he keep company with those awful old reprobates and go to Missy Thompson's place."

"She's a wicked woman all right and the Lord will punish her when he sees fit," Stan agreed. Then he outlined a proposition he had mulled over in his mind for some time, concluding with, "Now Mrs.

Morgan, why don't you think about coming here and working for me?"

Florrie waited for school to come out and as the kids passed Fleming's Store, she stepped out and joined the little group. She was afraid to go home alone after rubbing the filthy sheet on Dai's face. Meggie moved away from the other kids and fell in step with her mother. She sure was glad Simon had already left Primary School or her mother would have caught her with him right now. She only saw him after Sunday school since the big row, but this week she would see him on Saturday night as they had all been invited to a party at Griffith's that evening. It was a chance for all the Welsh folk who lived in the area to meet Jack Morgan. Tom Griffith had ordered home brew from Dai for the occasion. Meggie could hardly wait for Saturday to come around.

The kids all chattered and giggled on the way home and Florrie answered them absently. Her thoughts were still very much on the suggestion that Stan Fleming had put to her. He'd told her she could have a different life, free from drink related anxieties, if she would only surrender herself to the Lord. "Trust in the Lord," he had said, "and He will make life better for you." He'd suggested that she leave Dai and come to work for him. "Your girls will be welcome too," he had added expansively.

Once home Meggie began her after school chores. The chooks clucked enthusiastically as she threw the wheat to them. They had a big meal of household scraps and bran with hot water in the mornings so it was wheat in the afternoon and just enough to keep them occupied while she collected the eggs from the their nests. As Meggie gathered the eggs she wondered again what her mother had been doing at Mr. Fleming's shop so late in the afternoon and leaving without any groceries. She hoped it wasn't to do with Sunday school. Perhaps old Fleming had found out that Simon met her each Sunday and walked her to the Gully Bridge. Sometimes they'd go up into the pine plantation for a while, but never for too long because Meggie dared not be late home. Maybe old Fleming had told her mother that she left the Gospel Hall early every Sunday. Her mind was fearful with questions and she worried that if anything was wrong she wouldn't be allowed to go to the party at Griffith's on Saturday night.

Jack Morgan walked down the Gully Road feeling pleased with his efforts to establish that the coalminers were not shirkers hiding away in the valleys to escape serving overseas. He could truthfully report to Frances Langtry that they were brave hardworking men. He'd spent the morning conferring with the mine officials and had gone down to the coalface and talked to the men. With nostalgia he watched the lads swinging their picks and banjo shovels, each heavy shovelful lifted expanding their biceps twofold, as they hurled the coal expertly into waiting skips.

He'd watched sentimentally as the skips of coal rumbled slowly out of the mine mouth, through the Mac cutting, then gathering speed and guided by an endless wire ropeway, raced over the echoing viaduct and on to join those that were rattling more sedately from the black innards of the Glen Afton mine. He'd had smoko with the winchmen and rope boys, spent time with the screen lads and watched the as coal-laden wagons were marshalled into trains. He'd called at the Mine Office before lunching with the manager, Bill Stafford.

His concluding thoughts of the miners were that any man brave enough to go underground with the threat of being bombed while down the pit; any man who would enter those mines with the knowledge that he may be buried alive; any man that worked this hard, that man was not a coward. Most of the men working in these mines were past the age of war service anyway. As well had the authorities lost sight of the fact that these mines were keeping this coal fired nation going. Send them all to fight overseas and the country would come to a standstill. Tomorrow he would visit the Pukemiro Colliery and go back to Auckland with his full report after the weekend.

A shadow crossed his face as he recalled the happenings of the night before. Why did his first son have to behave this way? He began to perceive more clearly the sort of life that Florrie and the girls lived and that troubled him greatly. But what could he do, apart from appealing to Dai's better nature, to help them?

As he neared the houses close to the mine it struck him that little had changed from his days in the heart of a coalmining village. Everywhere there seemed to be coal. Spilled and dumped, coal dust in the wind, on your clothes, boots and hair. Coal smuts and soot from the steam engines on the women's white washing, on ledges and shelves, sills and mantelpieces throughout the house. The men certainly had better conditions but nothing much had changed for the coalminers' wives.

He turned his head taking in a forty-five degree of the landscape. The large pine plantation, grown to supply props and beams to support the underground mine tunnels, glinted green in the warming sun and whispered a song along with the breeze. Higher, on the ridges and running down the gullies, was the glorious native bush patch worked with a variety of green hues. Here at least, unlike his native Wales, man had not denuded every living thing. But nevertheless, the mine and rail yards where steam engines chuffed to and fro, and even the village to a degree, were man-made scars.

Jack stopped by the Railway Bridge and waited for the day shift men to come out of the bathhouse. Dai lit a roll-your-own when he saw his father, having immediately figured out why he was there.

"Look boyo," Jack started, but Dai put up his hand to signal quiet.

"Da. If yer going to give me a lecture we'll go down the club and have a drink while yer doin' it."

"No, Dai. I'll say my piece here and now. I'd be failing in my duty to my grandchildren if I didn't speak to you about your drinking, you see. You are a bad influence on your girls when you drink yourself into such a state. What sort of a life is it for Florrie?" He paused and frowned at his son. "Why do you need to drink so much, son?" he asked softly. "Can you not be satisfied with just a few and then go home?"

Dai quickly became defensive. "You seem more concerned about Florrie and yer grandkids than yer are about yer own. You were never around when we were growing up, were ya? What sort of a life do yer think that was for mum?" He stopped to take a long draw on his fag before he spoke again. His eyes glittered as he flung the next accusation at his father. "That's what killed her, wasn't it. That's what gave her the cancer, eh?"

Dai had hit his father's vulnerable spot. The guilt Jack still felt about Medwyn rose to the surface again. "Duw, mun. That's not fair. Times were hard everywhere then and a damn sight harder in the Welsh mines. What else could I do boyo? I came out here to give you all a better life than you could have had in Wales. And that is what you have if you would only value it. That was the reason, and well you know it," he finished lamely.

Dai was sorry. He knew he was being unfair. "Sorry Da," he said quietly. "I suppose it's everything. This bloody war goin' on so long and

Florrie and the kids get on me nerves a lot. I sometimes think I'm not a marrying man."

"Your probably right, son. But fact is you have got a wife and children and you have to take responsibility for them. Florrie shouldn't have to put up with that sort of behaviour from you."

"I know that, Da. I know. I don't know what gits inta me sometimes." Dai became confidential. "Yer know, I've always wanted to be someone, but nothin' ever seems to go right for me and I suppose I drink to blot out me disappointment."

"Well. It seems to be getting out of control, son."

There followed a silence, the only sounds the crunch of their boots on the metal road. "You're not all that strong, Dai, and working in the mine, even on top, is not helping your health."

"I know. I'd like ta git back in the open air. Might go back to farming at Mapiu if this bloody war ever finishes. That's if the Japs haven't finished us all off before then," he finished with a sigh.

Griffith's sitting room was warm and welcoming as the guests filed in. The kids were allowed to stay outside in the half-light for a while but as soon as the blackout curtains were pulled they had to come inside and 'behave themselves'. Meggie and Sarry went into Cissy's room to try on her clothes. She had heaps of them, even though fabric was scarce; many dresses had been handed down to her from her older sisters. Hazel Hutchins was showing off in the boy's room until Mrs. Griffith found her in there and shooed all the kids out of the bedrooms and into the sitting room where she could keep an eye on them. The men had drifted out into the large dining room where the talk had turned from politics and the coming election to the war in Italy where the 2nd Division New Zealanders were fighting.

"The Government's overcommitted the bloody country," claimed Ron Harmon, Brian's father. "How can they keep their promise to support three theatres of war, food for three overseas markets and maintain the bloody welfare state at the same time? Bloody impossible. We've only got a population of one and a half million. We just don't have enough people"

He looked around, much like his son would do, for the effect his statement had on the listeners. No one argued with him. How could they? It was the truth.

"Fraser's only brought the blokes home on furlough 'cause he wants their votes fer the election," added Ces Howard, looking furtively around to see if Girlie Whetu was present. "Must take us for a pack of galoots if he thinks he's fooled us."

Jack didn't like the way the discussion was going. It was clear Fraser wasn't liked in this solidly Labour area but didn't want to commit himself to any statement against the prime minister. He was grateful when someone else steered the talk onto the horrors of the Pacific war so close to home now. By now the young school kids had crowded around the men anxious to hear more about the war especially about the vile Japanese.

"Did'ya hear on the news about Sydney and Newcastle bein' shelled by those bloody little nips?" asked Tiny Anderson. "They're getting too bloody close fer comfort as far as I'm concerned."

The men all nodded and looked seriously into their beer glasses.

"Ya know they're still getting' bombed way up the top of Australia," added Bob Cochrane in his Scottish burr. "And they've started on Darwin now. Och and I don't know what we are going to do when they get here."

Tom Griffith didn't want to talk war anymore. "Let's not 'ave war talk for one night. Who's for a sing-song?"

The men followed him into the sitting room where the women were sipping sherry from tiny glasses. Tom lifted the lid of the old piano and began to play a lively tune. The guests gathered around the piano and sang all the old favourites. 'Someone like you, a pal good and true' … 'In your sweet little Alice Blue Gown' … 'Beautiful Dreamer awaken to me' …

Most of the kids knew the words, too, so they joined in. Simon stood behind Meggie in the crush and slipped his arms around her waist. She shivered at the feel of him pressing her from behind. None of the grown-ups noticed as they were all enjoying the singing but Hazel Hutchins did. She sidled up to Mrs. Griffith and told her to look at what Simon and Meggie Morgan were doing. But Rose chose to take no notice of her and carried on singing, pretending not to hear.

In the months since the big upset Rose Griffith had watched her son and become more sympathetic to his predicament. She knew her Simon was a good boy and she also knew that he saw Meggie Morgan every Sunday afternoon. She looked across at Meggie's pretty round face, her cheeks glowing with excitement, and took in her body, which was very over developed for her age. Her being so young is a problem, she thought, but Simon could do worse. She only hoped he would keep his head and not do anything silly. At least not until he's workin' and bringing in a wage, she thought to herself.

Jack Morgan began to sing 'All Through the Night' in his beautiful Welsh voice and the other Welshmen there joined in harmony with him. Then all the Welsh folks began singing in the Welsh language, their voices lilting high and low, and Meggie thought she had never heard more beautiful sounds.

Later that night, all the alluring voices sang on in her head again as she fell into an exhausted, but the happiest, sleep.

CHAPTER NINE

Full many a flower has bloomed unseen,
To wither and die on the village green.

Election Day dawned under a gunmetal sky. When the rain started it fell continuously, sometimes gentle, sometimes torrential. The men and women from the valley trudged in and out of the polling booth, set up in the local Hall, to cast their votes. By closing time the ramp and foyer floor of the hall was a carpet of sticky grey sludge from the wet gravel roads.

The men gathered at the Hogs Head that night to listen to election results coming in over the radio though it was hard to hear above the noise of the rain thundering down on the corrugated iron roof. Labour seemed to be ahead but it would be the middle of next week before they would know the true election results with all the votes from outlying areas still to be counted. They spoke of how they had all missed Micky Savage's phrase, 'Now then' from the campaign speeches at this election. It had been the battle cry and hope of the helpless. They discussed how different everything would have been had Mickey lived.

Later that week Labour's victory was announced and celebrated, though the Party had lost 8 seats. Six days after winning the election the Prime Minister ordered all single furlough men, who were fit, back to fight overseas. Florrie's brother was amongst those who had to go back to war. In the Pacific the Americans set up bases on the islands around Rabaul and the Marines and New Zealand's 'Coconut Bombers' moved in to take Rabaul from the Japanese. The war was getting closer.

But at Glen Afton and Pukemiro the interest was more on the wedding of Wilma Kalman and Bluey Aiken than the war. They were married in the Registry Office at Huntly one week before Xmas and Meggie and Sarry went into Huntly on the train to see the wedding. That night everyone attended the wedding dance held in the Pukemiro Hall. Simon and Riki arrived together early in the evening. Simon danced with Meggie twice but Florrie fixed them with such a stony glare that Simon disappeared and didn't return. Riki stayed and monopolized Emmie for dances most of the night causing Florrie to look even sourer. They made a lovely couple, with Riki having the natural easy movement of the Maori people, looking good as he and Emmie swept around the dance hall floor attracting admiring glances. They had the supper waltz and were still together when the band led off for the last dance and finished with God Save the King.

Meggie didn't see Simon again until after Christmas as the next Sunday was the break-up of Sunday school and the parents were invited to the concert and afternoon tea. Florrie, who now felt embarrassed about pouring her heart out to Stan Fleming, had been avoiding him. She hadn't taken up his offer to work for him nor did she attend the church services, but still made Meggie go to Sunday school. Today she couldn't escape him as he bore down on her full of goodness. After the concert she didn't wait for afternoon tea just grabbed Meggie and took off.

The long summer holidays that followed Christmas and New Year were hot and sultry and the intense summer heat turned the houses with coal ranges in their tiny kitchens into furnaces while the tin roofs cracked in the blazing sun. They didn't glow, those wives, they sweated like their miner husband's. Beads of moisture oozed on their lips and brows and they were forever wiping their flushed faces with their aprons. They opened windows and doors wide to create a draught but all that came in were fat lazy blowflies. And it was that scorchingly hot summer that Ed Hubbard's Store and the Hog's Head burned down.

There seemed to be heaps of fires that year, most of them caused by the sparks from the steam engines igniting the dry grasses and gorse that grew alongside the railway tracks. The day before Ed's store caught fire the weather had been ominous, as if sending a prophetic message that nobody in the valley picked up on. The air had been heavy with sultry heat and summer thunder grumbled constantly in the surrounding hills. That night the store caught fire. No one knew for sure how the fire started – perhaps it was too much heat on the tin roof or a flash of dry lightning starting something smoldering through the day. But the women of Glen Afton had no doubt that it was due to a cigarette butt dropped carelessly on the floor in the Hogs Head.

The whole of Glen Afton and many of the Pukeites turned out to see the fire as it raged in the early hours of the morning. The mine fire truck arrived late and squirted a bit of water at the burning shop but as Harry White said, "They might as well have pissed on it."

Maybe in some ways it was a blessing for Ed as rationing had hit his sort of general store hard. Many folks had their own hens, grew their own vegetables and some still made their own bread. But for the men who frequented the Hogs Head it was an out and out tragedy. They were devastated. Dai Morgan ran from his house when the popping and banging of overheated tins and bottles, which exploded like gunshots and echoed around the hills that embraced the valley, woke him.

"God spend me bloody days," he bellowed. "The club's on fire."

He gathered some wet sacks as he went but they were of no use. The Hogs Head members gazed at the fire through tear filled eyes as though seeking confirmation in its hissing embers. Florrie, Emmie and Meggie watched the shop burn down from the main bedroom window. And oh yes, burn it did. It burned so brightly it hurt their eyes to look. The sky glowed with searing light long after the building was no more than an untidy pile of smoking charred beams, scorched corrugated iron and mounds of grey ash that hid embers that smoldered on for days after the calamity. The smoke lay in a low mantle over the valley all week creating everywhere a hazy curtain of gloom. Meggie had stayed awake and watched until the last of the night shadows faded and daylight broke. Acknowledging that it was the first day without Ed Hubbard's Store across the road from her house gave her an empty feeling in the pit of her stomach. Losing the store caused Meggie to think about how much the little valley had changed. The kids weren't roaming the hills like they used to and Meggie couldn't go playing very often anyway with having heaps more jobs to do. Every Sunday was taken up with the awful Sunday school at the Gospel Hall.

Some of the older girls, like her sister Emmie, Biddy Stoutman and Hazel Hutchins, who would be joining Simon and Riki on the train to attend the Huntly District High when school went back and they, feeling superior in their new roles of High School girls, went around lording it over the younger kids. Meggie and Sarry still had another year at Pukemiro School and it was rumoured that they were to have a new Headmaster, a returned war veteran who had been invalided home and he would also be the teacher of their class. Meggie felt sure that all the changes were caused by the war.

Just after New Year there was news, by word of mouth that the furlough soldiers at the Frankton Railway Station were refusing to go back overseas and fight in the war. Frankton was quite near Glen Afton so there was much interest by the Glen and Pukeites in the stories. However, there was nothing in the newspapers to back up the rumour, nor was the story included on the local news broadcast on the radio.

The whole thing worried Meggie and she wanted to ask Simon if the war was coming here. Knowing all about the war he would know what was happening and it was all becoming so confusing to her. The Japs were supposed to have been coming for a long while now but they still hadn't arrived. Hazel Hutchins had frightened everybody with her story that when the Japanese captured us Hitler was going to kill all the dark haired people and only keep the blonde ones with blue eyes for breeding purposes. She said it was Hitler's plan to breed a perfect race of people. She told Meggie that she would definitely be killed along with all the Maoris and those with dark hair. This upset Emmie who became afraid for Riki Whetu. Hazel, having fine fair hair, would be saved and so would Simon with his blonde hair and blue eyes, Hazel had added. It was all very scary.

Early one Saturday morning, while Meggie was feeding the chooks, Simon hissed to her through the chicken wire. "Howja like to go out to Waingaro Springs for a swim in the hot pools this arvo?" Simon asked Meggie. "Chiz Barker's taking Mum out there in his truck to soak her arthritis."

"I'll have to sneak my togs out. Anyone else going?"

"Yer don't need togs. The mineral water rots yer togs."

"What do you wear then?" Meggie was puzzled.

"Yer altigether," Simon laughed. "And yeah. Sarry and Gerry are coming with us. We'll have to sit on the back of the truck."

It sounded like fun. Meggie asked Florrie if she could go with Mrs. Griffith and was pleased when her mother said yes but insisted Meggie wear her togs under her dress. At Waingaro the old corrugated iron shed, built on the side of the road above the hot water spring in the creek, served as a bathhouse. The shed was divided in two by another sheet of the iron riddled with rusty nail holes. One side of the iron was for the women the other side for the men. Once they'd sunk slowly into the hot, steamy water, Sarry reckoned they should look through the lowest nail holes to see if the boys really had nothing on. Mrs. Griffith, who was fully immersed and getting great relief from the water, called them a pair of scallywags. When they finally did get the courage to look through the holes all they could see was the boy's eyeballs looking at them from their side. They had been surveying the naked girls all the time. Sarry squealed loudly and Meggie quickly put her togs back on.

Returning to school after the holidays, Meggie and Sarry met Mr. Bowman, who would be their teacher for this final year in Primary School. It was Mervyn Bowman's first position as a Headmaster but that didn't faze him. He was more self-conscious of his ungainly gait as he dragged along his stiffened leg, a souvenir from his service in Egypt, as he walked.

God, likely he'd never forget Egypt, the foulest hole he had ever laid eyes on. Most of his time had been spent in the desert where they'd lived in sandbagged dugouts that were deep, dark and stuffy. The trenches swarmed with everything that crept, flew and wriggled and bull ants crawled all over the soldiers as they slept. But even worse than the creepy-crawlies was the lack of water to wash with. He felt the stench in his body and clothes, even in his soul. Filth had penetrated his being and he had become overcome with feelings of panic and hopelessness.

Mervyn Bowman was a gentle man and had long known that he was not meant for the battles of the world. Nevertheless, he had given three years of the best part of his life to the war and had been rewarded with a gammy leg. He had learned in that time the full horror of war and believed it nothing more than a mercy when his own dugout had been shelled. He hadn't remembered much after that and was invalided home as medically unfit.

After his Army discharge he'd been directed back into his previous profession of teaching and Pukemiro seemed like a green paradise to him after living in sand and filth and disease, and the putrid stench of death, for so long. Merv. Bowman had heard the rumours about the mutinying soldiers and was in full sympathy with them. 'Send the distinguished backsides of the prime minister and his cronies to live like swine and see how long they'd survive', was his opinion. Mervyn Bowman had come home to New Zealand a bitter young man.

"Wow. Isn't Mr. Bowman handsome," squealed Sarry, elbowing Meggie to look at the new teacher as they lined up for parade on their first morning back to school.

Meggie and Sarry had been split up as desk partners and Meggie shared with know-all Marian Holmes. In the desk behind them Mr. Bowman had, in his ignorance, sat the absolutely unpredictable combination of Jack White and Brian Harmon. The two boys hardly gave Marion and Meggie a minute's peace always prodding them from behind for answers to the sums or for Meggie to sketch illustrations for their Social Studies or General Science books.

Jack was always drawing naked female figures himself. These would have huge bosoms and once he'd drawn them he would fold the paper into darts, and scrawling 'Meggie's tits' in his untidy

137

handwriting on the tail of the arrow, he would fire these masterpieces around the room when the teacher's back was turned.

Meggie was deeply engrossed during one of Mr. Bowman's lesson about the origins of verse. Merv. Bowman had opened up a whole new world for her by introducing many of the arts to their curriculum and she began to take a whole new look at poetry and composition writing.

"For hundreds of years," Mr. Bowman continued his lesson; "rhyme has been the most popular poetic device because it is such an effective method of arranging words in a way that delights the human ear."

"Bullshit," hissed Jack White. Mr. Bowman didn't hear him. Meggie turned around. She didn't want anything to disrupt this wonderful subject. "Be quiet Jack," she hissed at him.

Mr. Bowman was writing on the blackboard as he spoke. "Onomatopoeia" he underlined the word several times, "is the use of word or words," he spoke slowly as he wrote, "whose sound imitates the thing being described." He underlined the whole sentence with his chalk. "For example: from 'The Highwayman'," he continued as his chalk squeaked across the blackboard, "'Over the cobbles he clatters and clangs in the dark inn yard ...'" He drew two thick white lines beneath the two words 'clatters and clangs'.

Jack White was totally bored with the lesson and poked Meggie in the back with his ruler. "Draw me a naked sheilah," he ordered through his teeth.

"Get out." Meggie pushed his ruler away. "Okay," she said, hoping it would keep him quiet. Quickly she sketched the outline of a naked woman and passed it under the desk to him. He poked her in the back again.

"Draw some tits on her – like yours," he hissed again, passing the drawing back.

Meggie sighed and drew the breasts on the body. She was just about to pass the picture back to Jack when Mr. Bowman's wooden cane slammed down on her desk. "And what, pray, is this?" Mr. Bowman asked as he snatched the paper from her. Meggie's face was crimson.

"You are obviously excellent at sketching," he declared, "but for the life of me I don't know why a nice girl like yourself, Megan Morgan, should be wasting your time, and mine, drawing such lewd subjects."

Meggie stuttered something unintelligible. Jack White sat stiffly eyes riveted on his desktop.

"Well if you have no clear answer you will stay in after school," Merv said over his shoulder, as he limped back to the blackboard taking the offending drawing with him.

At playtime the girls consoled Meggie, and Sarry called Jack White a stinkin' rat for not owning up to making Meggie draw the naked woman.

"Shut yer cakehole," Jack yelled back, and went off to join the other boys in a game of footie.

Meggie stayed on after the classroom had emptied and before long Mr. Bowman appeared. He sat for a long time at his desk just looking at Meggie making her feel more uncomfortable. The moments of silence hung in the room and she began to perspire with discomfort. Merv Bowman was returning to the teaching profession with a fresh perspective and could perhaps see things he may have missed earlier. He had a fine sense of justice and balance and could see in this schoolgirl a talent waiting to be developed. In his mind the young seeds of talent needed protecting. Here was something of beauty to contribute to the world, something he could build and develop, not bomb and destroy like most of the mad world was doing at present. She was too big for her age, her figure soft and attractive in a mature way and yet she was still only a child emotionally. In the main his school pupils were made up of children from working class parents who would become working class adults. But once in a while there arose a talented issue and he could see that Meggie Morgan was an artistic child and he wondered quite angrily why her parents couldn't at least supply her with some form of breast support. After a long silence he spoke.

"Meggie. Have you always sketched?" he asked in a soft tone. Meggie was surprised as she'd expected a real telling off. She nodded affirmation. "Have you any of your drawings here?"

Meggie nodded again. Mr. Bowman gestured for her to give them to him. Carefully he looked over the pencil and ink sketches. A long silence stretched out again before his thoughts went back to the issue of drawing a nude in class. Meggie's heart was thundering. Mr. Bowman spoke again. "Have you had any tutoring in art?" Meggie shook her head.

"Well," he said slowly. "I majored in art at university and I think your drawings are very good. You clearly have a natural talent" He paused. "I would like to give you some lessons. What do you think?"

She couldn't answer. It was like a dream, her being offered to learn to draw properly by the Headmaster. Finally she squeaked out, "Yes please."

"You'll need special pencils and brushes to work with. I'll give you a list of a few things that you'll need and you can get your mother to buy them. You can use the school paper and paints for watercolour. How about you stay back each Monday afternoon after school and I'll give you an hour lesson. But you'll have to practice at home too."

Meggie took the note and thanked him. She couldn't wait to start painting in watercolour.

Before she left the room Merv Bowman spoke again. "Meggie. Let me tell you an old Chinese saying. It goes like this. 'Everyone lives a hundred lives but only one to remember. This one may be yours. Don't waste it', he quoted. Do you understand what I am telling you, Meggie?"

"I think so, sir." She wasn't really sure and he could sense that.

"Well, you think about it on the way home. Goodbye"

Florrie was furious when she read the note requesting some additional materials for drawing at school.

"Is everyone doing this," she asked Meggie.

Meggie shook her head.

"Well I'm not buying these items. What does that new teacher think? That I've got a bottomless purse."

Meggie's bubble had burst. She should have known that she wouldn't be allowed to learn how to draw properly. Florrie wrote a really rude note to Mr. Bowman and Meggie cringed with embarrassment when she had to hand it to him. He said nothing after reading the contents but asked Meggie to stay in after school. The impolite note niggled him all day and interfered with his ability to impart the lessons.

During the poetry lesson he wrote on the blackboard two lines of verse:

'At midnight in the month of June

I stand beneath a mystic moon'.

The class watched silently as the chalk scraped across the blackboard surface. Mr. Bowman turned around to his surprisingly quiet pupils. "Now in your exercise books I would like you to finish this poem." He tapped the board with his long cane. "You have fifteen minutes and then I want them read out finished or not."

There was a shuffling of paper and clattering of dropped pencils before the class settled down to do the exercise instructed. Meanwhile, Merv opened the note from Florrie Morgan again and studied it. How could anyone be so lacking in interest in their child's future? He surely was dealing with working class ethics in this community. Not wanting to lose the chance to advance this girl's talent he was trying to work out how to handle this situation. He glanced at his watch.

"Times up," he shouted. "Put down your pencils now."

The kids stood up one by one to read out their verses and on the whole they were quite good. Brian Harmon stood and recited the first two lines followed by,

"I saw a big baboon, eating a banana". Brian looked around the class for their reaction. There were a few sniggers from the boys. Mr. Bowman was annoyed. Harmon was always trouble. But he kept his voice low as he stated, "But the verse does not rhyme, Brian."

"Yes it does, sir. Baboon rhymes with moon."

The kids all tittered. Merv couldn't tolerate Brian's stupidity especially when he had discovered someone who had real talent. So he didn't correct the poem, just called out "Next!"

At last the day was over. The children all filed out of the room and he was left alone again with Meggie Morgan.

"You know your mother has refused to purchase any art brushes."

Meggie flushed to the colour of ripe beetroot. "Yes," she said lowering her eyes.

"Do you still want to learn," he asked?

"Yes," she said again.

"Well, not a word to your mother. I will get the brushes for you and give you a lesson whenever I can. Okay."

Meggie could only nod and thank him.

That night at the pictures the Movietone Newsreel was of the Kiwi 'Coconut Bombers' blitzing the Japs in Rabaul, reminding the people at Glen Afton once again that there was a war on and it was not too far away.

CHAPTER TEN

GLEN AFTON 1944

The night the special film about the 3RD Division fighting in the Pacific was to be shown the picture hall filled quickly. After the whining episode of the current serial the film operator screened the movie that had been filmed under fire by the National Film Unit. There was complete silence as the patrons watched the grim pictures of New Zealand troops fighting, sweating and dying in the island jungles. The film, it was said, was to be shown around the country to remind those at home that any slacking on the home front would not be easily understood or forgiven.

Part of the hall had been partitioned off to accommodate Ed Hubbard's temporary grocery store. He intended to build again but due to the war building materials were hard to get and he might have to wait until it ended before supplies became available again. In the meantime everyone seemed quite happy shopping at the hall. It meant they could buy more things on picture nights than had been available at the tiny sweet hatch.

At half time there lacked the usual joking and the foyer was unusually quiet. The National Film Unit movie had brought the war in the Pacific to life in this little mining village way out in the sticks. Merv Bowman, now boarding at Griffith's, had come to the film with the older Griffith boys. Although it was a very different to the desert war he had fought in Egypt it was equally as horrifying. He didn't wait for the main movie. Instead he dragged his gammy leg down the hall ramp and in his bed he wept as another fit of shell shock ravaged his body.

A week later a happier crowd gathered outside the Glen Afton hall for the Women's Institute concert. They puffed on their cigarettes with an air of anticipation. It was a crisp cold night, the navy sky pinpricked with a myriad of flickering stars.

Meggie and Emmie walked haltingly towards the crowd with their father. It was unusual for Dai to attend a function at the local hall especially when it was a 'dry do'. With his father's words still fresh it appeared that he was trying to make an effort and the loss of the Hogs Head was helpful because as yet the drinkers had not been able to find another venue although occasionally some met up in the old powerhouse beyond the screens. Once inside the hall father and daughters parted company and the girls went to sit with their own special friends.

The tattered velvet curtain, held up by No 8-fence wire, scraped to the side of the stage indicating the performance was about to begin.

Pom! Ta Pom! Pom! Ta Pom! The piano burst out passionately as Mrs Josie Brown clomped onto the stage dressed as a soldier, complete with a large pair of black pit boots and a Home Guard wooden rifle on her shoulder. She looked mournfully at the audience but made no effort to begin her number.

Pom! Ta Pom! The pianist tried again. Apprehension floated through the darkened hall and Dai Morgan snorted with glee. He hadn't wanted to come to the Women's Institute concert in the first place but Florrie had really rounded on him when he'd expressed his intention not to attend. Florrie, being the producer of the show, had arranged most of the items as well as taking part in the concert herself. All he'd heard for weeks now, when he was at home, was Florrie warbling snatches of songs as she coordinated the concert in her head. Nah. He couldn't really complain though as she did have an exceptionally good singing voice.

"Stage fright," whispered Sarry to Moira and Meggie, inclining her head knowingly.

Pom Te Pom! Pom Te pom! The piano signaled again, this time with a hint of impatience. Josie made a thin squeak and the audience shuffled their feet. Knitting needles clicked at a faster rate.

A hand waved frantically from behind the curtain as the prompt hissed the first line of the song. Whether the hidden Institute member on the end of the hand was one to be feared the crowd would never know, but the sound was certainly enough to set Josie on the right path to sing her number. Without warning she flung back her head and emitted a terrible howl.

"In my arrmmmms... In my arrmmmms...

Ain't I never gonna have a girl in my arrmmms..."

Her right foot, encased in the heavy pit boot, plonked up and down on the stage in time to her singing.

Pom twiddle twiddle Pom pom. The pianist's fingers raced over the keys in an effort to catch up with Josie's eager singing. Glaring at the audience, and it seemed that the glare was particularly directed at Mrs Stafford who distributed the wool for knitting, Josie bellowed on,

"Ya can keep yer knittin' and yer purlin'

If I've a gotta go ta Berlin

Give me a girl in my arrmmms tonight."

The audience went wild, clapping and whistling, stamping their feet and shouting for more. Several other women, kitted out in make shift uniforms, joined her on the stage as the music changed tempo and the ladies sang a lusty rendition of 'Kiss Me Good Night, Sgt. Major.'

At half time May Ryan opened up the sweet hatch and the kids, giggling and squealing, crowded around the counter. Outside Meggie saw Simon and looked left and right to make sure of her father's absence before she smiled at him.

"Hi, Megs," he said, seducing her with his gorgeous smile. "Enjoyin' the show? Yer old lady's quite good, eh!" he went on without giving her time to answer.

Even in the half-light of the heavy blackout curtains on the hall porch Meggie knew he had been drinking. In one way it annoyed her that he couldn't seem to go anywhere these days without the Dutch courage booze gave him. Then, on the other hand, her own father was such a boozer that she felt she had no right to castigate anyone else. Simon threw down his cigarette butt and ground it into the shingle with his foot then sidled up to her.

"Reckon I could walk ya home tinight. Yer old man'll be going over to the old powerhouse after this."

Meggie nodded agreement then hurried back into the hall before the dimmed lights were extinguished. Most of the men had had a good skinful of what was in someone's car boot during the interval and were noisy for the second half of the show. The whistling and stamping feet quietened as the dusty brown velvet curtains slid slowly open to the tune of 'Give Me My Boots and Saddle'. The stage was set with dim lighting casting shadows on the campfire made of red cellophane and a torch glowing beneath the folds of paper. The women, wearing trousers, boots and plaid shirts, with wide-awake hats either positioned at a rakish angle on their heads or slung casually between the shoulder blades, were seated around the fire humming to the 78 record being played on the gramophone behind the scenes.

"I bet it's a cowboy medley," crowed Sarry loudly, so that most of the hall would have heard her.

"Reckon that's clear to the deaf, dumb and bloody blind," came a sarcastic shout from some bloke at the back of the hall.

Meggie didn't answer Sarry. Her mind was still on the encounter with Si and if she should meet him outside afterwards.

Mrs. Jean Rodgers rose from the circle and sang 'Old Shep' in a beautiful contralto. The hall was silent with expectation and clapping broke out as she sang the last wistful note. Sarry wiped her moist eyes. "Gee, I just love that song," she sobbed.

As the applause faded Florrie Morgan and Rose Griffith took the stage and began a truly magnificent rendition of 'White Cliffs of Dover', their voices blending perfectly. The Griffith boys and their mates shrieked and whistled through two fingers until old Mr. Raine, who was responsible for the hall, told them to shut up or he'd throw them out. Before the finale Dai Morgan slipped out of the hall and was already drinking at the old powerhouse when the Institute women danced and sang another medley of war songs. The whistling and shouts of applause were deafening as Meggie slipped out of the side door and waited for Simon. He was there within minutes and they made their way quickly behind the hawthorn hedge and along the well-worn path leading up one side of the hill then disappearing abruptly in a thick stand of pines.

"Dad's gone over to the powerhouse but Mum will only be about an hour or so cleaning up the hall, so I can't stay long." Meggie's breathless voice shook with apprehension.

"Relax, Megs," Simon soothed, as he eased her gently onto the coat he'd spread on the soft bed of pine needles. "I won't let ya be late."

"You know I'm not allowed to be on my own with you. Mum would kill me if she knew."

"Í know, honey. I know." There was a hint of defeat in his voice. "I only want to hold onto you for a few minutes. Then we'll go." He paused a moment. "Christ, I miss you, Megs. I think about ya all the time."

Meggie changed the subject. "How do you like working on the screens? Is it better than school?"

"My bloody oath! I couldn't wait ta leave bloody school. The old lady wanted me to finish the year out but it would just have bin a waste of time. I'd rather be earnin' some money."

Meggie relaxed and breathed out loudly. She put her arms up round his neck and raised her face to his cheek. He felt that surge of excitement that always happened when she touched him. Simon moved closer, his breath, scented with the tang of homebrew, was warm on her face.

Above them, through the pine's upper branches, a few stars pulsed around a now cloud-held moon. The pale light showed the black tracery of the boughs. Then swiftly the cloud grew thin for a moment and the moon shone through with a pearlised glow silvering the bush and pines with a mesh of shadows.

Simon looked down at her and his breathing quickened. Her lips, full and inviting, were disturbingly close. He wanted to kiss her but was afraid of himself. As Meggie pressed against him he could stand no more. The blood coursed wildly through his veins, beating in his heart so loudly he could barely hear the whine of the wind softened by the pine boughs overhead, as he exploded into a total loss of control.

For a moment he forgot his doubts, his caution. He forgot the trouble they'd been in and he groaned as he pushed her back on his coat, rejoicing in the feel of her body beneath him. Meggie thrust him away and he rolled part way down the slope. His passion killed he picked himself up and groped his way back to Meggie who was already giggling and they held onto each other laughing until the tears rolled down their cheeks.

Once the echoes of the concert audience tramping home faded away Meggie became fidgety. A halo of chimney smoke lay over the mine house roofs making the valley look spooky as they made their way back to the road and into their homes.

Meggie made it home before her mother but Emmie was already there.

"You've been with Simon Griffith, haven't you?" she accused.

Meggie went red. "We were just talking, that's all."

"I'll bet," Emmie said slyly.

"You can't talk. What about you and Riki? Do you just talk?"

"Riki's different."

Meggie hooted. "Different. Huh. Different how?"

"Well, he's not always drunk like Simon. Riki doesn't drink at all," she replied piously. "He says he's seen enough of it with his family." She hesitated before she spoke again, "Anyway, Mum reckons if you don't want to end up like her you'll stay away from Simon Griffith cause he's got the makings of a real boozer."

"Don't say that!" Meggie pushed Emmie just as Florrie walked into the kitchen. She was still on a high from the success of the concert and didn't want this aggro.

"What's going on here? Can't I leave you two for five minutes without you're fighting?"

Meggie was terrified that Emmie would tell her about Simon but she didn't. Florrie shooed them off to bed and sat down in front of the coalrange, with a cuppa, to hum the songs again as she replayed the concert over in her mind.

Next day Merv Bowman bumped into Florrie in the passage at the boarding house and stopped her. "That was an excellent concert Mrs. Morgan. I believe it was mostly your effort."

Florrie flushed with pleasure. Fancy the headmaster telling her how good her concert had been. She had momentarily forgotten about the rude note she had sent him just a few weeks ago.

"Thank you," she replied, in her special voice reserved for the doctor and Mrs. Stafford the Mine Manager's wife. She looked away coyly as she flicked her duster over the hall table.

"That must be where Meggie gets her talent from," Merv stated pointedly, hoping to get his message across. "I hope you realize just what a talented artist your daughter is."

Florrie's face went red. She remembered the rude note she had written to Mr. Bowman when he'd offered to tutor Meggie in artwork.

"Well. Yes. I used to draw myself so I expect that's where Megan gets her art from," she replied in her posh voice.

"Well, if that is the case I would have thought you'd have been keener to support her talent. Help her make a career of it," he finished with an edge to his voice.

Florrie was really embarrassed, but annoyed, too. Fancy him speaking to me like that, she thought. Who does he think he is?

Mr. Bowman and Meggie continued the painting lessons in secret and Merv often took her out of class to sit in the staff room and paint. They collected foxgloves and daises and berries and she painted them superbly.

"Can you get away on Saturday morning if it is fine?" he asked her.

Meggie looked up from painting a stroke on the stem of foxglove flowers. "Yep. I think so. Why?"

"Well I would like to start you on sketching some native ferns and bush plants. I've noticed there are lots of specimens close to the edge of the bush behind the bathhouse so I'll meet you by the Maori baches at ten o'clock and we'll gather some."

Though the autumn had been exceptionally wet by Saturday the rain had died away and the May sunshine shimmered in a cloudless sky. The bush behind the baches ran high onto a ridge and a patchwork of greens dotted with nikau and ponga fronds glistened in the morning sunshine. Meggie ran up the incline where Mr. Bowman was waiting for her.

"I can't be too long," she puffed at him. "I've got to help Mum preserve the last of the eggs for winter. She thinks I've gone to Moira's."

Merv felt sad that she had to lie about everything. They made their way slowly along the track through the prickly gorse and manuka and soon came to the native growth. Merv's leg prevented walking any faster and it was still quite wet and slippery underfoot from the autumn rains.

Soon they were under a forest canopy of rata and rimu and the bush floor was lined with ferns and creepers. Merv sketched the ferns, the supplejacks and bush lawyers and even the fungus and lichen that sprouted from the trunks of some trees, carefully shading the drawings to illustrate to Meggie the subtle tones of light and shade on the bush vegetation.

Meggie was rapt. She had always loved the bush with its curious mixture of soil and things growing. Now she was looking at its vegetation through totally new eyes. The time sped by and before long they had moved right along the edge of the bush to come out at the stand of pines already being cut and used for props in the mine. The sun was directly overhead. Meggie realized it was midday. She panicked.

"I'll have to go," she called, as she scrambled through the edge of the pines and onto a metal track that led out to the main road. The terrain was much too difficult for Merv to manage with his bad leg so he wandered slowly back towards the bathhouse enjoying breathing the special fragrance that smelt of damp earth and leaves. It helped take away the stench of the rotting bodies in the desert that seemed would stay in his nostrils forever.

At home Florrie was greasing the eggs ready to start packing into the isinglass preservative jelly that filled the kerosene tins. She growled at Meggie for being so long but soon the tins were filled and covered with heavy wooden lids, then stored out in the washhouse beside Dai's home brew.

Dai came in late for his tea. The Home Guard had been drilling out at Matera Beach so he hadn't had a drink all day. He knocked the top off a bottle of home brew and drank it straight down.

"The jokers were telling me that Fraser spewed his guts out when he visited our troops in Cassino," he told Florrie, after expelling a loud belch. "Couldn't take the stink of joker's lyin' dead all over the place they reckon. Serves the bastard right."

Florrie felt sick at the news. Her brother had been sent back to fight at Cassino. Maybe he was one of the dead bodies. And she hadn't even seen him when he was home on furlough leave, or more correctly, brought home to vote in the election last year!

Merv Bowman snorted at the news. He doubted there'd be one furlough soldier; the heroes Fraser had labeled deserters, who would sympathize with Fraser's predicament. He remembered again the other ludicrous activities done at the battlefront. The hypocrisy of praying before each battle. Fancy saying prayers before the battle and over on the enemy side they were praying for the same victory, too. How would God choose? Was he to pull straws for whom he would side with? What a farce! The longer the war went on the more absurd the whole thing became, Merv thought.

It was reported that the Kiwis fighting in Italy were very tired and discipline was at an all-time low. He could understand that only too well. Now the war had moved on into Burma, tales of the absolute inhuman treatment by the Japanese to the POW's working on the Burma railway were filtering out into the backblocks. Merv thanked his lucky stars, and not God, for where he was in this little valley, safe for now, where he could hide away when his trembling fits of shell shock and panic overcame him. He refused to thank God as he no longer believed in a God regardless of that crackpot Fleming trying to lure him into his little Church. He felt very sorry for Meggie Morgan forced to attend every Sunday because of some silly misdemeanor she was supposed to have committed.

Throughout New Zealand the latest craze with the young ones was the new beat of American music. 1ZM had become the American radio station so the tunes soon reached the outbacks and the Andrews sisters' hits, 'Boogie Woogie Bugle Boy' and 'Don't Sit Under The Apple Tree' and 'American Patrol' played by Glen Miller and his Band, took over from Vera Lynn's more sedate 'White Cliffs of Dover' and 'We'll Meet Again'. For the young ones jitterbug and jive replaced the waltz and foxtrot. Florrie thought the American dances and jazzy songs were disgusting but Dai liked the new sounds and argued with her. The Maoris with their natural sense of rhythm danced up a storm on a dance night, which were fewer now due to the blackouts.

In late October that year the Americans re-took the Philippines after a battle lasting three days – the biggest naval battle in history. 'Japan lost almost all their aircraft and their Navy is believed destroyed,' relayed the radio news broadcaster. 'Meanwhile New Zealand's 'Coconut Bombers' are still mopping up Japs in the Pacific.'

CHAPTER ELEVEN

In December 1944 the BBC news announced the start a new offensive, which soon began to be referred to as the Battle of the Bulge. It was reported to be Hitler's final attempt to save Germany but by Christmas it was apparent that his last ditch had failed. The big question on everyone's lips now was, 'Is the war coming to an end at last?'

In the Pacific America's 'might' seemed to be winning the war. Walter Nash made a 'price of the war' speech but it hadn't gone down well and people, by now becoming weary of war, turned their wirelesses off. Weary yes, Merv Bowman thought, as he switched off his radio with an angry click. But not half as weary as those poor bastards still fighting in Europe and in the Islands. And never as weary as those miserable skin and bone prisoners starving and dying in German and Japanese POW camps. Let alone all those men left limbless, disabled and scarred, the thousands already dead and the innocent women and children killed because they just happened to get in the way of a war. Here in New Zealand no one has any idea, he thought bitterly. And especially the bloody politicians in this country. They have no idea at all.

Merv turned his attention back to the task of writing out the end of the year school reports. He was only up to H and already half the day was gone. It was going to be a long Saturday he could see. Some of the children hadn't passed the end of the year exams. Like Brian Harmon for instance. Merv wanted to pass Brian Harmon as the thought of another year trying to teach that smart arse lad wearied him! The boy was a bit of a wit, he supposed. When Merv suggested he get his long straggly hair cut Brian had replied that he was waiting for wool prices to go up. Smart mouth and totally class-disrupting boy. His excuse for not joining Mrs Holmes folk dancing class was that he had 'sore shoes'. No, he couldn't possibly pass him as he'd not learnt a thing, and worst of all for Merv he knew that Brian didn't care. He was just waiting for the day when he could leave school and start work at the mine. Merv wrote in the comments section on the bottom of the report, 'Brian is a clever boy but will not apply himself'.

He would like to write that the boy was a smart aleck and a disruption to the other students in the class and a totally frustrating child to teach. Merv did suspect that somewhere in Brian's snowy tousled head, there was a brain but it seemed that no one could reach it.

The next report was that of Davy Howard. Well, this lad was a different story. A sad story. The kid wasn't the full pound that was clear. He hadn't passed one single exam subject. There was no way he could send a boy like Davy off to a secondary school. He'd be picked on and ridiculed by town children. Davy's only salvation was for Merv to keep him here in the safety of the valley, amongst those who accepted him, until he was old enough to go into the mine. Then God help the miners.

The thought of another year with Davy hurtling around the classroom shooting people with rulers, dribbling all over the place, and of girls constantly squealing because Davy was climbing up their toilet wall to look over and scare them was almost enough to send Merv back to Egypt!

Merv had observed Davy's home life and concluded that he wasn't privy to the most salubrious family in the Glen. The trouble lay with his rat-faced father, Ces Howard. Big drinker and thoroughly obnoxious man who knocked his wife and kids around when he was full of booze.

For some reason Davy got the worst of it and it was rumoured that Davy wasn't Ces's child, that Vee Howard had brought him along with her when she came to housekeep for Ces some years ago. Vee had borne four children to Ces so where was she to go. Like most women of the era she was trapped and just had to make the best of it. A pale-faced thin woman, Vee Howard looked as though someone had wrung all the life out of her. The family lived in a shack partway in the bush with no electricity or conveniences of any sort.

162

"Bad fer the kids eyes," Ces had argued when it was suggested that the power lines be taken to their dwelling. Strangely, he had never worried about his own eyes when he'd sat under electric lights, night after night, in the Hogs Head before it burnt down. Merv's heart went out to Vee Howard, but more so to Davy when the boy arrived at the school battered and bruised, black eyed, face swollen and discoloured, but still happily rat-tat-tatting around the classroom as if nothing unusual had happened. And for Davy nothing unusual had happened! This was the norm; this was all he knew. 'Another year at Pukemiro would benefit David,' Merv wrote at the bottom of the report and placed it on the pile of already completed reports.

He was up to Megan Morgan's report when Olwyn Griffith tapped on his door.

"Lunch is on the table," she called, before moving on to hail the other boarders.

Merv had a soft spot for Olwyn but never showed it as she was walking out with Roddy McLaughlin from the Junction. Olwyn worked at the potteries through the week and helped her mother in the boarding house at the weekends so she didn't see Roddy that often. Roddy would walk the mile or so down the railway track most Saturdays or Sundays, depending on what shift he was on, and stay over if there was a dance or for the pictures on Sunday night. Mervyn saw her every day and they often had long intelligent conversations.

Merv thought Olwyn was pretty, clever, obedient and sweet natured and could have gone places if she hadn't been manpowered into the potteries to work. She was typical of her generation of girls who were worked hard and rarely disobeyed their parents. Merv made his way slowly down the passage to the big dining room and the smell of fresh bread and meat roasting for the evening meal made his mouth water.

After lunch Merv resumed work on the school reports. He wrote that he strongly recommended Meggie Morgan do her secondary education at Hamilton Technical College. Here was a child who would really benefit from the Art and Graphic Design Course run at that college and there was nothing of that kind at Huntly District High. By evening dinner he'd finished. He stacked the reports into his portmanteau and was glad to see the back of them. The next thing he had to deal with was the finalizing of the fancy dress ball arranged for the school break-up. He was glad to be busy so as he didn't have to think about the long Xmas break when he had no travel pass to go anywhere but also nowhere to go.

"And what are you goin' to be for the fancy dress ball?" asked Mrs. Griffith, when Meggie Morgan delivered eggs to her kitchen that same Saturday afternoon.

"I'm not going as anything," Meggie answered flatly.

"Oh! No, that can't be. What is Emmie going as?"

"Emmie's not dressing up 'cause she goes to High School. But Mum says I'm too big to dress up as anything."

"Ooh. We can't 'ave that," Rose Griffith squeaked. She was quiet for a few minutes while she thought about a costume for Meggie. "I'll talk to Jimmy the Islander. He's got a grass skirt hangin' on the wall in his room. You can go as a Hawaiian dancing girl."

"Gee. That would be great." Meggie was quite excited. "But I don't think I'll be allowed."

"'Ere, you leave it to me, Megan Morgan. You'll go dressed up all right," she finished with a determined nod of her head.

There was only Merv and Jimmy the Islander for the delicious roast dinner that night. The boarders not on back shift at the mine had gone pig hunting on Canon Ridge out Waingaro way and they were staying out all night. Merv envied them. They had asked him to go with them, and while he was conducive to the idea, his gammy leg prevented him from climbing up ridges. Again he felt bitter about the war.

Mrs. Griffith placed their pudding in front of them and then sat down at the table.

"'Ow about lending me your island skirt?" she asked Jimmy the Islander.

Jimmy laughed. "What you want my skirt for?"

"For Meggie Morgan to wear. I want to dress her as a Hawaiian girl for the Fancy Dress Ball next week."

Merv pricked up his ears.

"She no good for Island girl. Her hair too short," Jimmy answered laughingly in his broken English.

Rose hadn't thought of that but Olwyn had an idea. "What about all that old black wool in the cupboard, Mum? Couldn't we make it into a wig of long hair?"

That week they sewed the cut lengths of wool onto a cap formed from an old stocking, and then dyed an old bra red. With the grass skirt the outfit fitted Meggie perfectly. Jimmy the Islander said they would have to darken her skin on the night. Meggie could hardly wait for the ball now. Sarry was going as an Egyptian Princess and Moira's mother had made her a super cat suit, with a long fat tail, out of her father's old suit.

On the day before school broke up Merv Bowman handed out the school reports. Meggie was excited to see he had recommended that she go to Hamilton Tech and take the Art and Graphic Design Course. She hurried home and gave the report to her mother. Florrie read it and sniffed, "It'll be up to your father," she said.

That night Dai read out loud Mr. Bowman's recommendations for Meggie's future in art. After he'd finally absorbed what the teacher had written he snorted, hoicked and spat into the coal range firebox. The globs of mucous dangled from the grate, hissing and hardening, leaving silvery deposits on the red hot metal.

"Nah," he drawled, after what seemed an eternity. "Waste of money sendin' a girl for flash trainin' at a college."

"Please, Dad," she begged. "Please can I go."

"Nope. Costs extra on the Hamilton bus. Yer can go to Huntly High fer free. And yer can stop snivillin' cause that's me last word on the subject."

Meggie knew it had more to do with having less to spend on booze if he had to shell out a bit extra for bus fares to Hamilton. Young as she was she knew deep down that there would never be any chance to develop her talent as long as she lived with her parents. Mr. Bowman's tuition had all been for nothing. Not for the first time she thought about running away. That night she felt sick with disappointment as she cried herself to sleep.

"Never mind," said Sarry when she told them next day at school. "You'll be coming to Huntly with us so we can have some fun on the train."

Florrie felt a bit sorry for Meggie and even thought about defying Dai and paying the extra bus fare out of her wage from the boarding house. But at the same time she wasn't very pleased that Rose Griffith was dressing Meggie for the fancy dress ball that night. But she held her tongue as she needed to keep her job.

Meggie gulped down her dinner then ran over to Griffith's where Rose and Olwyn dressed her for the Fancy Dress Ball. They covered her shoulders, arms and legs with a mixture of old face powder and cocoa and had borrowed heaps of shell necklaces and a lei for around her neck. Lastly they placed the wool wig, with crepe paper flowers sewn onto it, on to her head. Jimmy the Islander nodded his approval.

Meggie was disappointed that Simon hadn't waited to see her dressed and had gone off early to drink at the old powerhouse. When she was finally dressed they all walked over to the hall, which was already crowded, and the dancing had begun. After the parade of costumes Sarry was announced winner with her beautiful Egyptian outfit that had belonged to her mother. Meggie got second prize. The Griffith's all cheered when her name was called. Jack White yelled out that Meggie only won second place because of her big tits and Mr. Bowman ushered him out of the hall.

Later in the evening Merv Bowman asked Meggie if she would be going to Hamilton Tech and wasn't surprised when tears welled up in her eyes as she shook her head. He looked around for her parents thinking a word to them might help change their minds, but neither was in the hall. Typical, he thought. Merv felt so angry that his prodigy would not get a chance. "Typical of this earn not learn society," he fumed, "that I as an educator have to deal with."

Christmas at the Glen wasn't as exciting as past Christmases with Ed Hubbard's shop gone. The older kids already attending Huntly High School were acting superior and there were no art lessons from Mr. Bowman. Simon was either working or drinking at the old powerhouse. The miners worked on through the holidays. Extra rations of sugar and flour were available for the women to make a Christmas cake but there was little else to buy from the shops.

"I hear old Arch Bell wants to sell his farm," Dai announced one morning at breakfast. "Wouldn't mind havin' that place and getting' outa the mine. Fer me health's sake," he announced, drawing heavily on his roll-your-own which immediately started a paroxysm of coughing.

Florrie didn't answer. There was no way they could afford to buy a farm so she didn't think much more about it until after Christmas when Dai told her he was going to Auckland for a few days. "I want ta see the old man," he said, looking furtive.

Florrie was immediately suspicious. "Oh yes. And how are you getting there?"

"I'm takin' the truck. I've got enough gas to see me there and back."

Florrie knew he was up to something but she didn't know what. "Well, you can take Meggie with you," she said. "She's still pretty upset about not going to the Art College at Hamilton."

"What. She's still grizzling about that?" Dai seemed genuinely surprised that Meggie should still be upset about what he considered a small thing. However, he agreed and set off with Meggie early next morning. Maybe he is turning over a new leaf, thought Florrie. She had noticed he hadn't been away on escapades with Bill and Snowy much lately.

Meggie was excited that she would see Granddad Morgan. She intended to tell Granddad about not being allowed to go to Hamilton Art College. Meggie hadn't been to Auckland since before her Nanna Morgan had died and that was a long time ago, even before the war had started. She remembered her Grandparents taking her and Emmie to the Zoo one day where they watched the Chimps having a tea party. They had been so funny and then they'd had a ride on Jumuna the Elephant.

Another day Granddad and Nanna had taken them the Farmers Trading Company, and while they'd had morning tea, she and Emmie had ridden in pedal cars on the rooftop of the building. It had been a bit scary being up so high but she remembered the holiday with great pleasure.

Meggie also had aunties and uncles and her cousin Evan who lived in Auckland and she might get to see them. Her uncles were wharfies and always had lots of tins of special kinds of food like you never saw anywhere else. They brought them home from out of the boxes that arrived broken at the wharf. It would be fun to see them all again.

The drive was long and bumpy in the old truck and quite scary when they drove up the winding razorback road and down the other side. Finally they reached the outskirts of Auckland and Dai drove straight to his brother's house at Otahuhu and they stayed the night with Uncle Rees and Auntie Mollie.

"I'll take yer ta yer Granddad's tomorrow," Dai promised, when Meggie wanted to go straight there.

Next morning Dai and Rees argued with Auntie Mollie because they wanted her to take Meggie to see Granddad at Grey Lynn but Auntie Mollie had arranged to spend the day with her friends at the Ellerslie Races. Uncle Rees was really annoyed with her.

"Yer a miserable bitch," he called after her, as she backed their Hillman Humber car out of the garage.

They didn't want the nuisance of taking a child with them for a day at The Star Hotel, Charlie Nick's pub in Otahuhu. Meggie wasn't allowed in the hotel so they told her to sit on a bench outside.

"We'll take ya to yer Granddad's after we've had a few drinks," Dai promised her.

Every so often one of them would come out and buy her an apple or a sweet from the Indian shop across the road, though there was little choice with rationing. By midday the sun was scorchingly hot and Meggie realized that she was getting very sunburned. She stood in the shade for a long time but kept going back to the seat as there was nowhere else to sit. She wanted to go home and thought of taking a tram into Grey Lynn but then realized she had no money for the fare. Several times American Marines came up to her and once she went with two of them to a milk bar down the street and they bought her a milkshake. They were real nice asking her about her life in New Zealand and gave her some chewing gum in long packets like she'd never seen before.

At four o'clock that afternoon she was still waiting for her father and uncle to take her to Granddad's. By then the sun had crossed the sky and she could at least sit in the shade. But her face and arms were red and burning. She was exhausted and ready to cry when she looked up and her Auntie Mae and Uncle Bill were getting out of a car in front of the hotel. Meggie jumped up and called to them. They were surprised to see her and aghast that their niece should have been sitting outside a hotel on her own all day.

"How long have you been here?" asked Auntie Mae.

"We came about eleven o'clock, I think."

"Well, those brothers of mine need shooting. Go in and get them Bill," she ordered her husband. "I'll give them the length of my tongue."

The men staggered out and Auntie Mae gave them a real telling off. But they were too drunk to comprehend what she was saying. Finally Auntie Mae bundled Meggie into their car and took her back to her place.

"You're not risking your life in a truck with those drunken lunatics," she growled as Uncle Bill drove off.

Next day a very hungover Dai came to pick her up at Auntie Mae's and take her home.

"But I haven't been to Granddad's," she wailed.

"Shut up and get inta the truck," Dai snarled, red-eyed and ill-tempered from his binge yesterday.

He'd seen his father in the morning and asked if he would help him with money to buy Arch Bell's farm. But Jack Morgan hadn't been very receptive, especially after he'd heard about yesterday's drinking spree at Charlie Nick's and leaving his granddaughter outside a pub in the sun all day.

"You'll have to prove you can stay off the drink, boyo, before I invest any money in a farm for you," Jack said crossly. "And leaving Meggie outside all day. Anything could have happened to her. Those Casanova Cowboy Yanks could have molested her, you see. No. Dai. You'll have to show me you're more responsible before I put any cash in."

His bloody sister Mae had to open her big mouth, Dai thought sourly. And he hadn't wanted to bring Meggie with him anyway.

Dai took all day to drive back to the Glen calling into the pubs at Drury, Mercer and Rangiriri on the way. Meggie vowed as she sat in the cab of the truck waiting for him that she would never go anywhere with her father again.

CHAPTER TWELVE

GLEN AFTON 1945

Huntly District High had only three courses in their curriculum. There was General and the other two courses were Commercial and Academic. None fitted Meggie's talents so she went with Sarry and Moira into General. There was more teaching about the events of the war than there had been at Primary school and Meggie found herself becoming more interested in the war in Europe. In mid-February bombers turned the German city of Dresden into an inferno and an estimated 60,000 people died. Twenty New Zealand Lancaster bombers had taken part in the operation so it was ardently discussed in their Social Studies lesson.

The Pacific war raged on and the Americans along with New Zealanders, Aussies and British troops pushed the Japanese further back towards their homeland. Bomber raids over Japan destroyed a quarter of Tokyo and on April 1st the Americans began raids on Okinawa that were to last for the next three months. More news was filtering through about the cruelty and huge death toll of our captured soldiers working under Japanese rule on the Burma railway and in all an estimated 14,000 men were to die building the bridge and railway in Burma.

One morning Huntly High school was called to a special assembly. Mr. Clifton, the headmaster, looked grave when he stood on the rostrum to address the pupils.

"We have received the sad news that America's President Roosevelt has died." He paused to allow the significance of his statement to sink in with the school kids. "As we teeter on the brink of victory in this Second World War, the great President of the United States of America has been taken ..." His voice broke. "... taken before he can taste the victory we all know we will enjoy. So many of America's sons have lost their lives in the Islands while defending our shores from the Japanese."

The headmaster stopped, seemingly overcome with emotion and the kids shuffled and twitched as they waited for him to continue. "We will now have two minutes silence to remember President Roosevelt and give gratitude to all those American servicemen who have lost their lives defending our country." After the assembly was dismissed a sense of gloom descended over the school.

Towards the end of April the BBC news announced that Russian and American troops had put Berlin under siege. Seeing the war going against him, Adolph Hitler committed suicide five days later. Eva Braun, his wife of just 24 hours, killed herself, too, by taking poison with him. New Zealand received the news of Hitler's death with great joy and everyone said the war was 'as good as over.'

On May 8th Huntly High students were again called to a special assembly and Mr. Clifton announced – with a broad smile this time – that the war in Europe was over. That night Florrie allowed the girls to sit up and listen to the BBC news from London, as Prime Minister Churchill was to give a victory speech. Winston Churchill announced that the war in Europe was officially over. "Advance Britannia. Long live the cause of freedom. God save the King," he stated, as he ended his VE speech.

Over the next month troops, who had been serving in Europe, began returning to New Zealand. With them came stories of the Nazi horrors in the Concentration camps, revelations about people being burnt in cremation ovens, and of a German Holocaust on a scale like nothing known before, began to shock the whole world.

Alf Bredeson was the first of the mining valleys' soldiers who had survived the war to arrive home. The only thing on his mind when he landed in Auckland was a good feed of New Zealand tucker so he set out for The Silver Grill in Customs Street. By God, a man needed this, he thought, as his meal was placed on the table before him. A steak nicely browned, that covered more than half the plate, the egg on top staring at him like a blinded eye, and onions and chips still sizzling from the deep fat they were cooked in. Worcester and tomato sauce mingled together on top, then followed by a smoke with the cup of tea. Five bob the lot and, he considered, it was bloody worth it.

At Glen Afton a welcome home dance was arranged for Alf Bredeson who had served in the 3rd Echelon in Fiji and gone on to fight in Egypt and the Middle East. The hall had been decorated with nikau palms and decorations from the Women's Institute concert props.

Alf looked handsome in his army uniform as he whirled around the floor giving all the young girls a dance. Bob Cochrane gave a welcoming home speech and when Alf replied he announced that he had married an English rose in London and his bride would be arriving at Glen Afton as soon as she could get a passage out from England.

The older girls were visibly disappointed. Meggie's disappointment was that Simon chose to go drinking at the powerhouse rather than attend the dance. Maybe her mother was right. Maybe he did have the makings of an absolute boozer and she'd be better to forget him.

After three months of solid bombing Okinawa finally fell and the American and New Zealand troops crossed to the mainland of Japan. Then in

August of 1945 America dropped an atomic bomb on Hiroshima and another on Nagasaki. The Japanese surrendered and the Pacific war was over.

Sarry and Meggie knew nothing of the end of the Pacific war until they reached Huntly High that morning. There the kids were running around out of control. There were no teachers in sight and the pupils continued to behave in a barbarous way until finally the teachers appeared and restored order. The kids were lined up and given white satin ribbons, with VJ painted in bright red to pin onto their uniforms.

Later they were marched through the main street of Huntly and then allowed to go home. It had been raining and the slush from the metal road splashed up onto the back of their long black stockings. But regardless of the rain people in the street were shouting and hugging each other. Everyone seemed to be floating on air.

The girls were able to catch the earlier train back to the Glen. Meggie wished she could share the wonderful news of victory with Simon. She knew he was on backshift so she went straight from the train to Griffith's Boarding House. Everyone there was acting as if they were drunk and Florrie and Rose Griffith were in the kitchen sipping sherry from tiny glasses. Meggie suspected they'd been sipping for quite a while, as their noses were very red. They didn't notice her as she slipped down the passage and when Simon saw her he whirled her off her feet.

"Hav'ya heard the news? We've won the bloody war." His mouth found hers and for moments they were swept away in the joy of victory forgetting all else. Then Simon pushed her away and looking at her for a second or so, growled, "How much bloody longer have you got at school?"

Before Meggie could answer he spoke again. "Ya know yer old lady's in the kitchen, don'cha?"

Meggie nodded. "Yep. But they didn't see me come down here."

He grabbed her arm and pulled her towards the front door. "C'mon. Quick. Out the front door before they see us now."

They dashed out the front door and ran down the road through a fine drizzle of rain and were up in the bush behind the baches before anyone could have noticed them. Once there, they fell breathless onto a damp bed of bracken and leaves. The bush whispered to itself with a faint patter of soft misty rain on the leaves blending with the subdued rustle and rub of leaf and branches. They could hear the muffled clatter of skips running from the mine mouth and spilling their loads onto the screens. The surrounding hills were lost in a bank of mist giving nothing of the appearance of what this victorious day should be.

Simon buried his face in her hair, now sprinkled with tiny beads of mist. He lifted her face and his mouth gently explored her lips, then, as he became more passionate, twigs snapped beneath them in the bed of leaves they lay on. And as their mouths continued to caress they became suspended in a place where neither time nor consequence existed. Meggie began to feel physically different. She couldn't think; she could hardly breathe. Simon lay across her, his face hot on her breasts, his breathing quick and uneven.

Then the bush suddenly became very cold and a small spiteful whirlwind, as though having been sent to cut across their passion, whipped the dead leaves into spinning vortices. The mist from the hills came down lower and spread over the bush floor like a thin layer of icing on a cake. Simon raised himself and there were tears in his eyes. He blinked them away but made no attempt to hide them.

"How long did ya say before you leave school?" he asked again.

"I didn't. But I've got another year and a bit," she answered.

"Jeez, girl. That's too long for me to wait. I can't wait that long," he repeated. "I want you now."

Simon knew he could so easily take this child who already had a woman's body right now if he wanted to, but he knew that he would not. "C'mon," he said, pulling her up roughly. "Ya'd better get home."

They ran back up the road with puddles splashing under their feet. Simon left her and ran on ahead and she knew instinctively not to follow him back to the boarding house. No one was home when she arrived at her house so she fed the chooks and did her jobs then went to the bedroom to sketch pictures of what she imagined VJ Day should have been, but it was not. Somehow making believe relieved her disappointment on the cold drizzly day.

A victory dance was quickly arranged for the next Saturday night and was to be held at the Buffalo Lodge Hall at Pukemiro. Merv Bowman asked Meggie to draw the posters for the shops to display and she got many compliments about her art. The young jokers cut nikau palms from the bush in the morning to decorate the hall. Everyone searched their back rooms for red, white and blue ribbons and crepe paper, and by that evening the paint flaked interior of the old hall looked dazzlingly festive.

Because of the rationing the women had limited supplies but nevertheless they managed to prepare a sumptuous supper. Arch Bell, from up on the farm, donated a pig for roasting and oodles of fresh cream and old Edgley the butcher at Pukemiro supplied other cuts of meat. Florrie and Dai gave eggs and home brew while Ed Hubbard contributed tins of fruit that he had kept under the counter for special customers.

The whole of the residents of Glen Afton and Pukemiro, from the youngest to the eldest, turned out for the Victory dance, including the mine managers and deputies from the mines. Mrs. Stafford had on a long dress that Sarry reckoned she had made out of her old sitting room curtains.

Olwyn Griffith, feeling sorry for Meggie, had given her a sundress that had a sort of a built-in bra. Meggie wore the dress to the Victory dance.

Merv Bowman escorted Olwyn to the dance, as Roddy McLaughlin was on backshift at the Mac mine. Once the dance had begun there was the usual crowd of young jokers, smartly dressed in sports coats, collar and tie, skulking around the door looking the girls over. Correct procedure was for the girls to sit lined up along the walls of the hall. Something like a market with the girls as produce and the blokes the buyers.

There were a few new faces as some of the Huntly jokers, who had heard about the Victory dance out the back, had pooled their petrol coupons and driven out in a couple of cars. One of them approached Meggie for the Destiny waltz.

"Howdja like ta cut a rug?" he asked with a gorgeous grin.

Sarry poked Meggie in the back as she got up to dance with Jamie Forbes, reputed to be the local Casanova in Huntly. They won the Destiny waltz, the prize being a box of chocolates and when they were opened, the chocolates were white with age.

Jamie sat down beside Meggie indicating he was her escort for the night. Sarry poked her again and nodded towards the entrance. Simon had just come in and was glaring at Jamie Forbes sitting with his girl. The band struck up again and old Raine, the emcee, announced take your partners for a maxina.

"C'mon darlin'. Let's trip the light fantastic again," Jamie shouted above the band as he pulled her to her feet.

Simon lurched towards them but was too late. They were already in the circle dancing the maxina. Meggie knew he had been drinking before he came and looked as though he was already pretty well tanked up. He hadn't been in touch since they had been in the bush on VJ Day and that really hurt her so she shot him a tight glance as she turned and swayed to the rhythm of the maxina with Jamie.

After the maxina Rhys Evans took the stage and the emcee announced Rhys would sing 'Trees.'

"Gawd Dammit mun," yelled Totty Dunsborough. "Di ye no' know another song?"

A snigger spread around the hall and Meggie, Sarry and Moira covered their mouths as they giggled. But Rhys took no notice and just carried on. The piano twiddled the intro and he began to sing in his lovely Welsh voice.

"I think-a that I shall nev-a see-a, A poem as lovely as a tree-a …"

The girls were in fits and old Raine told them to shut up or he'd put them out of the hall. Dai was standing near the stage crooning away with Rhys.

"Beeyoutiful. Bloody beeyoutiful," he cried, as Rhys's voice faded away on the last note.

Taking another huge swig from his bottle he leapt onto the stage and began singing 'Red Sails In The Sunset." The piano caught up with him and the rendition was great. The men whistled and stamped the floor until the dust rose to mingle with the cigarette smoke.

"Jeez. Didn't know yer had it in ya, Dai," they bellowed.

The supper dance was announced and Jamie claimed Meggie again. Simon was nowhere to be seen and Meggie felt her heart sink a little. Then the hall was cleared and the men set up trestles down one end of the hall by the stage. The hard working women laid out the meat, and the sandwiches and cakes they'd prepared in the back room behind the hall and everybody bogged in, especially the young kids. After the supper was cleared away the emcee sprinkled powder on the dance floor and the little kids pulled each other up and down the hall on sacks to work the powder into the boards.

Alec Porter, the drummer, announced the dancing was about to begin again by banging on his drums loudly. Everyone hooted and all the mine officials left the dance. Things seemed more relaxed after they'd gone and the men concentrated on getting coarsely drunk.

There was a series of items in the second half of the evening. Sarry's father sang 'Begin the Begin', and Sarry said she was so humiliated she could die. That was followed by 'Among my Souvenirs', 'I'm a Lassie From Lancashire', Danny Boy', and finally Terry Best sang his usual 'I'm Alone Because I Love You', and wept with emotion throughout the song. Everyone in the hall joined in to help him through the last verse and the girls giggled uncontrollably. Jamie Forbes laughed and said he thought the entertainment was quite unique.

Soldiers who had survived Japanese Prisoner of War camps began arriving back in New Zealand. Ben Highley and Sid Stamp's kin did not recognize them when they stepped down onto the Glen Afton Railway Station platform. Mrs. Highley from Pukemiro cried bitterly when she saw her skin and bone husband.

Sarry told Meggie that Sid Stamp had been young and really good looking when he went away to the war, and now he returned from the Changi POW camp a bent and broken scrap of humanity.

The people in the mining valleys were shocked. They'd seen the newsreels at the pictures about the atrocities in the POW camps, but seeing their sons return so frail and emaciated showed them the reality of the war, a war that had so nearly reached them!

CHAPTER THIRTEEN

1946

As the soft greenness of spring settled over the raw countryside things were about to change dramatically for the Morgan family. Once the euphoria of VJ Day had lessened and the Home Guard was disbanded Dai Morgan felt he'd lost his importance in the village.

However, he already had his heart set on Arch Bell's farm on the hill and negotiated with Arch to leasing the land with the option to buy. He told Florrie only when the deal was settled and signed. She was furious and Meggie's heart sank to the ground when she was told. Emmie, with her aptitude for figures, already had work at Ed Hubbard's temporary store in the hall and it meant a lot further for her to walk to and from the shop.

The October morning was sunny when the Morgan's shifted their belongings into the farmhouse on the hill above the pottery. Meggie knew instinctively that she would hate life on a farm and she was right. She'd been as near too happy as possible living in the mine house near Sarry and across the road from Simon although she hadn't seen him since the night of the Victory dance. The weather had returned to winter-like conditions by November. On the farm everything was horribly wet and mucky. Now, when Emmie and Meggie went out, they needed to wear gumboots through the muddy, wet paddocks and put their dry shoes on by the hawthorne hedge that bordered Rhys Evan's paddock. Sometimes in the rain, they were saturated by the time they reached the village, with Dai never offering to drive them in the truck when the rain was heavy – as other fathers seemed to do. Both girls absolutely hated this new way of life.

It was raining, and had turned cold, that November afternoon when Meggie stepped onto the railway platform at Glen Afton. The strong southwest wind swept down the gully, creating whirlwinds that hit both the station and the goods shed full on. It swirled around the alighting passengers, buffeting them with hot sulphurous smoke and steam that spewed from the huffing steam engine. Meggie had no coat to keep out the biting wind. Her second hand gym frock of well-washed serge had little warmth and she shivered. She didn't want to go home today. She never did nowadays if it came to that, but it was worse on wet and gloomy days and today's leaden skies made her feel she couldn't cope with the work that was waiting for her at home. She speculated that there'd be a note on the kitchen table telling her to go straight to the milking shed. God, how she hated the cowshed. The awful stink of cow urine and droppings nauseated her as did the steamy sweat from the cow's wet coats as they bustled and pushed waiting their turn to enter the cow bales for milking. She hated the feel of her aching shoulder caused from forcing the cows haunches back in order to leg rope them. She hated the splits on her hands from caustic soda in the water from washing the cows' udders. Just thinking of the prospect of the shed, hot needles began prickling her skin. More than ever, she did not want to go home today.

She walked slowly up the ramp, fought her way against the wind on the overhead Railway Bridge, and then turned onto the main road running through the Glen, the sodden gym frock slapping against her thighs leaving red welts on her flesh, Meggie found herself veering towards Griffith's Boarding House on the rise. She opened the back door of the big house and the heat from the sizable coal ranges, and smell of cooking food, swept over her.

"'ho's that now? Is it you, Simon?" Mrs Griffith called from the pantry. Meggie felt better already just for hearing the Welsh lilt. It reminded her of Granddad Morgan. She knew full well she'd be in trouble for not going straight home but a short time in this safe cosy home would make the punishment worthwhile.

Mrs. Griffith looked aghast when Meggie entered the pantry, water dripping from the hem of her gymslip and her wet hair flattened against her head.

"Oh, lordy, lordy, Megan Morgan isn't it. What are you doing with no coat on your back? I wonder you will catch pneumonia, you will."

She bustled Meggie next to an open firebox.

"I'll make you some hot cocoa, now," she called over her shoulder as she hobbled away, her arthritic limp even more pronounced with the inclement weather.

The brass handle on the back door rattled as it opened again. Simon stamped his feet on the concrete step and shook off the oilskin that had protected his black singlet and baggy work trousers.

"Jeez! That's some bloody storm out there," he yelled to his mother.

"Yes. And there is Megan Morgan wanderin' around with no coat. You can stop that swearin' in my kitchen, too. In front of a young girl and all."

Simon jerked his head around the corner, at the same time slicking down his wet hair. His eyes took in Meggie, her thin school uniform sticking to her body. The bumps of her nipples were quite visible under the wet fabric and the sight stirred him. For a while he just stood looking at her. Meggie lowered her eyes. She hadn't seen him for ages and she hated him seeing her like this and wished now that she hadn't come.

"You okay, Megs?" he asked softly.

She nodded. He stepped close and wrapped his arms around her. "Christ Meggie. You tear my heart out when I see ya like this."

Mrs. Griffith startled them by coming in shaking out a heavy maroon coat.

"'ere. Take this, lovey. None of mine wear it now." She shrugged Meggie into the coat. "Simon. You take Megan part of the way. It's gettin' dark so don't be too long now, mind."

Meggie, snug in the coat and with Si's arm around her felt happier than she had done for weeks. Since Dai had shifted them all onto this hateful farm, in fact.

They sloshed through the wet grass in the sodden paddocks, then at the top of the hill stopped, and sheltered under the belt of pines that roared loudly in the wind scattering millions of needles. Simon pulled his oilskin around them both, and then lifting her wet face he turned it up towards his own. He brushed his lips softly across hers, and his warm mouth caused Meggie to move instinctively against him. He then pressed with an urgency that sent a thrill tingling through her body and his hands stroked the nipples standing high on her breasts. Suddenly, roughly, he pushed her away, muttering, "For Chrissake, girl."

Meggie started to shake again.

"I'm sorry," he said after a few minutes. "It's not your fault. I won't come any further with you in case yer old lady spots me. You go on, honey, and I'll watch to see you get home okay."

Meggie picked up her saturated schoolbag and ran quickly down the other side of the hill towards her house. It stood stark and alone in the centre of a paddock and looked spooky in the gloom of the fading light that encompassed the wooden structure.

"Megs," Simon called after her. "I'll meetcha off the train tomorrow. I want to talk to ya."

Meggie just nodded. She was concentrating on the trouble that would be waiting for her arriving home at this time.

The next afternoon on the train home Gerry Dunstan was holding everyone attention with the graphic coloured pictures in the Peoples Pictorial magazine. The huge plume of an exploding atomic bomb was all colours, not just white or grey smoke, but purples, reds and blacks. There was even a tinge of yellow in the smoke and that made it look really sickly. Meggie felt a pang of fear when she looked at the photos. But she didn't dwell on them the way Sarry did as her mind was on what Simon wanted to talk to her about when he met her from the train.

"If one of those landed here I'd go straight up the bush and stay there," stated Sarry.

"That wouldn't do ya much good," sniggered Gerry. "There'd be no bush anyway. This thing flattens everything for hundreds of miles around. You'd be fried to a little cinder in one second flat."

Sarry was scared. "Shut up. Yer only trying to scare me. Isn't he Megs?"

Meggie just shrugged.

"What's eating you?" Sarry asked Meggie. "You've hardly said a word to us all day."

The train had gathered speed once leaving the lakeshore and Sarry had to shout over the clacking wheels to make herself heard.

"Nothing." Meggie answered. "I'm just not allowed to go to the pictures for a month."

"Jeez. Why?"

"I didn't go straight home last night and Dad was mad as a meat axe. He had to finish milking the cows on his own."

"Where didja go then?"

"Into Griffith's to dry out. And Simon walked up the hill with me."

"Jeez. That was asking for it, wasn't it? Didja mother see him?"

"No. He left me by the pines. But he wants to meet me off the train. Reckons he's got something to tell me."

Sarry was quiet for a long time while she thought about the situation. She really loved her friend Megs and hated the way she was made to work. Since they'd moved onto Bell's farm, above the pottery, Meggie wasn't allowed to go anywhere. She'd always had work to do, even when they lived in the mine house, but then at least, they had some time to play together. Nowadays, Sarry only saw

Meggie at school or at the pictures sometimes. There'd been that big blow up after old Ma Stafford, the mine manager's wife, had pimped on them going up the Mac track alone and that was years ago. After that, Mrs Morgan had forbidden Meggie to ever be on her own with Simon again. She had, of course, and Sarry had been their alibi on several occasions. Now, if they were starting to meet again, she thought Meggie was playing with fire.

"Whatja reckon he wants to tell you?" Sarry asked at last.

"Dunno," Meggie replied.

The engine whistle squealed announcing the train's arrival as it chuffed through the last cutting before Glen Afton Station. Meggie sat glued to the window as they clattered past the baches and the bathhouse. Relief filled her as she spotted Simon on his own walking down towards the road bridge.

Yesterday's storm had passed but the afternoon was still dull. A mist was low on the hills, and already there was fine drizzle in the air, as Meggie ran back up the railway tracks to meet Simon. They clasped hands and headed up to the bush behind the baches. Riki Whetu was stretched out on the veranda strumming softly on his guitar. He stopped playing to wave to them, handsome as any film star with his dark easy eyes and wavy jet-black hair.

"How ya going, Riki? Don't see much of ya now yer workin' over the other side."

"I'll see ya at the dance on Saturday if yer going. Crikey, you two are taking a risk, aren't ya? Yer old man drove around towards Puke about ten minutes ago. Yous had better get out of sight before he comes back."

Simon pulled Meggie quickly into the scrub behind the baches. From there they could watch the road and not come out until Dai had passed on his way home. The ground was too damp to sit so Simon leaned against the thick trunk of a Miro tree and drew Meggie against him for a moment. His body was still warm from the bathhouse and he smelt soap scrubbed clean. Fine drops of mist had settled on their hair making them look shaggy. Simon laughed at her look, at the same time burying his face in the mist beads that sprinkled her hair.

"What happened last night?" he asked.

"Aw. I'm not allowed to go to the pictures or to the dance on Saturday night but what did you want to tell me, Si?"

"Nothin'". I just wanted to see ya."

"Really! I thought it was something to do with Hazel."

"With Hazel. What about Hazel?"

"Well, I thought you were going steady with her."

"Go steady. Cripes, what made yer think that?"

"Well. You always sit with her at the pictures now. And she told Sarry you two were going steady."

Simon laughed. "Ya mean she always sits with me."

They were both silent for a while, each a bit tongue-tied as to what to say next. Simon broke the silence. "Cripes, I'll be glad when you leave school, Megs?"

"Why?"

"Ya know why. We can go steady. Yer old lady can't stop ya seeing me then, eh?"

"Dad says I'm not allowed to go back to school after Christmas. Reckons he needs me to work on the farm."

Simon was shocked. "Jeez girl. You can't do heavy farm work."

"Dad reckons he's not going to pay a farmhand when I can do the work for nothing."

"Well, stone the bloody crows. I knew Dai was a miserable bastard but that takes the bloody cake." He shook his head in disbelief. "What's yer old lady say?"

Meggie shrugged, but before she could answer the murmur of a vehicle sounded up the gully. "That'll be Dad coming now."

They stood in silence watching the road below as the growling engine came closer and Dai's truck chugged past turning off onto the clay and metal side road that led to the farm.

"Mum must be doing the milking on her own," Meggie observed, with Dai being on the road at past milking time. "I'd better get home."

Simon didn't want her to go. "Aw, jeez, Megs. Yer can't let them do this to ya. What about yer drawing and all that?"

Meggie shook her head and turned away; unable to think about the art lessons she was missing or about being with Simon. Tears filled her eyes as she ran down the track past the Maori baches. Sometimes she wished the war was still on as life seemed to have become more miserable for her since it had ended.

CHAPTER FOURTEEN

Following the end of the war the Glen experienced many changes. Manpowered miners from out of the district were free to return to their hometowns and without the military orders for sanitary ware, and with domestic pottery from Great Britain beginning to filter back into New Zealand's market, the pottery works closed down. The drinkers from the powerhouse were quick to claim the building for a new club, which they called 'The Blueroom'. Materials became more available and Ed Hubbard was able to build a new store opposite the railway station, this time in concrete hollowstone blocks hoping not to risk another fire. Rationing continued on many foodstuffs, but other things, like dress material, wool and cosmetics became available once again. Alf Bredeson's wife, Sally, arrived from England and the young girls thought she was absolutely beautiful.

Although the move to Arch Bell's farm had been difficult for both the girls the advantage for Meggie was being closer to the bush. She loved the smell; it was different to any other smell she knew. As often as she could she would sneak away to the gully of native bush where she felt safe. Away from the sweet sickening smell of booze, no vile stink from the pigsties and cowshed and it was so quiet. It was the sort of a hush like one would imagine if the world stopped turning. Her little gully was a soft place where there was no bellow of threatening voices, nor the sounds of rats that kept her awake at night as they scrambled and scratched in the walls of the old house. Little by little she had carried bits and pieces down and formed a sort of art studio where she kept her paper and pencils in a Bycroft biscuit tin to keep them dry. There she would sit on a mossy log and sketch the leaves and ferns shading the subtle tones of light in the bush, the way Mr. Bowman had taught her. The only sounds were of the birds and trickle of the stream below. It was her own little paradise and the only place she had to escape to.

The first Christmas on the farm was a miserable affair. Though Dai had kept his promise to stay off the booze he made an exception on Christmas Day and spent it at the Blueroom. Florrie and Meggie did the evening milking and again next morning when Dai didn't return home. In fact, it was three more days before he came back to the farm.

Meggie stopped scouring the separator and watched from the cowshed as her father's truck chugged and bounced over the rough farm track then came to a spluttering halt in front of the house. Dai staggered from the cab, a butt hanging from his lip, muttering something in a voice thick with drink. Her stomach knotted with fear as she observed his crumpled person lurch into the house. After three mornings of carrying heavy full cans of cream half a mile out to the gate so as not to miss the cream lorry, her arms ached so much they felt as though they had been pulled from their sockets. Only Dai could drive the horses and koneke, but they couldn't leave the cream, as it was their only source of income now.

The skin on her hands was broken and weeping from caustic soda and as she looked at her father she knew in that moment that she hated him for bringing them onto this farm. Ever since he'd made her leave school and the end of last year she'd been hounded to do this or do that. No time to sketch or draw. She was not allowed to go to any school now to finish her education, yet he could go off to who knows where, spending money on the booze, and sometimes not come back for days on end. Anger filled her and she raced down the track to the house. Inside Dai was snarling at Florrie and Emmie

"…Man works his fingers to the bloody bone and you lazy bitches sit around drinkin' tea …"

Meggie went straight for him and he hit the wall with a thud. "I hate you," she screamed, as she went for him again. "I hate you … hate you." She pummeled her fists at him hitting anywhere they found a mark.

Florrie screamed, "Stop it, you stupid little cat! Don't talk to your father like that!"

Dai, taken off guard with the attack, began to retch and too helpless to restrain himself he spewed stale vomit onto the floor.

Meggie turned in disgust and ran out of the house, stumbled through the chook run, across the cattle race and down into the bush gully that ran down to the Pukemiro road. Down to her own private place. For a long time she just sat and cried. She hated her life so much and decided to live in the bush and never go home again. It was no use trying to draw, for one thing her arms and hands were too sore and another she was too upset. Late in the afternoon she walked out of the bush to wash her face in the creek

"Hey! What ya up to, Megs?"

Meggie jumped with fright, and then looking around saw Riki Whetu hopping over the stile and into the paddock. He sat down on the bank beside her.

"Hey. What's the matter, girl?" he asked again.

Meggie began crying again and sobbed out what had happened since Christmas day. Riki nodded, at the same time putting his thumbs together on either side of a blade of grass and concentrating on pulling it up slowly by the roots, as he listened. The grass blade came free of its sheath with a tiny squeaking sound. He chewed the sweet tip thoughtfully before speaking.

"Yeah. I knew old Dai was on the piss," he said quietly when Meggie stopped talking. "Ya should have yelled out and I would have come up and

200

helped with the milking. Actually I've been worried about Emmie but yer old lady puts me off coming up to yer place."

Meggie laughed.

"That's better, girl." He chucked her under the chin.

"Emmie's okay. Mum won't let her do any milking anyway."

"Well if yer really gonna live in the bush I'll bring ya round some tucker," he said, raising his eyebrows in slight amusement. "But I reckon yer'd be better to go home. Yer old lady'll be worried."

"S'pose your right. I wish I could go and live with Granddad in Auckland."

"I'll come up in the morning to get some milk and see if yer all okay," Riki promised.

"If Dad's sober enough he's starting the haymaking on New Year's day. Come for that, please." Meggie paused. "And thanks, Riki," she said self-consciously.

Riki called in at Griffith's on his way home and told Simon about finding Meggie so distraught in the bush. Simon was furious but felt helpless. Riki suggested that they both turn up for the haymaking.

New Year's Day dawned clear with air like chardonnay and the sky so blue you could drown in it. Alf Bredeson and some of the local men, including Riki and Simon, came early to start the haymaking. Sally, Alf's new bride from England, came to the house to help out. Florrie and Meggie

201

were kept busy carrying heavy milk cans of lemon and barley water and food to the men in the hay paddock, while Emmie and Sally baked endless scones and pikelets, and they all made huge plates of sandwiches when it came to lunchtime. Meggie loved Sally on sight. She was blonde and wore her hair rolled up at the sides just like the film stars did and she talked with a quaint accent.

As well as feeding all the haymakers, Florrie and Meggie came in for doing the milking too. God, how she grew to hate the chug chug of the milking machines and that whining separator. Dai took the jokers out to the Waingaro Pub to shout them drinks for helping with the haymaking. Riki and Simon stayed and helped with the milking. Florrie wasn't very pleased but left them to clean up the shed so for a while they joked about and had a bit of fun. Simon got Meggie to one side.

"Riki told me what happened the other day. I could kill the fuckin' bastard." He shook his head angrily. "Christ, Megs. I feel so goddamn helpless."

Dai took another week to return from Waingaro, or who knows where, and the heavy manual work was sapping Meggie's energy. She was always tired yet she lay awake at night aching all over and she hated her father more than ever for bringing them onto this awful farm. And in some of her self-pitying moods she even thought of killing herself.

Rose Griffith missed Florrie working at the boardinghouse but when the pottery closed down she wasn't needed as Olwyn took over Florrie's work. As well, with the manpowered workers gone, there wasn't so much to do so she and Olwyn could manage. Merv Bowman was still boarding at Griffith's and he and Olwyn became engaged at Easter weekend. There was to be an engagement party so Rose sent Cissy Griffith up to Morgan's farm to invite them to the party to be held at the boardinghouse on Saturday night. Meggie hadn't seen Simon for a couple of months, since the haymaking in fact. With the heavy manual work she was even too tired to go to the pictures nowadays. Besides, she had no money as Dai didn't pay her anything for her labour.

Merv Bowman sat down beside Meggie on the couch in Griffith's sitting room. He was shocked at the look of her. This girl, who he had seen as his prodigy, looked thinner and was quiet and nervy. She should still be at school, he thought, not getting up at all hours in the morning and in all weathers in to milk cows. He didn't know how her parents had got away with taking her away from compulsory schooling.

The rumour was that they'd got a certificate from a Huntly doctor saying that Florrie was ill and needed help at home and the Education Board had accepted that. Doctor Willis at Pukemiro would never have given them such a certificate. Merv had a fine sense of justice and it made him fume every time he thought about it. There weren't a lot of talented children in the area and to think Meggie had the misfortune to belong to a drunken father and an insensitive mother incensed him.

"How are you, Meggie," he asked, observing she was wearing one of Olwyn's dresses that was now too big for her.

She didn't answer, just looked at him with eyes that were tight with unshed tears and he imagined she would have looked this way when she had been a little girl with hurt feelings but refused to cry. The look unnerved him. He was at a loss at what to say next. "How do you like the farm?" he asked in desperation.

This time she answered. "I hate it."

She spoke in monotone with no life in her voice at all. They've broken her spirit, he thought. She's far from the girl who got up to mischief with Sarry Adams. Merv looked around for Simon then remembered that he and several others had sloped off to the Blueroom straight after the speeches had finished. It was damn rude of them, but he knew it was because of Florrie that Simon had gone. Perhaps he could have a word with Florrie Morgan, appeal to her better self, about Meggie finishing her education at least.

"Are you keeping up your artwork?" he asked only to break the strained silence. "Wasn't your father going to send for an art correspondence course for you?"

"He never sent for it. But I go down the bush and draw when I get time," she answered flatly.

Merv felt he could weep. He stood up to go. "Take care, Meggie," was all he said as he made his way through the celebrating crowd and outside into the warm still night. His leg dragged more than ever. It always did when he was upset. He looked around the valley, and the lights that flickered from the windows splintering the darkness, reminiscent of a glow-worm cave. The night air was scented with late summer flowers and filled with the whirr of cicadas. This should be the happiest night of my life, he thought, looking up as a stringy cloud whispered across the face of the moon. He'd won Olwyn's heart, was warmly embraced by the Griffith family, and yet the encounter with Meggie Morgan had plummeted him to the depths of despair.

The returned POW's who were there were upsetting him too. They looked wasted and gaunt sitting cross-legged on the floor. Nothing would entice them to sit on a chair. They only felt comfortable sitting on the ground as they had done while in those disgusting POW camps. Gods' truth, he thought, whatever has happened to the gentle things of life I knew before that goddamn bloody war started?

Dai arrived back at the farm at noon the next day. They saw him from a distance at first silhouetted against the sky poised on the high ridge at the back of the farm. He was riding a young mare.

"My God, it's the Lone Ranger," muttered Florrie sarcastically as Dai galloped down the slope and dismounted before her. She was furious. "We can't make ends meet now without you paying out money for something that will eat feed that should be for the milking stock." With that she burst into tears.

Dai looked abashed. "I bought her fer the girls to ride," he lied.

They all knew it would have been a drunken deal over the bar at the Blueroom.

"C'mon, Emmie," he called, feigning good humour. "I'll giv'ya a leg up."

Emmie went over to the horse, which was snorting and looking around with wild eyes. Dai positioned his hands to leg her up saying, "Yer farm girls now and should be ridin' horses."

He jerked Emmie's foot with his clasped hands but she didn't manage to straddle the horse. He tried again this time giving her foot a mighty boost and Emmie went right over the top falling onto the ground on the other side of the horse. Dai hid his annoyance. He wished he'd never bought the horse, too, but had to brazen the situation out now. He hoped this wouldn't take too long as his head was throbbing like a drum.

"C'mon Meggie. You'll get on okay."

But Meggie was just as unathletic as Emmie and couldn't get astride the horse either. Dai lost his patience. "What the bloody hell's wrong with you two?" Dai yelled at her. "Yer got lead in yer arses or what?"

Meggie started to cry, too, and made off for her hideaway in the bush with Dai's voice following her.

"Buy ya a bloody horse and what do ya do. Yer nothin' but bloody millstones around a man's neck."

Next morning when Meggie carried the swingletrees out of the implement shed, Dai attempted to apologize to her. She didn't answer. Now all her thoughts were concentrated on ways of escaping from this awful place of misery.

In no time Nick Handisides, from the next farm along the road, turned up at Morgan's after hearing about the new riding horse. Nick and his brother were bachelors and Nick had been waiting for an excuse to visit the farm and see the Morgan girls. "I'll teach ya ta ride the horse," he offered Meggie, with a lecherous smile.

He mounted the horse with ease and stopped her beside the wooden gate. "Here. Climb up on the gate and get on behind me."

Meggie had no trouble getting on the horse that way and holding Nick tightly around the waist they set of at a gallop along the farm track, then down the road to the Handisides farm. Nick was great fun joking with her all the way and making her laugh.

The Handisides' farm was a real tip with broken and rusting implements lying around everywhere.

Nick invited her inside the house for a cup of tea but once Meggie saw the state of the kitchen she declined. Huge blowflies buzzed around like bomber planes after the rotting food and overall filth of the room. Dirty dishes overflowed on the tiny bench and the coalrange was covered in grease and scraps of food. Seeing her distaste didn't seem to bother Nick. "Yep. What we need around here is a damn good wumun."

His expression, as he eyed Meggie over, left no doubt that she was his number one candidate for the position. Meggie felt uneasy. "I'd better get home. It's nearly time for milking."

"Yep." Nick said good-naturedly and they galloped back to the farm just in time for afternoon tea before starting milking. Nick invited himself in and looked hungrily at Emmie's baking set out on a plate. He emptied the plate in record time and Florrie glared at him.

"I hope he's not going to make a habit of coming here for afternoon tea," she said, as soon as he had gone home to milk his own cows.

Nick did become a daily visitor much to Florrie's annoyance, always timing Meggie's riding lesson to finish at afternoon tea time.

Meggie liked Nick. He was funny and could whistle and sing like Tex Morton. They would sing cowboy songs as they rode and Nick would whistle the choruses. Within a week Meggie could manage the horse on her own. She became quite fond of the horse and called her Poppy.

Poppy liked Nick, too. When she saw him coming she would whinny and start blowing through her nostrils. She hoped that he would have an apple for her and she would look at him with big anxious eyes and ears at a slightly forward cock. Her soft velvet lips would pluck the fruit out of Nick's palm and flick it back between her huge molars where it vanished in one juicy crunch. Nick still continued to call at afternoon tea time but after two weeks Florrie decided to put a stop to his visits. She buttered a plate of dog biscuits and set them out on the table.

"These look great," Nick said as he crunched hard on one. There followed an awful crack as Nick's front tooth snapped off and fell into his lap. Nick was in a lot of pain and Dai had to drive him around to Dr Willis at Pukemiro. That meant Florrie had to do the milking with Meggie so in a way things had backfired on her.

"You're a miserable bitch," Dai berated Florrie when he got back from the doctors. "That poor bastard had to have that tooth pulled out."

Florrie didn't answer and Nick stopped coming for afternoon tea.

A letter from Nana Bowen cheered the girls up. She and Granddad Bowen were coming to stay for a few weeks in June. Florrie was pleased but apprehensive too. She hadn't seen her parents since she had left Mapiu in '42. Dai drove the truck to the railway station to pick them up and at first it was exciting to have them staying. Nana Bowen was concerned about the heavy work Meggie did on the farm. "She should still be at school, Florrie," she commented.

Florrie didn't answer. She'd already had a tongue lashing from Merv Bowman, the headmaster at Pukemiro, and was feeling a bit guilty about taking her away from school. She didn't want extra aggravation from her parents.

After a week Dai felt desperate to get away from Florrie's parents with their veiled dislike of him so one afternoon he sneaked off through the front door and down to the Blueroom. No one knew he had gone until Florrie called him for afternoon tea before the milking. Florrie and Meggie took Granddad with them for the evening milking leaving Nana to cook the dinner. Florrie usually cooked at night now that Emmie was working at Ed Hubbard's store.

They'd just finished milking when Dai appeared, drunk and in a terrible rage. He lashed out at Granddad and Nana Bowen. "Yer nothin' but a pair of scroungers and yer can get out now," he bellowed at them.

Florrie began to cry and Nana comforted her. "It's all right, Florrie. We'll go. We know what Dai's like and should never have come."

Florrie wrote a note to Rose Griffith and sent Meggie, still in her gumboots, down to the boarding house with it.

"Oh my goodness. Oh Megan Morgan are you all right?"

Meggie nodded, not trusting herself to speak, as she looked at Mrs. Griffith through a stinging mist of tears.

Rose called to her eldest son who had an old Essex car. "Roland, come 'ere."

Roland appeared in the kitchen doorway. Meggie hoped Simon wouldn't come home and know about their shame.

"Roland. I want you to drive Megan home and bring Mr. and Mrs. Bowen here for the night."

Roland raised his eyebrows. "Never you mind, boyo" she ordered. "Just do it for me."

Next morning Roland drove the grandparents from the boarding house to the railway station. Florrie and Meggie walked down the hill early to see them off as they started their long journey by train back to Mapiu.

Meggie cried as the train pulled out of the station. She had so looked forward to her Nana Bowen's visit and once again her father had spoiled everything. Everything seemed so hopeless and for this she hated him more than ever if that was possible.

"Why do you let him do these things, Mum? Why don't you leave him?" she asked, as they walked through the heavy dew-laden grass back to the farm.

"If it wasn't for you two I would have left him years ago."

Meggie knew that, as that was one of her mother's constant complaints.

"Besides, he'd end up in the gutter if I left," Florrie added. Meggie sensed the reason was more than that.

When Dai sobered up and became aware of what he had done he was full of remorse and tried to apologize. He worked hard on the farm and in an effort to make amends and excused Meggie from many jobs that he previously made her do. But it was no use. Her mind was continually full of wild ideas of escape but she was always too exhausted and had no wherewithal to follow any of them up.

Winter brought frosty nights and freezing mornings with water pipes frozen, and then followed by clear, sparkling days. The atmosphere on the farm remained icy too. Dai Morgan was beginning to realize that his daughters were growing up and developing minds of their own. He felt that he was losing the power he had held over his family for so long and he didn't know how to deal with it.

"I'm jest goin' down the mine fer a load of coal," Dai shouted, as he left the house after the evening meal.

No one answered. The continual icy silence was getting him down so he called into the Blueroom for a quick drink on his way home with the coal. It was well past midnight when, bellowing and shouting, Dai hounded them all out of bed.

"Get up yer lazy bitches and unload this bloody coal."

Meggie and Emmie huddled together as they stumbled out of their beds into the midwinter night clothed only in their thin pajamas. The huge moon cast ample light for them to work by, their bare feet scrunching on the heavy frost already well set in the early morning hours. They both shivered violently as they shoveled the coal from the truck's tray into the coal shed.

"Do somethin' to earn yer bloody keep. A man's nothin' but a meal ticket..."

His voice trailed off as he staggered indoors and fell onto the settee in the kitchen. Both girls were crying now and urine dribbled involuntarily from Emmie sending up thin wisps of steam as it trickled onto the frost-covered ground.

Next morning Emmie packed her belongings and Meggie helped her carry them down the hill to the boardinghouse where Mrs. Griffith let her have a room. Meggie was upset as it meant she was alone on the farm now.

"Emmie. What will I do now? At least you were there with me."

"I'm sorry, Meggie. But I'll never give him the chance to humiliate me like that again."

She left Meggie and went to her work at Hubbard's Store and Meggie walked slowly and reluctantly back up the hill to work another day on misery farm.

CHAPTER FIFTEEN

The winter that Ronnie Holden bought the 'passion wagon' from Andy Niesmith was cold and crisp. Andy, now respectably married, had no further use for the machine. The first owner of the grotesque lime green vehicle had set a tradition that it could only be sold to someone who was seriously courting. No one could rightly remember who the first owner of the notorious wagon had been, only that it had been introduced to the district sometime before the war had begun. What was known for sure was that many proposals of marriage had been made within the square chassis of the nauseous green wagon. However, the passion wagon was a bad choice for Ronnie Holden who made no secret of his liberal ideas about sex before marriage.

Ronnie had begun trotting out Cissy Griffith, Simon's younger sister. Mrs Griffith showed her disapproval with pursed lips each time Cissy left the house on a date with Ronnie. Cissy ignored her mother's warnings about older men with liberal ideas.

"'Ere, you are too big for your boots, Cissy Griffith," Mrs Griffith called after the wagon, as she watched it skid away amid a storm of metal and dust. To her the one saving grace was that Simon was with them. Rose Griffith felt sure that her golden haired boy would see there was no hanky panky from Ronnie Holden.

The air was sharp and stars crisp in a dark velvet sky when the four young people arrived at the dance at the Rotowaro Hall. Ronnie sniffed with appreciation as he helped Cissy down from the high running board. She smelt corker, he thought, kinda musty like pressed flowers in a book. Cissy certainly had been generous with her new bottle of 'Evening in Paris'. Ronnie felt elation surge through him. The conditions were favourable, as it was his experience that the sheilahs were more forthcoming on cold frosty nights so that his prospects for tonight looked good.

Simon's mood wasn't quite so optimistic. He was annoyed that Ronnie had fixed him up with Hazel Hutchins to make a foursome. Ronnie had an ulterior motive. If Simon was concentrating on Hazel he could hardly object to anything happening with Cissy. Strangely most blokes thought all girls were fair game – except their sisters!

The dance turned out to be a hoot when two of the local drunks staggered into the dance, circumnavigated the hall for a girl to dance with but were refused all the way. They left disgruntled only to return minutes later with the poor goat that had been tethered outside the hall for keeping the grass down and began dancing with the terrified creature. They were all thrown out.

Ronnie's foursome left the dance after supper and drove out onto the Waingaro road. The glow from the huge golden moon cascaded across the landscape lighting the countryside, as daylight would have done, causing native bush and the gurgling creek to take on a mystic look. Romance was in the air and Ronnie intended taking full advantage.

Simon was cheesed off with both Ronnie and Hazel. Hazel had been all over him at the dance, making out they were now a couple. Simon didn't want people to think that. He wished Ronnie had set him up with Meggie. But that was unlikely, as Meggie never went anywhere now.

On the drive out to Waingaro they'd done a good bit of drinking, talked a lot of nonsense, and laughed about the drongos at the dance. But once Ronnie had parked and turned off the engine he was ready to get down to serious business. Passing his half-empty bottle to Hazel he began heavy necking with Cissy. Hazel put the bottle to her lips and drank long and hard.

"Jeez, girl! You can't half put it away."

"That's not all I can put away," she answered Simon pertly, making little cooing noises as she snuggled closer into him.

Simon supposed he'd better make some sort of an effort, though God knows, he hadn't felt like anything since Meggie. He tried to blot her out of his memory as he lifted Hazel's face and kissed her at the same time running his hand over her bra.

Shit, she doesn't need a bra, there's bugger all there to put in them. Not like Meggie, he thought. Hers swelled round and high even without a bra to hitch them up. Her image danced before him now. Wide green eyes and a body begging to be seduced. As his heartbeat quickened he pulled away from the kiss and looked over the back of the front seat. Even with such hindrances as the steering wheel and gear stick Ronnie was making good progress. Simon knew he should say something but Christ, they depended upon Ronnie to get back to the Glen. Too bloody far to walk on a freezer like tonight.

Hazel, afraid Simon was cooling off, placed her hand between his legs. He felt a flicker and his limp penis began to stiffen slightly. She took hold of the shaft at the same time kissing him passionately. Within seconds his shank dwindled and lay limply on his thigh. Hazel tried to hide her annoyance but she still persevered. Simon was annoyed with himself now. Here was a sheilah handing it to him on a plate and this was the best he could do. If this were Meggie offering no way would he be turning her down.

Suddenly the whole night's activities seemed coarse and seedy. The wagon's interior stank of sweat and beery farts and their breath had fogged up the windows. Simon pushed Hazel away and fumbled in his pocket for his tailor-mades, at the same time buttoning up his fly.

Inhaling deeply on the first drag his mind wandered back to the days before Meggie had gone onto that farm. There had always been a chance that he would see her, talk to her, even if only for a few minutes. The days seemed sunnier then than they were now. He remembered the times when they'd gone off together; those rare times when they could manage to meet in secret with Meggie being forbidden to see him. Times when he would walk her as far as the hawthorn hedge after the pictures or a dance and they would just stand holding each other for a long time. Other times their blood ran hot and it would have been oh, so easy. But tonight, as he smoked, he glimpsed some understanding of Mrs Morgan's anxiety about him and Meggie. It wasn't that she didn't like him; it was more that she was afraid he would impregnate her daughter. But it was her accusations of them doing things that they had not done that stuck in his craw.

He glanced sideways at Hazel noting she was still partly undressed. She was writing on the steamed up window with her finger. 'Simon Griffith is a party pooper.' Little rivulets of water trickled down the window from the bottom of the crudely formed letters. Silly bitch, he thought, as his emotions took another dive. He lifted the bottle from the floor and took a long swig, draining it, then picked up another lifting off the top with his teeth.

A cold blast of air hit him as he wound down the window to throw out his butt. He continued to drink while Hazel made another attack at his fly. He turned his head and covered Hazel's mouth with lips now well slackened from booze. Hazel's fingers pinched and scratched in her haste to draw his penis through the narrow slit in his jockeys. It remained limp.

Ronnie opened the driver's door and the bright ceiling light flooded the interior of the car. "Shit Si". What the hell's that? Ha! Ha! Ha!" He snorted with laughter. "Is that the best you can do? You'll need a bloody bike pump to get that bastard moving tonight."

He slammed the door cackling with laughter. Simon was furious. Furious with Ronnie because he knew he would relate the incident to all his workmates on the screens on Monday morning, and furious with Hazel for exposing him in this way. He pushed her away.

"Let's get home," he said as calmly as he could manage.

The whole night had been a goddamn washout. He wished he'd gone to the Blueroom with the boys instead.

It was late and all the house lights were out when Simon made his way to the bedroom he shared with his brothers. There was usually little privacy for him to fanaticize about Meggie but tonight as he lay listening to the snores and grunts of the other sleepers in the house, he acceded after the catastrophic night with Hazel that he loved Meggie Morgan and no one else would do.

Hazel Hutchins was as mad as a hornet. After the disaster last Saturday night she'd promised herself she'd have Simon this weekend, come rain, hail or shine. Hazel had long ago earmarked Simon for her husband. If she could manipulate him into fatherhood now she could be sure of him. He was easily the best looking joker in the district and she would have had him hooked long before now if it hadn't been for that stupid Meggie Morgan. Though what he saw in someone who looked older than her age was a mystery to Hazel.

So tonight, as Ronnie skidded away in the passion wagon, throwing out a shower of gravel, to pick up Simon and Cissy, Hazel pledged that no matter what it took, tonight would be the night.

Ronnie tooted loudly outside Griffiths' big house. Within seconds Cissy came running out skirting a huge mound of black, shiny coal heaped in the gateway. Her mother's high pitched voice, shouting totally ignored admonitions, followed her path. She jumped in the wagon with a breathless, "Let's go," as she slammed the door.

"Where's Simon," Hazel yelled, as the vehicle shot into first gear.

"Not coming," Cissy answered. "Gone down the Blueroom with the boys."

Hazel was devastated. This wasn't how she'd planned it! "Go to the Blueroom, Ronnie," she demanded, pulling roughly at his new nylon blend shirt. "We'll pick him up from there."

"Hey! Get off. Yer ruinin' me good shirt."

Ronnie swerved the wagon around to park beside the main entrance to the club. He patted his shirt smooth before entering, but within minutes he'd returned, without Simon.

"He doesn't want to come and I can't make him," he brayed through the open window.

Hazel began to cry.

"Aw, c'mon, Haz. If he doesn't want to come he doesn't have to."

Cissy turned around. "I told ya, didn't I?"

She didn't like Hazel all that much and also felt sorry for her brother, knowing his feelings about Meggie. Besides Cissy was afraid to put pressure on Simon or he might spill the beans about her and Ronnie. After a while, with only Hazel's sniffs breaking the silence, Ronnie turned the passion wagon around and drove Hazel back to her house.

"What sort of a bloody mate are ya?" Ronnie snarled at Simon over smoko on Monday morning. "I heard yer tied one on Saturday night."

He paused to take a swig of tea from his bottle. "Look. Why don't yer forget about that Morgan sheilah and get yer end away with Hazel. She was heartbroken ya know."

Sammy Hunter, overhearing the conversation, began imitating Hazel's lisp.

"Put your hand under my thkirt and give me a good feel up," he stammered in a high falsetto.

Simon was furious. He picked up his crib tin and made for the bathhouse with the sounds of the miners' rude cracks and laughter echoing across the screens behind him.

Meggie was happy when she learned that Granddad Morgan was coming to stay on his way back from the Labour Party Conference in Wellington. To Meggie there seemed less interest in this Election than there had been during the war. Granddad confirmed this.

"Now look you," Jack said as he jabbed his finger in the bowl of his pipe. "Labour is only keeping office by retaining those four Maori seats. They are holding on by the skin of their teeth and it's not good, you see." he told Dai, as they sat in front of the coal range discussing the state of the country. "The people want to enjoy life now that the war is over."

"Well, why are they keeping on with bloody rationin' then," Dai asked. "They'll go out next elections if they don't loosen up control."

On the nine o'clock news the newscaster reported that while there were happy homecoming scenes as soldiers from the New Zealand

Expeditionary Force returned to their country, other servicemen were preparing to leave for Japan as part of the British Occupation Force.

Dai had stayed sober for the whole of Granddad's visit but after he left he went off the deep end again. He came back the following Sunday looking very bedraggled and abusing them both for their laziness.

"Man work's like a bloody slave. Can't even have a bloody drink without yer lookin' down yer snotty noses," he snarled.

Meggie looked at the raw skin on her hands. As well that she'd picked up cowpox from the herd and the large pussy sores looked repulsive. She could feel the fury rising in her at his unfairness. In a flash she picked up the shovel from the hearth and as he came towards her she brought it down on his head. Florrie flew out the door and Meggie tried to follow but Dai caught her by the arm. She managed to wriggle free and stumbling over the doorstep she tried to catch up to her mother. Dai was quick in pursuit and deftly grabbed the axe as he passed the chopping block. They ran like the wind along the rough farm track and down the dusty metal road towards the mine houses. As they neared the village Dai gave up and still shouting all sorts of obscenities at them he turned back towards the farm.

Florrie and Meggie were exhausted and breathless by the time they reached Bredeson's house. Sally opened the door to them. Alf didn't seem surprised.

"Dai gone orf his rocker again?" was all he said.

Sally made them tea and insisted they stay the night.

"We can't do that," Florrie protested. "The cows will be in agony. We've got all the new calver's bursting with milk."

"If ya want ta get an axe through yer skull, then go back," Alf said frankly. "I'll go up and see them milked."

He put his arm around Meggie's shoulders. "Never mind, sweetheart," he said kindly. "Stay here with Sally and she'll cook ya a good feed."

Alf took them back next morning before he went to the mine. Everything looked normal. Dai had finished the milking and the full cans of cream were out at the gate. Once Alf was sure they were safe he left them and went straight to the mine. He caught up to Simon, who had just started working underground, as he walked out of the daylight and down the dark sloping tunnel.

"Yer still got tickets on young Meggie Morgan?" he asked.

Simon was embarrassed but curious. "Whatcha want ta know for?"

Alf told him about the events of yesterday. Simon was upset but again felt helpless. "I could kill the bloody pisshead," he told Alf.

Alf smiled, as that was choice coming from Simon who was getting quite a reputation as a boozer himself.

"Well, we'll have ta keep a closer eye on them in the future," said Alf as he left Simon to take up his position with his mate at the coalface.

Simon drank himself legless at the Blueroom that night and he did it because he didn't know how else to handle the tremendous anger that filled him.

CHAPTER SIXTEEN

Meggie loved delivering eggs to Sally Bredeson on Saturday mornings. Sally had served in the English Land Army during the war and with Meggie she could regale her tales of the Land Army and England to a captive audience. Life in England sounded so glamorous, though some of Sally's stories were quite hard to believe, even for a devoted listener like Meggie. Florrie reckoned they were all lies. "Filling your head with all that nonsense. You must be half-witted to believe them."

Well, at least her stories don't harm anyone, Meggie thought.

Alf and Sally had become regular visitors to the farm, and when the evenings lengthened out, they walked up to the hill at least one night a week. Alf was determined to keep an eye on Dai as he felt with the axe incident that things were getting serious. Sally felt sorry for Meggie as she always looked so shabby in the ill-fitting hand-me-downs she wore. She made her a nice dress refusing to take money for the material. Not that Meggie had any money to give her, but ideas of how to earn some and get away from the farm were still forming in her mind.

Meggie loved the lilac georgette blouse that Sally was fitting her for now. It was to be her birthday present as she was turning fifteen on Friday. She found that she was spending less time in her bush bolt hole and all the spare moments she got visiting Sally Bredeson. She confided in Sally about most things. Emmie and her were growing apart as Emmie would not come to the farm if Dai was there so Meggie only saw her at the Ed Hubbard's store and sometimes when she delivered eggs to Griffith house. Simon was never at the boardinghouse these days and Emmie told her that he spent most of his leisure time down at the Blueroom boozing.

"Mum said I can go into Huntly for the day on Friday," Meggie told Sally. "So I'm going to get a job while I'm in there."

Sally secured another pin into the side seam of the blouse before she replied. "Eeh. What's your Mam say about that?"

"I haven't told her about getting a job."

"Well, would you like to wear your blouse? I'll have it finished by then."

"Gee, that would be great. I'll call in here on my way to the station and put it on."

Next Friday Meggie boarded the midday train to Huntly. She decided to try her luck first at the underwear factory where Sarry worked and was shaking all over when she stepped inside the foyer of the big Berlei building. Through the glass doors she could see rows and rows of women hunched over the long wooden benches and the noise of the whirring sewing machines echoed out into the foyer. She was peering through the doors when a voice startled her from behind.

"Can I help you," asked Jamie Forbes, who, unknown to Meggie, was the foreman at the factory.

Meggie jumped and then was relieved to see someone she knew. "Oh … Hi … Yes … Can I have a job?"

Jamie looked surprised. "Hey, I remember you. Meggie from out the back. Glen Afton."

Meggie nodded.

"Yeah. I remember you from that night we came out to the Victory dance. That was a great night," he reminisced. "How'ya been then?"

Meggie became tongue-tied but managed to squeak out, "Okay."

"Yeah. I asked Sarry Adams when she started working here where you were and she said you were working on a farm."

Meggie blushed scarlet, then nodded again. After an awkward pause Jamie spoke again.

"So you're wanting a job here, eh? Can you sew?"

"A little bit."

Jamie noticed the broken skin on her hands. "Jeez. What you done to your hands. You'll have to cover those. We can't risk getting any stains on our superior fabrics," he half joked.

Jamie was silent for a while. He seemed deep in thought. Meggie's heart was beating so fast she thought she would faint. She prayed silently, for the first time in ages, 'Please. If there is a God. Give me this job.'

"Well. You'd better get something to cover your hands until they heal. When would you like to start?"

Meggie couldn't believe her ears. "You mean I can have a job? I can start anytime," she squealed.

"Yep. OK .Come in on Monday with Sarry. We'll get you started."

Meggie couldn't believe her luck. She didn't even think about her parent's reaction when they were told. She spent the rest of the afternoon looking at all the new merchandise that had come into the shops since the war had ended, then met Sarry outside the Berlei factory to get the train home together. Sarry hadn't been working long but it was ages since they'd had a chance even to talk so it would be great them working together.

Hazel Hutchins boarded the train and sat down in the same carriage. She threw Meggie a drop-dead look. "What are you doing in Huntly?" she asked in a snooty voice. "Shouldn't you be up to your elbows in cow muck at this time?"

"I've got a job at Berlei," Meggie answered, still too excited to be nasty back to Hazel. "I start on Monday."

"Humph! I suppose you'll be making eyes at Simon again. That's if you can prise him away from the bottle for long enough," she remarked spitefully, still smarting from his rejection of her.

At home Meggie's bravado had disappeared when it came to telling Dai and Florrie that she had a job at the Berlei factory and started Monday. Both her mother and father looked at her with accusing eyes and she felt as if she was in a silent, swirling mist. The silence lasted for an indeterminable time and for the second time that day Meggie's heart raced to bursting point. Dai was first to speak. "Well, I'm real disappointed in ya, I am," he said around a mouthful of rice pudding. "Real disappointed."

Florrie said nothing and the silence hung like icicles in the air. Then Dai spoke again. "I thought yer'd be the one who'd stay here and help me git this farm earnin'."

Meggie wanted to reply that it might pay if he didn't spend so much on booze. That he never gave her a penny piece for all the heavy work she did on the farm. That he'd deprived her of a social life when he'd forced them onto this farm. And why shouldn't she be like Emmie, and friends Sarry and Moira, earning wages and getting nice things. But she didn't say any of this because she was afraid of him. When the silence continued Dai spoke again. "Well missus. Yer'll have ta help me with the milkin's now that she's desertin' us."

He rose from the dinner table, hoicked, and spat into the firebox. "Man works like a bloody demon fer the family and this is all the reward he gits."

Dai picked up his tobacco tin and in silence began making roll-your-owns.

Florrie glared at Meggie. Her eyes were narrow and flinty. "So this is what you do when I let you go to Huntly for the day. You always were a sneaky little cat, and this proves it."

Meggie didn't answer. She was close to tears and wondered if she should just forget the idea of working in Huntly all together.

Florrie spoke again. "How much will you be earning?" she asked in an icy tone.

Deep down Florrie was scared. She hardly saw Emmie nowadays and now her second daughter was leaving them. She felt as though her insides were shattering but she was too proud to show it. The truth was that she, like Dai, just didn't know how to handle their daughters who were becoming adults with minds of their own.

Meggie found her voice. "Seventeen and six a week," she answered.

"Well, if you're not earning your keep here you'll pay me ten shillings a week board."

Meggie quickly did the sums in her head. Five and sixpence for a weekly train ticket and ten bob to her mother left her two shillings and sixpence to spend each week. Her heart sank to her boots as she realized it was going to take her ages to save enough for the train fare to Auckland if her plan to live with Granddad Morgan was to eventuate.

Dai went off on the booze that weekend and had a huge argument with Rhys Evans because Rhys had called him a communist. He rolled home earlier than usual and attacked Meggie physically because of her getting work in Huntly. She struggled with him as he pulled her arm up her back in a wrestler's hold, at the same time forbidding her to leave her gumboots, which she wore through the wet paddocks to the metalled road, on Rhys's back porch where they kept dry if it rained.

But Meggie stuck to her guns on the Monday morning, and after lighting the coal range and leaving the cooked breakfast on the stove, she made her way through the paddocks still wet with dew to the train. Heeding her father, after changing into her dry shoes at the bottom of the hill, she pushed her gumboots under the hawthorn hedge. But Rhys Evans was waiting for her.

"ere girlie," Rhys called in his musical Welsh accent. "Your Da telling you to put your gumboots in the hedge, isn't it?"

Her face flushed scarlet with embarrassment as she nodded. She hadn't expected Rhys Evans to be watching out for her.

"Well, ere girlie. You'll leave 'em gumboots on my porch, you will, and your Da need never know, you see." He chuckled as he took the gumboots and patting her on the shoulder he remarked, "Indeed to goodness, a braf girlie you are these days."

She was breathless when she reached the railway station but once aboard the train her feelings of liberation were stupendous. She allowed the rhythmic clatter of the carriage wheels on rails to take over and help her overcome her guilt of leaving her parents to cope without her on the farm. When she arrived home that night Dai had sold her horse Poppy to Nick Handisides for only half of what he paid for her. Meggie was upset but not surprised. In the week that followed Dai was away drinking so that Florrie was still milking late in the evenings when Meggie arrived home on the train. The days were longer than ever for her as she was up early to get the coal range going and help Florrie carry the cream to the gate. Then she went straight to the shed when she came home in the evening to help Florrie finish the evening milking. They fell into bed most nights without a meal.

The next Sunday they were finishing off milking the herd when above the chugging of the machines there began a terrible low rumbling.

"Oh, my God," wailed Florrie. "It's an earthquake."

Though the rumbling went on and on becoming louder the ground didn't appear to be moving. Florrie hurried to the end of the yard railing to look in the direction of the deep thundery sound. "Oh, my God. Come and see what this half-witted buggar is doing now."

Florrie never swore as a rule so Meggie knew it was serious. She let the last cow out of the bail and ran to the end of the cowshed yard. All they could see was a large ringed water tank being rolled across the swede paddock. Finally it arrived at the shed and Dai and his latest drinking mate, Barney Wheal, staggered out from behind the tank. They were both puffing like steam engines and were a lather of sweat.

"What der yer think of this, missus," Dai shouted over the combined milking machines and separator noise.

Florrie didn't answer. She knew the tank was mine property and she was worried.

"Get 'us a drink, Missus," Dai called again. "Mouth feels like the bottom of a birdcage.

Florrie saw red. "Want a drink, do you. Well here you are." She picked up a bucket of filthy water that had been used for washing the cow's teats and fired the contents over both men. Dai returned the tank next day and was fortunate that the mine took no action over the theft.

Meggie told Sally Bredeson about the incident when she delivered the eggs on the next Saturday. "I think I'd better give up working," she said. "It's n—"

Before she could finish Sally rounded on her. "No, you will not give up working in Huntly. If you go back now he'll know he's won and you'll never be free again." She paused for a breath. "Oh, sweetheart. I'm not growling at you. I just want to make you see you're letting him win if you go back and work on the farm. Your mother lets him win all the time! That's why he gets away with such bad behaviour, that's why he sold your horse, can't you see? To get you back as free labour. I know it's hard for you now, but at least you are earning a wage. Now be strong, darling and you'll benefit in the end."

She hugged Meggie and sent her home. Meggie heeded what Sally had said. The days were still long as she was up early to rekindle the fire and leave a cooked breakfast for Dai and Florrie when they came down from morning milking. At the weekends she was still expected to milk and help with the farm work. There was no time left to do any drawing and she didn't see Simon at all as he spent most of his time at the Blueroom.

At the Berlei factory she began earning a small bonus each week that she banked towards her train fare to Granddad's in Auckland.

Berlei were having their annual Christmas break-up dance in the Huntly Miners Hall. Moira's mother said that Meggie and Sarry could stay overnight at her house for the dance.

Jamie Roberts leaned across her sewing bench. Meggie looked up from her work. "How about coming to the Christmas dance with me?" he asked.

"I don't know if I'll be allowed to go."

His eyebrows shot up on his forehead. "Well find out and let me know. I'd really like to take you."

Florrie said that Meggie was doing what she liked these days anyway so she could please herself. It meant a new dress so that was her savings gone again. She bought some green-flocked nylon from the drapery shop and Sally Bredeson made it into a lovely party frock.

It was raining when Jamie called for Meggie at Moira's house so the three girls crammed into his little car and arrived at the Christmas dance reasonably dry. Inside, the Miner's hall which was decorated with streamers and holly, was crowded with girls wearing full can-can skirts with yards of petticoat beneath.

It was a great night and passed all too quickly as the whirling dancers glided to the waltz and Valletta, bounced to the schottische and polka and marched to the military two-step. American music had increased in popularity and when the band played a set of 'Boogie Woogie Bugle Boy', 'American Patrol', 'Working for the Yankee Dollar' and 'Don't Sit Under the Apple Tree', the crowd sang loudly as they bopped to the jazzy sounds. It was the most exciting event since the Victory dance. Jamie was a super dancer and as they swayed to the music in the last dance he drew her to him and they danced cheek to cheek.

Unfortunately for him, Moira's father was waiting up for them when they arrived home at midnight and invited Jamie in for a cup of tea, much to his annoyance. Being the local Romeo he'd planned a good snog session with Meggie after the dance.

CHAPTER SEVENTEEN

GLEN AFTON 1947

Many of New Zealand servicemen had brought home their English brides and several parties of New Zealand war brides who had married American Marines had left on passenger liners for the United States. Sarry envied the girls who were going to America to live.

"Lucky devils," she lamented. "I wish I was old enough to marry a Yank."

Clothing coupons and lack of fabrics, as well as the urgency of the times, had cheated those women married during the war out of their white weddings. Most war brides had to make do with a Registry Office wedding wearing a plain costume and matching hat. Seldom could enough food coupons be saved for a reception to be held afterwards.

Consequently wedding bells seemed to be the order of the day when Merv Bowman and Olwyn Griffith were married in March that year. Mrs.

Paxton made Olwyn's wedding frock in the new hailstone nylon blend fabric. The girls were all raving about the material because it didn't need ironing. As Merv had no family in the area the Griffith boys were his groomsmen and Olwyn's sisters were her bridesmaids. Olwyn had chosen a rainbow wedding, which were all the rage after the war, and the bridesmaids all wore different coloured watergrain taffeta dresses. Chief bridesmaid Cissy looked gorgeous in her powder blue and the other sisters were in lemon, soft green and lavender, with floral headdresses to match.

The day dawned gloriously sunny, but not too hot, and the bridal party looked a picture as they posed for photographs outside the tiny church on the flat land at the bottom of the Pukemiro hill. It was a wonderful setting with pale yellow trumpets of honeysuckle clinging to the fence and climbing up the side of the building. The stream from Glen Afton continued its way past the little church, steering the shallow water over a stony bed. And today dragonflies, a deeper blue than the sky overhead, hovered near the stream as if having been hired to add splender to the wedding décor.

"Aren't they gorgeous? Gee, I can't wait to get married," Sarry, overcome with emotion at the occasion, half-sobbed to Meggie and Moira.

Sarry looked gorgeous herself in a Ming blue straw cloth suit that Moira's mother had made for her. Meggie had thought she would be the shabby one but Sally Bredeson came to the rescue and made up the corn-coloured ever glaze material that Meggie had paid off in installments at Allen's Drapery.

"Hey. Doesn't Si look spivvy in a suit?" Moira nudged Meggie.

Meggie had been aware of how gorgeous he looked, in the dark navy pinstriped suit, from the minute she'd entered the church. With his blonde hair and long dark lashes, Simon had grown to be very handsome young man. Probably under threat from Olwyn, he had managed to stay sober for the wedding. Simon approached Meggie after the Bridal waltz at the dance that night and asked for the next dance.

"I haven't seen ya for ages, Megs. How do ya like working in Huntly?"

"I love it," she answered. "But I hate coming back to the farm every night. I'm thinking of getting board in Huntly."

Simon's face dropped and he was silent for a long time as they danced on through a maze of swirling circular skirts.

"Can I walk yer home tonight?' he asked apprehensively.

She shook her head indicting 'no' making dozens of pincurls dance.

"Moira and I are staying at Sarry's tonight."

"Well, can we go for a walk later, Megs? I need to talk to ya."

Meggie was tempted. Just moving against his lithe physique, muscles now well hardened with swinging a heavy banjo shovel at the coalface, were unnerving her.

"What about?" she asked, in a voice as near to normal as she could muster.

"Come with me and find out," he said a mite mischievously, as he walked her back to her seat, then disappeared out the side door of the hall.

Meggie's heart sank. It had been so lovely dancing with him, sober for once, and she knew he would be going outside to drink. But as soon as the next dance was announced Simon was beside her leading her onto the floor again.

"Wow. Si's keen on you tonight," Sarry said, as Simon approached Meggie for the supper dance.

His heart hammered as he asked her again to go for a walk with him after supper. Outside the hall the night was magic. The sky was clear of clouds and there were stars, layers and layers of stars, which went down and down until they appeared to fall behind the hills. Meggie pulled her jacket around her against the chill night air as they walked in silence beside the roadside grasses. In the distance was the deep throaty crouck crouck of frogs in the swamp beside the horse paddock. They were opposite Griffith's house when Simon finally broke the silence.

"There's no one home. Come on up ta the house and we'll talk."

"What's this all about, Si?"

Meggie was curious by now as this behaviour was out of character for him. Normally he would be legless by now and having to be helped home. He took her hand and she followed him up the bank and through the front door of the boardinghouse. The warmth from the two big coal ranges, which were kept burning night and day, was very welcome. Steam gushed endlessly from the kettles that sat on the stovetop beside the chimney flue. In the sitting room he reached out and brushed aside a wisp of hair that clung damply to her cheek before he spoke. "Jeez, girl this is bloody hard fer me."

Meggie looked puzzled. "What is?"

"Megs. I'm tryin' ta ask yer again ta be my sheilah." He rushed on before his courage failed him, "Megs. I reckon I love ya and I need you. I'm in pain, honey, and it won't go away on its own. Do ya understand?"

Meggie wasn't sure she did understand fully about the pain but she did know what he was getting at. She was really browned off that he had only brought her here to try and make love to her.

"Is that all you brought me here for? Well, no, Si. And I'm really disappointed in you." she snapped, picking up her jacket to go.

"Aw. Shit. Yer've got it all wrong, Megs. I've said it all wrong. Jeez, I'm no bloody good at this." He knew he should be caressing her with words of love but somehow those words would not come out. Meggie suddenly felt sorry for him as he looked like a little boy about to burst into tears. "I want us ta go together and get hitched pretty soon. Yer know I'm earning good money now at the pit face," he blurted out, as he came to her and took her hands.

Looking hard at her for a second or so, and then pulling her tightly to him, his mouth found hers. The kiss made the core of her melt. She felt a wave of intense desire with the taste of his wonderful mouth crushing her own. They fell together onto the chesterfield suite. Simon was the first to come up for air.

"Come on inta the bedroom," he cajoled. "I won't do anything, I promise."

They moved off quietly, each unwilling to say a word that might break the magic of the moment. Simon led her into the bedroom he shared with his brothers. It was a long barrack type room with a corner wardrobe with lots of hooks but no doors. There hung slacks and sports jackets and a selection of gaudy ties.

"Take yer dress off so it doesn't get crumpled." Simon suggested when they reached the bedroom. "Bloody oath, ya know yer looked great tiday?"

He carefully laid her dress over the high wooden bed end next to his suit. With Meggie in just her petticoat, they lay together saying nothing. This was the closest they had been since that day, long before, when he had scared her and then had to explain the birds and bees to her. That all seemed so long ago now.

The dance music from the hall throbbed around the valley as they lay together. Then soft as a moth's foot Simon gently found her mouth. They locked together as though they belonged to one flesh.

"Couldn't we, honey?" he begged. "It would be so easy."

"No. Please, Si. Don't."

"Okay, honey. I won't do anything against yer will. But jeez, if only you knew the effin bloody agony I'm in."

Meggie ignored him as she began to worry about how long they'd been away from the hall.

"Si. We've been gone ages. There'll be talk. We'd better get back to the dance."

"Honey. You never said whether we should, yer know, get hitched or not. What do ya reckon?"

Meggie laughed. "Yes. I want be your girl-friend."

"Great," he whispered, as he kissed her. "But yer know what's gonna happen, don't ya. I won't be able to stop every time."

"You'll have to, Si. I don't want the shame of becoming pregnant."

"I'll get some protection," he mumbled, as they walked back over towards the hall of celebrating people. "Can I see ya tomorrow?" Si asked, as they entered the hall.

"No show. I'll have to go home in the morning and make up for what I didn't do today."

"Jeez. I don't know why yer don't get out. Ya do a week's work in at Berlei and another bloody week's work on the farm at the weekends. Why do ya stay?" he asked angrily.

"I told you, Si. I'm thinking of getting board in Huntly."

"Why don'tcha get a room with us, like Emmie does. She's happy and sees Riki all the time."

"Yeah. And after just now I can imagine where you'd be sneaking in every night."

Simon nodded and laughed. "Yip. Bloody oath I would," he agreed.

They reached the hall and Meggie went back to sit with Sarry and Moira. Hazel Hutchins had seen them go out and was watching for them coming in again.

"Look at that," she nudged Jan Anderson. "No prize for knowing what they've been doing."

She was still eaten up inside from his rejection of her and to see him come in with that cowhand, as Hazel called Meggie, looking like the cat that drank the cream, added fuel to her fire. The emcee announced a Ladies Choice.

"What the hell does he see in her?" she elbowed Jan again.

"Well, here's your chance to find out. It's a ladies choice. Go and get him for a dance if you want him back."

Meggie was dancing with Gerry Dunstan and Hazel looked around for Simon but he had gone from the hall.

Simon arranged to meet Meggie off the train on the next Friday night and they'd go to indoor bowls at the hall. Meggie had told her mother that she was having tea with Sarry and going to bowls from there.

He felt awkward, as he hadn't seen her since the wedding. All week down the pit he'd felt an unusual tenderness inside that humbled him but he really didn't know how to handle this heavy romantic stuff. He wanted to talk to someone about it but there was no one. Tender emotions were not something discussed among pitmen.

They walked up the road to the boarding house where Mrs. Griffith had a meal for Meggie keeping hot in the oven. Meggie loved the feeling of being part of their family.

"Buggar the bloody bowls," said Si, now nicely settled in the warm sitting room. "Let's stay here."

"Stop that swearin' inside the house," Mrs. Griffith reprimanded. "You can stay here but don't you be getting up to no good, mind."

Simon laughed. "As if we could with you spyin' on us every few minutes. And it's just as well yer not down the pit or you'd really know what swearin' is."

"Well, I don't want to be hearin' such vulgar language in this house."

They ended up playing five hundred on the big dining table with Tom and Rose Griffith. It was quite late when Simon walked Meggie up the hill as far as the stand of pine trees. The night was dark but not still. When Meggie looked across at their house it seemed unusual that the lights should still be on so late.

"I'd better get going. There might be something wrong."

Simon's blood was running hot and he felt the packet in his pocket. He was annoyed that her attention had turned off him and on to something else. Exasperated he growled, "Jeez, Megs. When are yer going to stop kowtowing to yer family? You don't owe them anything, my bloody oath yer don't."

But passion spends itself quickly when fear or worry enters the equation. She gave him a quick kiss goodnight and as she ran across the home paddock she could not shake the feeling that something was wrong.

"So you've decided to come home, have you, Lady Muck," Florrie shouted at her as she came in the back door. "You're never here when you're needed."

Dai turned around from where he was sitting in front of the stove with his feet in the oven.

"What's happened?"

"It's yer Granddad. He's had a stroke," Dai uttered, with tears in his eyes. "We got word from Mae this mornin'."

Meggie's heart turned over. "He's not de …"

"No," Florrie cut across her question. "Mae says it's only a mild stroke and he's out of hospital and at home. Jack wants you to go up and stay with him in the house until he can manage on his own again."

Meggie's mind was whirling. This was happening too fast. Now she knew why she'd had that overwhelming feeling that something was wrong. She shouldn't have gone to Griffiths with Simon when her dear Granddad Morgan was sick with a stroke. Strokes were where you got all paralyzed, she remembered, and couldn't bear to think of her Granddad all paralyzed.

"Well. Are yer gonna go?" Dai asked. "We can't leave the farm."

"Yes. I want to go. But I haven't got enough money saved for the fare."

"Well, if you didn't spend so much on clothes for weddings and dances you'd have more, wouldn't you," Florrie argued.

"Shut up, Florrie," Dai yelled. Then in a lower voice he told Meggie, "Mae sent money for your fare with the letter."

Meggie couldn't think clearly. She'd have to give notice at work. She'd be leaving Sarry and Moira, her best friends. She remembered the commitment she'd made to Simon to be his 'sheilah'. What was she to do?

Maybe there was a God after all, she thought, and things did take care of themselves. After all living with Granddad was what she had been saving for. Meggie told Si the next day. He was stunned.

"Well, bloody oath. Wouldn't yer bloody know it. Just when things were goin' right fer us this happens."

"I won't be gone forever," she assured him. "Just 'til Granddad gets better."

"Oh yeah! Dad's old man had a stroke and he never got better. Lived fer bloody years with everyone fetchin' and carryin' for him," he said sourly. "Well, I can't stop yer, but jeez, I'm gonna miss ya girl."

Sarry took a message to Jamie Forbes at Berlei factory that Meggie had been called urgently to Auckland. Monday morning saw Meggie struggling down the hill through the wet paddock grass with her suitcase to catch the train to Huntly. Though Dai had the truck he had never been guilty of driving his daughters anywhere whether it be rain, hail or shine. At Huntly she crossed from the branch line to the main railway station and from there caught the express to Auckland. By the time the train hissed to a halt at Auckland Railway Station Meggie was exhausted and so pleased to see her Uncle Bill waiting, with his car, to drive her to her Granddad Morgan's house at Grey Lynn.

Sarry's first letter to Meggie in Auckland was full of the Royal wedding of Princess Elizabeth to Philip Mountbatten in November 1947. Included was a picture cut from a magazine of the Princess in her beautiful ivory satin dress that had been designed by Norman Hartnell.

"Gee, look at this, Granddad. Doesn't she look beautiful? It says here that her dress is decorated with 10,000 seed pearls." She poked the picture under Jack's nose. "And the veil is made of gossamer silk."

Jack looked cynical as he glanced over the magazine photo. His mind fled to memories of his own Mam worked to death to provide luxury for the likes of this one.

"A bloody poor specimen she would be not to respond to her pampered life, isn't it? And did they pool their clothing coupons for that garment, I wonder?" he finished sarcastically. A scowl flickered across his face. "That lot would be doing without nothing during the war. They sat back in their air raid shelters while the Commonwealth fed their nation." He ended with a loud poof of disgust as he dismissed the subject. "Turn the radio on, girlie, and we'll get the evening news."

CHAPTER EIGHTEEN

GREY LYNN 1947

Granddad Morgan was not nearly as sick as Meggie had expected him to be. It had been a mild stroke, a warning, the doctor had said. His right side had lost strength so he needed help with his food and personal washing. Uncle Bill came around once a week to bath him.

Meggie loved being in the old house she remembered with affection from her childhood. There were the same heavy velvet curtains with fringes and tassels making the rooms look dark and mysterious. Meggie did everything in the house and loved it. Every morning she walked the short distance to the Surrey Crescent shops and bought meat and other daily supplies. In the afternoons she sat with Granddad in the sunny bay window while he talked. Mercifully his speech hadn't been affected and to talk was what he enjoyed most of all.

"Why look you," he would say, puffing great clouds of pipe smoke into the air as he told of the Cilfynydd pit explosion in Wales that had killed 251 men and boyos.

"Conditions were so bad then, you see. We worked with naked lights underground and they caused explosions that took many a pitman's life. And not much better for the Huntly Ralph Mine disaster here in 1914. I worked in the Extended Mine in those days and we could hear the barges swishing above our heads as they sailed down the Waikato River. That's how greedy the mine owners were to put our lives at risk with not a care. As long as they made a profit." He ended the sentence with a loud poof and an extra-large puff on his pipe.

He talked about the past with such fire, about the cloth cap days of Unionism, and his association with Kier Hardie back in Wales. He remembered well Kier Hardie ploughing his lonely furrow at Westminster for Jack had shared that same burning sense of injustice. And he'd caught up with Hardie again when he visited New Zealand. Kier Hardie's book, 'Reflections of New Zealand', was like a bible to Jack and he closed his eyes as Meggie read to him from the book each day.

Jack had a captive audience, as Meggie loved hearing the stories, which were about the struggles and hardships in Wales, told to her in his beautiful musical lilting accent. She could visualize the snow low on the mountains around the little mining towns, the songs bursting from the Rhondda villages, and the women carrying baskets of coal from the mines balanced on their heads.

He spoke a lot about his beautiful mother who had died so young, and the remnants he had been told by his Uncle Taff the Rail of his own roving Romany father. Jack would nod off while telling the stories, so then Meggie would sketch the houses in the street with an array of pencils she had found around the house. Jack loved the drawings and sent her cousin Evan into the city one Friday night to buy a full artist's kit. The kit included canvases, oils, and even an easel. Meggie was rapt and took to the oils as though she'd been painting with them all her life.

Meggie's Aunts, Mae and Bronnie, called several times a week bringing fresh baking and they helped with the house cleaning. Cousin Evan called in the evenings in his newly acquired Prefect car. Granddad was always pleased to see his family.

One weekend Evan took Meggie to the pictures at the Civic Theatre in Queen Street. They saw *The I Don't Care Girl* starring Mitzi Gaynor. Evan thought the movie was a bit wet but Meggie fell in love with the beautiful dancing star and wished she could be like her. She'd never been to a cinema before and was fascinated with the flickering stars on the Civic Theatre ceiling and was totally awestruck with the exotic décor. Life in Auckland was busy and exciting. Nevertheless, Meggie wrote to her parents every week as well as Sarry and Simon. Sarry and Moira shared the letters, and wrote back a combined letter. Simon never answered any of her letters.

At Glen Afton Simon was bitter that Meggie had gone off to Auckland. He thought about her daily and at night he ached for her. There was no comfort in his work. Underground in a coalmine is a heartless place with its black walls and coal dust caked oil floor. Going down the pit every day meant putting the sunlight behind you for eight hours. Sometimes Simon wondered, as he picked his way down the rails, guided only by his lamp lit helmet, whether he would see the sun again that afternoon. There had been casualties over the years, none so big as the disaster in '39. Though Simon had only been a boy then he well remembered the day the Glen had hushed as dead miners were carried from the mine.

But now he didn't care whether he saw the light of day again, or at least that's what he told himself. Without Meggie in the Glen there was no sunlight for him. But despite his personal pain he still retained his pit sense while underground. He was still aware that an error of judgement could cause danger to the safety of the other miners, so his mine mentality still prevailed while at the coalface.

He drank more than ever and when his mates teased him about not having a regular sheila, he'd laugh and answer glibly, "A joker can't drink piss and run a woman too."

He looked forward to her letters each week but they were no consolation for not being able to see her, hold her, love her. He'd made many attempts to answer her letters, acknowledge his love for her, put down on paper the thoughts he had about her, but try as he might he was unable to pen a letter back to her. He just didn't know what to say. He had asked Cissy to write for him but she had no time now that she and Ronnie were married with family and had moved into a colliery house up the gully.

There were plenty of events in the country to write about. In May that year the whole country was agog with the awe-inspiring spectacle of Mount Ngauruhoe erupting. All the newspapers had photos of the mountain throwing out huge red-hot boulders as big as houses, along with great masses of smoke. The Weekly News had photos of the explosions taken from the air and Meggie poured over the pictures in wonderment. They reminded her of the pictures of the bombs going off during the war, particularly the A Bomb that had destroyed the Japanese cities of Hiroshima and Nagasaki. But Simon would never think to write about national events. His world began and ended within the bounds of Glen Afton.

Meggie wrote to Sarry telling her about visiting His Majesty's Theatre, with her aunts, to see Sir Laurence and Lady Olivier. Lady Olivier, Vivien Leigh, was absolutely beautiful, she wrote. Meggie hadn't really understood what the play was about but it was just so exciting to have seen a real film star and the beautifully ornate theatre.

Meggie often thought about the Glen especially when she received letters from there. She missed the air in the bush that smelt of cool, damp moss, the antiseptic smell of the bruised manuka that they rubbed on their wounds, and the earthy smell of decaying leaves. There was no razor sharp bushlawyer or stringy supplejacks to swing on in Auckland. She missed the star laden night skies and brilliant country moons. In the artificially lighted city full moons rode pale and only a scattering of stars could be seen. She missed the ancient brooding hills that kept the Glen protected from the outside world. But for all that she missed, she wasn't ready yet to leave the excitement of city life, and she prayed every day that she could stay on with Granddad for a long, long while.

CHAPTER NINETEEN

AUCKLAND 1949

The two years since Granddad Morgan had taken his stroke had passed quickly. He was really well now, getting around with the aid of a stick, and doing most things for himself. Meggie began to fear she would be sent back to Glen Afton and it would be hard to go back now, even to Simon. She'd had no word from him since she'd left the Glen. Sarry had mentioned once that he drank more than ever, so though she missed him still, maybe she was better off. Evan took her into Queen Street most Friday nights for late night shopping and they would eat at The Silver Grill, and then go to a movie. Granddad always made sure she had some money of her own. Sometimes in the daytime he allowed her to catch a tram into town or to her Aunt's in Ponsonby but on the whole Granddad didn't like her to travel around the city on her own. He still had visions of the oversexed Yanks prowling the streets of Auckland so was inclined to be over protective of her.

Christmas had been wonderful. The family gathered at Granddad's house on Christmas Day, bringing with them heaps of food. Rationing of some foodstuffs was still on, but luckily her Uncles access to the contents from the boxes that fell and broke open on the wharf made a big difference! There had been salmon and mackerel, tinned ham, canned strawberries and peaches, and plates of cold meats that her Aunts had cooked. Uncle Trevor was the gardener in the family and from his small vegetable plot he had produced mounds of salad vegetables, new potatoes and peas.

Evan teased Meggie as they sat on the back steps shelling the peas, eating more of the juicy green legumes than ever reached the pot. Inside the women laughed and chattered speaking Welsh as they prepared the food in Granddad's tiny kitchen while the men sat in the sitting-room drinking beer, waiting for the Christmas dinner to be served.

After the dinner Auntie Bronnie played the old piano and they had the usual singsong. Meggie was in awe of the beautiful voices of her city relatives. She wondered if her father missed this family closeness, as he had certainly lost his accent more than his sisters and brother. Maybe that was why he drank so much. Once the family had all gone back to their own homes Meggie and Granddad sat in the bay window and listened to the King's speech, although Granddad said it was a load of rubbish.

"Granddad, now you're better do you want me to go home?"

Jack looked surprised. "Duw, cariad. Homesick and wanting to go home, isn't it?"

Meggie felt guilty about Simon but she shook her head indicating no.

"Well, let me be ill a little longer, cariad," he chuckled. "I'll be ill just a little longer."

Meggie took a deep and grateful breath as the late afternoon breeze billowed the sprigged muslin curtains into the room.

From Sarry's latest letter Meggie learned that Davy Howard had cut off his fingers while working on the screens and had been paid out a huge amount of compensation, which his father had taken off him and bought himself a flash American car. Gerry Dunstan had left the Glen and was training with the Air Force to become a pilot. Ruthie Smith, from up the Gully, was expecting Brian Harmon's baby so he had to marry her. Sarry had included a photograph of Merv and Olwyn's lovely fat baby boy. And Hazel Hutchins, she wrote, had finally given up on Simon and left the Glen to work in Auckland.

Well, that's one person I won't be getting in touch with, Meggie thought, as she read about the changes in the Glen.

Florrie wrote a sad letter telling Meggie that Emmie and Riki had been married in the Registry

Office at Huntly and were living in one of the new State houses built in Harris Street. Meggie felt sad that she had not been asked to be at her sister's wedding but neither had Florrie and Dai. Emmie's hurt was apparently still with her and so deep that she had cut her parents out of her life. Meggie's heart raced with guilt.

Florrie had got the job of postmistress at Glen Afton to make ends meet and suggested Meggie should come home and help on the farm.

At the same time as Meggie worried about her family at Glen Afton, her Grandfather and cousin, Evan could talk of nothing other than the All Blacks who had left for South Africa to play the Springboks. "The Boks came here before the war, 1937, you see, when you two were only nippers and they cleaned up the whole country. Our boyos will clean them up this time, of that I am sure."

Later that year Jack was disappointed that he wasn't well enough to attend the Labour Party Conference in Wellington. With it being an election year he had grave doubts about the Party which seemed to have been torn apart by a referendum to restore peacetime compulsory military training. "Can't he leave it alone," Jack growled to Frances Langtry, who had called to visit him one wet afternoon. "A lot of damage was done to the Party allowing those furlough soldiers to be Court Martialled in '44. Gawd dammit, man. They were bloody heroes and he labelled them criminals. Aw, no. They'll not forget he cost them their service pensions and rehab rights. And the bloody RSA refused to recognize them as returned soldiers to boot." Frances Langtry paused as Meggie brought the two men their afternoon tea. "Yes. I reckon you're right, Jack," he said, as he sipped his tea and took another scone. "We only squeaked in last time. This election I reckon we've had it."

Just as Jack and Frances predicted Labour were defeated in the 1949 elections. Sid Holland's National Party swept into power with 46 seats to 34 and Sid Holland chose his new cabinet.

New settlers began arriving from the Netherlands. "Next year hundreds of single Dutchmen are expected to arrive by assisted passage," the radio announcer reported. As Meggie Morgan listened to the newscaster she had no inkling that one of these new Dutch immigrants was about to change her life in ways that she never could have imagined.

Auntie Mollie and Uncle Rees came in from Otahuhu, and along with the rest of the family, gathered again for Jack's 70th birthday. Uncle Rees had made apricot brandy years before and they opened the bottles to celebrate Jack reaching seventy.

"Here's to you, Da," they all shouted, and then sang, For He's A Jolly Good Fellow, and Jack's eyes filled with tears.

"Thank you all," he answered, in his musical Welsh. "I may be older but I am no wiser, you see."

Among his gifts of mostly tobacco and whiskey, was a new pipe from Evan. Meggie had done for him a painting of a Welsh landscape that she had copied from a calendar picture. His eyes misted over again and he disguised their wetness by packing his new pipe.

"It's to the Art College that you should be, isn't it," he growled.

His mind sped back to the last visit he had made to Dai on the farm at Glen Afton. How they'd taken this child from school and worked her like a man on the property. He'd wanted to take her with him then but there was little he could do at the time. Then came the stroke and, he thought, it's an ill wind that blows no good at all. He saw the opportunity to get her away from the Glen and he took it. He loved having the girlie with him. Not only was she efficient in the house but she was great company, too. Meggie cut through these thoughts.

"You know I can't get in, Granddad. I never finished High School so I haven't even got my School C. Anyway, I'm too old now."

"More's the pity, cariad. More's the pity," he sighed.

He looked and felt sad. Hadn't he fought all these long years of his life for better conditions, better education for the children, and here was one of his own, not cheated from adverse conditions in society as he had been, but from the hand of his own son. A son who appeared to have no sensitivity or recognition of talent. A son who couldn't seem to see past the bottom of a beer glass. Jack felt far from happy on this day of celebration for his birthday.

CHAPTER TWENTY

GREY LYNN 1950/51

Evan called for Meggie on Friday night. He had another bloke in the car.

"Meet Kees," Evan introduced the thin looking joker sitting in the back of his little car. "This is my cousin, Meggie Morgan."

"Ya. Dag juffrouw. Dunk u," Kees nodded several times and extended his hand across the back of the seat. Meggie noticed that he had a special sort of Nordic good looks, his fair hair was trimmed short and he spoke in a European voice that was soft and deep.

"Kees has just arrived from Holland," Evan explained. "He's another sparkie. Working with me down the wharf."

"Ya. Ya." said Kees, his head bobbing up and down so swiftly that Meggie wondered if he had an affliction.

They pulled into parking in Customs Street and walked across to The Silver Grill for their dinner. Rationing had finally ended giving more choices on the menu.

"What'll you have, Kees?" Evan asked, knowing he couldn't read the menu. "There's steak and onions ..."

Before Evan could finish reading the menu Kees had nodded with a loud, "Ya."

Evan continued, "Sausages or bacon and eggs ..."

"Ya," said Kees, nodding furiously.

Evan tried again, "Fish and chips with bread and butter ..."

"Ya. Ya," said Kees, smiling and nodding.

The waitress wrote down the order as Kees nodded and a huge plate piled high with everything arrived and was placed before him.

"Goed, goed," he drooled, as he crammed the food into his mouth.

Meggie and Evan, and most of the other diners in the restaurant, watched in amazement, as Kees levelled his enormous plate of food in minutes.

"Dank u, het was een uitstekende maaltijd," he thanked them, and still nodding he wiped his mouth. The food seemed to give him new energy and he leaned across the table to take Meggie's hand.

"Mijn naam Kees Roobeck." He shook her hand so vigorously. Meggie wanted to giggle but she daren't.

After the meal they went to see *Casablanca*, the new Humphery Bogart film. It was Evan's choice, as Meggie didn't like 'Bumphery Gocart', as she and Sarry had nicknamed him. Their favourite male star was Tyrone Power and they both thought he was a dream. Kees sat quietly not understanding any dialogue. Afterwards they dropped Kees off at his boarding house in Symonds Street.

"Goed wegrestaurant. Dunk u, dunk u. Waar kunnen we gaan dansen?"

Meggie and Evan looked blank, as they had no idea what he was saying, so Kees began to dance around the footpath, his arms stretched out as though he was holding a girl. Meggie couldn't hold back her mirth any longer and burst out laughing. Tears ran down their cheeks as she and Evan laughed all the way home. They had Granddad in fits too when they relayed to him the evening's activities. But for all the amusement, Meggie had noted that Kees cut a fine figure, slim hipped and wide shouldered and wore his clothes well.

Meggie and Granddad were having their lunch at midday on Saturday when there was a loud knocking on the front door. Kees was standing outside looking for all the world like a dog anxious to make a friend. He was dressed immaculately again the creases in his slacks as sharp as any razor blade. Meggie's heart went out to him and she invited him in.

"Granddad. This is Kees from the pictures last night. Kees. Granddad Morgan."

"How do you do, mun," said Jack.

Kees nodded furiously as he shook hands with Jack. He accepted their offer to eat lunch with them and emptied all the plates in no time. Later Kees took a piece of paper from his pocket.

"Dansen Horange," he said.

Meggie took the paper from him and read out, "Orange Dancehall Saturday nights."

Kees nodded in agreement. "We uitgaan dansen?"

With that he struck the pose of dancing with a girl in his arms again and whirled around the room several times. Granddad laughed loudly. He liked this young man.

That was the beginning of the foursome of Meggie and Kees, Evan and his girlfriend, Shirley Wallace, who was a telephone operator at the Wellesley Street Tollroom. Movies and a meal Friday nights and dancing at the Orange Dance hall on Saturday nights. Saturday nights were wonderful with the sweep and frenzy of motion as the guys danced with girls wearing yards of skirts and petticoats. Kees proved to be a super dancer teaching Meggie heaps of new dance steps that were already all the rage back in Holland. He was in great demand when a ladies choice was called.

Kees had been fascinated since his arrival in Auckland by the windmill that sat on Auckland's skyline that had supplied flour for the city for over a hundred years. The old mill was an historical landmark and could be seen from all points around Auckland. Kees's first glimpse of the old Partington Mill had been as the passenger ship had steamed into Auckland Harbour and was thrilled to see something so familiar to what he had left behind. When the council began to demolish the old landmark he was horrified.

"Why do they break this up when they have no other wind-molen to see?"

Jack shook his head. He hadn't thought much about the old mill until Kees had brought it to his notice.

Each day Kees walked up from the wharf to watch the old mill come down. First the heavy machinery, huge metal cogs and wheels, were removed from inside and taken away on waiting trucks. Then the small fantail was lowered from the top of the tower followed by the sails.

"You in New Zealand seem to break so many things up. In Holland we break nothing. We have the buildings still there from hundreds of years ago." He shook his head again in disbelief. "In Amsterdam we have building still stand that were made … dertiende, oh how do you say, dertiende eeuw."

He was lost for the correct English but eventually they worked out that he meant thirteenth century.

Lastly the gallery was removed and Kees watched the huge metal ball crash into the sides of the brick tower transforming the enchanting old landmark in a matter of minutes into nothing more than an ugly pile of bricks and mortar. It was almost as though he was losing a close friend and tears joined the dust that filled his eyes.

In no time Kees had a good grip of the English language. They often laughed over the many faux pas he had made when he'd first arrived in New Zealand. He lost his leanness and filled out from the good New Zealand food. He and Granddad became great friends and talked at length about the war and politics. Kees explained that even now, five years after the war had ended, there were still serious shortages of almost everything in Holland. Life there during the German occupation had been horrendous and as well Kees had spent a year in a German work camp before the war had ended.

Meggie feelings for Kees were growing but becoming nothing like those she'd felt for Simon. He amused her with his great sense of fun and she supposed it would be hard for any girl not to fall for him. He was now a regular visitor at Granddad's and they spent a lot of their time together. Kees always left her smiling and putting her slippers on the wrong feet and Meggie wondered how he could retain such a wonderful disposition when he had seen such horror at the hands of the Germans in his childhood and youth. Sometimes she would let her thoughts roam on to comparing Kees's soft gentleness with her father's violent temper. Surely they'd both suffered similar deprivation, both knew the taste of hunger, so what made one of them one thing and the other another.

"Duw, so serious you look?" Granddad would break through those thoughts and Meggie would just smile but give no answer.

A letter from Sarry reported that Moira had left Huntly and gone Karitane nursing. Her letter was also full of news about the Dutch immigrants who had arrived in Huntly to work on the railway. Sarry had been going out with one called Hans who she thought was a dream. There was no mention of Simon in the letter. Meggie had stopped writing to Simon a long time ago, as he had never answered one of her letters.

Jack was becoming frailer and in need of more care. Kees presented his 'alien card' at the Grey Lynn Police Station to advise them of his intention to change his address, and he moved into Granddad's spare room. He was wonderful with the old man doing all the jobs that were too heavy for Meggie.

When the former Prime Minister Fraser died in December that year Jack wasn't well enough to attend the State funeral in Wellington. Frank Langtry, retired now from Parliament, visited him on the day and the two solid old Labour men listened to the funeral as it was relayed through the radio. Crowds paid homage but both men agreed, as they sipped whiskey, that there wasn't the fervour amongst the crowds that had accompanied Michael Joseph Savage's funeral. The people had revered Mickey Savage. They trusted him because he had taken their miserable lives and transformed them. Turned the working mans' mean existence into a secure one, well paid and well fed. Mickey Savage had made it possible for the common man to live comfortably.

"The young ones have gone soft. They forget the Government that gave them these conditions was Labour," Jack commented, as they discussed the downfall of the Labour Government at the last election.

"All the young lads want to do is play billiards, fill their guts with beer and go to the pictures," reflected Frank. "Too many years of security with a Labour government. Mickey's welfare state has become the too bloody well fed state."

Jack nodded in agreement. "Yes. Well, they've got the good wages and better conditions all right, but they spend as fast as they earn … throw it away on booze and the races." He nodded knowingly. "Unless they begin to see the value of the unions and support them they'll be back to long hours with pittance wages and huge profits for the wealthy."

"Well, they won't do that 'til their bellies are empty, Jack. Just like ours once were. There's nothing like the sides of your stomach flapping together to fan the fire in your guts."

They filled their glasses again and continued to reminisce about the old days and each predicted who they thought would lead the Labour Party now that Fraser had gone. Jack began singing, in his still splendid Welsh voice and Frank joined in

"The people's flag is deepest red …" the two lovely male voices blended beautifully. "It shrouded all our martyrs' dead …" and Meggie, having learned that song before learning Baa Baa Black Sheep, sung along with them. Afterwards, she covered the two old warriors with rugs as they slept soundly in their chairs.

Christmas came around again and Kees bought Meggie a diamond engagement ring. "We'll marry and go back to Holland when your Grandfather has gone," he told her frankly, but not unkindly.

Meggie was thrilled with the ring, sad at the thought that it was as inevitable as the rising and setting of the sun that her dear Granddad would die sometime soon but not sure about going to another country on the other side of the world to live. She'd never been out of the North Island, nor further than Mapiu one way and Auckland the other. As well, because she had accepted the engagement ring, she developed huge guilt feelings about Simon. After all, he had asked her to marry him first and she had agreed. But because he didn't keep in touch she didn't know where she stood now. No one wrote about Simon anymore. Perhaps he was seeing someone else and her friends didn't want to tell her or maybe they just assumed that he kept in touch with her. Should she write to Simon one more time and ask him if he still wanted her when he hadn't responded to her letters at all?

She asked Granddad what he thought about her commitment to Simon.

"Kees is a good man, cariad. But you must let your soul take you to where you should be," was all he said.

So she tried to put Simon to the back of her mind.

While the days of falling in love with Kees were heavenly and Meggie wished that life would stay just as it was right now, there was also a lovely quietness about the relationship. Something Meggie had never experienced before. Kees kissed her a lot but never became hot blooded like Simon had done. But sometimes Meggie did worry that he didn't find her attractive enough. The closeness they had and his acceptance at Granddad's house seemed to be enough for Kees.

1951 had hardly arrived before Kees and Evan, along with all the wharfies, came out on strike. Kees hated being at home doing nothing and was also concerned about losing money as he could see his precious savings dwindling and that was the money that would take them back to Holland. Things looked really bad when the Government brought in the military servicemen to work on the waterfront.

WAIKATO MINERS OUT. THREAT OF A LONG STRIKE.

The newspaper headlines glared out at Jack. He jabbed the paper with his finger as he addressed Meggie and Kees at the breakfast table. "These are only the start of strikes now the Tories are in," he said, shaking his head knowingly. "I won't be here to see them but you mark my words," he nodded towards Kees, and puffed great plumes of smoke from his pipe. "This is the beginning of many more."

All day Meggie's mind was on the strike at Glen Afton and she wondered if she should make it an excuse to write again to Simon. But she knew in her heart that he wouldn't answer so she put the idea away, satisfying herself with just following the strike in the newspapers, and radio news broadcasts. Jack used up too much energy following the strike and by Christmas that year he had been confined to his bed.

At Glen Afton the village had taken little notice when the screens stopped rattling before the whistle blew for crib. But when the miners came trudging up the hill there was a clutch of fear amongst the women. Had there been an accident? Most of the men looked grim with their smeared faces and staring eyes still blinking in the bright sunlight, but some were grinning, with their teeth gleaming white in their black faces.

"It's a bloody strike," yelled Harry White, to relieve the anxious looking wives who watched the miners marching towards the bathhouse. "One out, all out," he called back over his shoulder.

Immediately the women began to worry about no wage coming in. As the strike wore on a relief store was set up in the Blueroom and the local farmers donated sheep and pigs. The men filled their days playing darts, drinking, and digging coal for their own use from the seams that thrust up through hillsides around the valley. Other times they congregated in clusters, smoking and talking, around the Post Office and the picture hall.

Florrie was still working as Post Mistress when the strike came. She'd taken on the job after Meggie left because without her board the farm didn't bring in enough. She cast a disdainful look at the groups of men loitering outside. I'd like to go on strike too, she thought. Working here all day and there was plenty waiting to be done when she got back to the farm. Oh, yes. They earned a lot more than she did with no study at all. If she hadn't had her Proficiency Certificate she wouldn't have been eligible for this job. And they had no responsibility. Look at the way they stood around idle now outside the Post Office and the shop while she didn't know whether she was coming or going.

There was only her here to receive communications and people waiting at the counter, some with marked impatience, others gossiping loudly while she tried to connect a telephone call over a crackling connection. She'd finish that only to deal with the grumbling knot of people waiting. Bloody miners, she thought. They'd never cope with this pressure. They don't know what real work was.

She often thought about old Stan Fleming, gone five years now, and wondered how different her life might have been if she'd taken up his offer those years ago? She would have inherited his shop and been quite well off now, instead of working all the hours God sent for a miserable living. Florrie sighed, and once more decided she'd been born on the dark side of the moon.

CHAPTER TWENTY-ONE

GREY LYNN 1952

Two important men died in 1952. One was King George the Sixth of England; the other was Meggie's beloved Grandfather, Jack Morgan. Jack had grown fragile over the last year and began living most of his days in the past. He reminisced about his youth in Wales which seemed as near to him as if it was yesterday. He talked to, and about, his Mam and at those memories smiles and scowls flickered across his face. He muttered about the Unions and the Party and eventually drifted into a semi-conscious state. Nature's way perhaps, of protecting the old when their spirit and fire of youth are gone.

For weeks he lived a life that seemed no stronger than a spider's thread before he finally gave up and let go. Meggie stayed with him day and night and when he passed over a yellow sun was riding a perfect blue sky. That sunlight shimmered through the narrow gap in the curtains and lit up the drifting dust motes like showers of golden rain. The slender ray shone onto the tears that slowly squeezed like diamonds through Meggie's lashes. To her it didn't seem right that the day outside could be so bright when inside this house were the saddest people.

Everyone was there the day Granddad died. Dai and Florrie had come up from Glen Afton the day before. Alf Bredeson and Nick Handisides were doing Dai's milking while he was away and Florrie had arranged a relief at the Post Office. The next three days were fully occupied with the aunts feeding the crowd and the family arranging the funeral.

Emmie and Riki, with their baby son, arrived the morning of the funeral. It was the first time Meggie had seen her nephew and she immediately fell in love with the cutest little fellow. Black curly hair and long dark lashes like Riki but the image of Emmie in facial features. Emmie was pale and didn't look well to Meggie who had not seen her sister for five years.

The day of Granddad's funeral dawned clear, but within minutes of the family leaving for the church, the sky grew bruised and angry. Despite the inclement weather it was a big funeral with a full church. The air stayed cold and charged with moisture while the funeral cortege moved slowly out to the Waikemete Cemetery. So it was beneath a leaden sky remincent of the days of his youth that they laid Jack Morgan in his final resting-place. The minister said a last prayer at the graveside and the mourners breathed a soft ... "Amen".

A large crowd returned to Rona Avenue where the table was laden with food prepared by the aunts. Plenty of drink flowed and Frances Langtry toasted his old friend and fighter for justice with a large glass of whiskey.

"Here's to Jack, a fighter whose motto was always 'a fair day's work for a fair day's pay'."

"Here, here," the crowd cheered, and they all drank to Jack Morgan.

The day had been emotionally draining for Meggie. She was clearing empty plates when Dai sidled up to her. "So the old man left ya the house, did he?"

Meggie felt uncomfortable but nodded in agreement.

"Well yer going ta sell it, aren't ya and come back to the farm."

These were the very words Meggie had dreaded to hear in the last five years. Granddad, when updating his will two years ago, had told her that he was leaving her the house, but she had told only a few. Not even Kees knew that she was now the rightful owner of the Rona Avenue house and all the contents. Meggie looked straight at her father. He was fairly well tanked up and the old fears crowded back and settled in her mind. "No," she said bravely. "I'm staying here."

"If ya sell the place the money will make the farm freehold fer us. Yer know ya mother's working at the Post Office ta make ends meet?"

When Meggie didn't answer Dai became nasty. "Yer've got a bit big fer yer boots haven't ya." Again she didn't answer but ran to her bedroom and fell sobbing onto the bed. Dai's request had been just too much on top of burying Granddad that day. Kees followed her in and shut the door. He rubbed her shoulders and back and made soothing noises. His own sadness at the loss of Jack was great so he could imagine how absolutely devastating it must be for Meggie.

The weather continued to deteriorate and the wind rose as the long day wore on. Finally everyone had gone leaving only Kees and Meggie in the house. They'd never been alone in the house before. There had always been Granddad.

"I need to get out of the house for a while," Meggie told Kees.

Regardless of the strong wind that almost toppled them off their feet, they ran up to the tram stop and getting off at Pt. Chev. They walked around the cliff tops where a few sturdy pohutukawa had somehow managed to find a toehold. There she told Kees about Granddad's will and that she now owned the house. Kees was happy for her.

"So I hope you will not, how do you say, kuck me out," he laughed.

"No. But Dad wants me to sell the house and put the money into the farm."

Kees was alarmed. "But you won't do that?"

"I don't want to but if they need the money to make the farm freehold … Mum looks so tired and I feel guilty that I don't want to go back and help them on the farm" Her voice trailed off in the wind.

"Is that why you were so upset this afternoon," Kees asked.

Meggie nodded. "What do you think I should do?"

"Well. I give it to you straight. I don't think you should ever sell the house. I think Jack left it for you because he knew you must have always some security. If you give in to your vader you will be foolish."

They walked on in silence, down the rough track of slippery ginger clay to the lower land at the water's edge. The waves were high and grasping as they clawed at the shoreline. Kees held her as they stood with their feet apart rocked by the strong winds as they attempted to defy the elements.

"Show me what I should do," Meggie called into the wind. Without hesitation it scooped the top from a swollen wave and threw the spume into their faces. They were both thoroughly wet when they jumped down onto the tram zone and ran home with the wind behind them. Evan had returned to the house with his mother and Auntie Mae. They were stacking dishes to take home and clearing up.

"Get your things together Meggie. You'll come back with me tonight," said Auntie Mae. "You can't stay here on your own with Kees."

Meggie shook her head. "No. This is my house now and I want to stay here just as Granddad wanted me to."

Both Aunts were shocked. "What about Kees? You two can't stay in the same house before you're married."

A mean stubbornness gathered in her and she spoke coldly. "Thank you, but no. Kees stays and I stay,"

Her aunts tut tutted about what the neighbours would think, and be it on her own head, but Meggie said she didn't care. Kees was proud of her.

After they'd gone she cried again. Kees comforted her and that night he took her to his bed. She didn't object. After all, warmth and acceptance were something she had sought all her life and that night she needed that comfort more than ever before. Afterwards, as she lay warm and safe in Kees's arms, they talked.

"Why did you never want me this way before? Si—" she stopped.

"Finish. What were you to say?" Kees asked.

Meggie realized her slip of the tongue and tried to rectify what she had been going to say about Simon always wanting sex. "Just that some of my girlfriends say their jokers are always trying it on so I thought you didn't find me attractive enough."

He laughed. "No, no, my lieveling. I always wanted your sex, but you were still a caterpillar, so I must wait."

Meggie looked puzzled. "What do you mean I'm a caterpillar?"

"Real love is letting the caterpillar grow into the butterfly," he explained. "And today, you became my butterfly."

A warmth spread through her at his words. She hadn't known until now what it was like to be properly loved by a man and she savoured the sensation. They slept, and Kees woke her sometime in the darkness. Slowly and tenderly he made love to her again and for the first time in her 21 years Meggie felt no guilt about what she was doing. As long as she had strong and gentle Kees beside her she would care less what the world thought. Meggie applied and got work as a telephone operator at the Wellesley Street Tollroom

"We will work hard and save our money to go back to Holland to live," Kees told her. "And there we shall be married with my family all around us."

Meggie didn't object for what did she have to stay in New Zealand for now.

CHAPTER TWENTY-TWO

ALKMAAR, NORTH HOLLAND 1953

Meggie's mind kept fluttering like some crazy moth as she prepared for their departure from New Zealand. To contemplate travelling halfway around the world to live in Holland was surely the biggest event of her life. She felt like she was in a movie and being swept along each day in another episode. There seemed so much to do. The packing; what they would take and what to leave behind, gifts to be bought for the relatives in Holland, photos and acquiring her passport. She was in a whirl.

At times, when her heart was racing too much, she would sit and wonder if she ever would hear again the rattle of screens endlessly emptying coal into the wagons below, smell the sulphur from a steam engine's smoke stack as it huffed into the village, and by complete contrast, breathe in the fragrance of native bush and with its carpet of mouldering leaves. She'd remember gathering the late summer berries and the crisp white frosts that froze the water pipes, and the farm. And when she remembered the farm she would go about the business of preparing to embark on a life in foreign country.

Finally, all the arrangements came together and Evan solved the problem of the Rona Street house by moving in as the tenant and caretaker.

Some of the wanderlust inherited from the Gypsy ancestor came to the fore in Meggie as their liner called at exotic ports on their way north. Singapore, Ceylon, Aden and the Suez and past the breath-taking Pyramids that Merv Bowman had taught them about at school. Meggie drew in her breath sharply in awe at the huge structures, and in wonderment at the turn that her life had taken. Portside, Naples and finally, on a warm day in the late northern spring, they rounded the Hoek van Holland to disembark at Rotterdam. Here Meggie was to learn about another aspect of the war that had raged here a decade ago.

"The city is so modern," she said, surprised. "Didn't you say Rotterdam had been badly bombed by the Germans?"

"Yes, it was reduced to a wasteland by the Germans. Everything was destroyed. Hospitals, churches, schools, shops, they said 28,000 buildings over an area of 640 acres."

Kees had tears in his eyes as he looked around the new ultramodern city. "Just before the war ends the Germans blew up the piers and the harbour and blocked the Maas River with sunken ships. Never have I seen such a broken city," he continued, as he wiped his eyes and his face worked with emotion. "But we must be thankful. It has been rebuilt," he cried, as he stretched his arms out to take in the fresh setting of steel and glass, brick and concrete and the fine new shopping pavilions.

Only once before had Meggie ever seen Kees so emotional and that was when Partington's Mill had been torn down. She realized now that she had much to learn about the suffering of the Dutch people during that last World War. She held tightly to Kees as they window-shopped in the traffic free malls.

"Tomorrow I will take you to see the statue of Mei, 1940," Kees whispered as Meggie lay in his arms that night.

Meggie looked quizzical.

"It is the monument that commemorates that black Tuesday on May 14th in 1940 when the Germans bombed Rotterdam to ruins," he explained.

Tears filled Meggie's eyes as she gazed at the tortured face and body of a bronze female figure, looking up at the sky in agony, holding her palms aloft as if shielding her home against a rain of bombs.

"How privileged we were in New Zealand. Compared to this we knew nothing," she wept, so moved was she by the suffering that the statue radiated. "Nothing at all."

They boarded the train the next day on their way to Kees's home at Alkmaar. Meggie felt she was floating in a dream world as she took in the flat and orderly landscape dotted with windmills, like nothing she had ever seen before. Seeing the windmills, and after viewing the museum photographs of the devastated ruins of wartime Rotterdam, Meggie at last understood why Kees had been so passionate about the demolishing of Partington's Mill in Auckland.

As the train neared Amsterdam the landscape spread out in magical mosaics of breath-taking blooms, criss-crossed with canals, each square growing a different colour. Meggie found herself seized by a longing to draw and paint. Not so much to be an artist or to show in exhibitions, but a desire to record the beauty she could see around her.

At Amsterdam, after Meggie had stopped exclaiming at the seas of bicycles parked outside the railway station and in all other nooks and crannies, Kees took her on a waterbus cruise along the network of waterways that wound through the city. They passed under centuries-old bridges, beneath the branches of tall elms and past stately homes built in the seventeenth and eighteenth centuries. They saw old churches and heard the tinkling chimes of the carillon as they cruised. Later they visited the Rijksmuseum and saw Rembrandt's Night Watch. Meggie kept stopping to stare at the wonderful old buildings that were so ornately decorated. By the time they reached Breede Straat 21 in Alkmaar Meggie was totally captivated by the radiance of this beautiful country. Kees's parents, Arnika and Jaap Roobeck were waiting to greet them.

"Welkom, welkom," Kees's mother and father cried, as they embraced Meggie in a huge bear hug.

Though Meggie had learned some basics of the Dutch language from Kees, it was difficult at first to converse with his family. But they were kind and loving people and so delighted to have Kees home again.

"Don't go away again, zoon. It was too big mistake," his moeder told him every day without fail.

Meggie and Kees married at the Town Hall in Alkmaar with all Kees's family attending. Their son was born later that year and they called him Jack after Granddad. The next year they were blessed with a beautiful little girl and they called her Arnika after Kees's mother. Kees had set up his own electrical shop and worked long hours. Soon the business was thriving and he was able to expand.

Meggie explored Alkmaar fascinated by its wonderful old and so well preserved buildings. She would stand and stare for hours at ornately decorated buildings that had 1305 or 1487 etched into the stonework. How could these structures still be standing after 600 years? At weekends they visited Petten and walked along the top of the dikes. At Bergen aan Zee, Jaap told her of how it had looked during the German Occupation when dead bodies of British soldiers and airmen were regularly washed up onto the beach. "The young boys from the town were sent to collect the identification tags from their bodies each day," he said.

He told of how the Germans had knocked down many beautiful old buildings in the area just to get a better view of the sea and enemy ships approaching The German bunkers that remained in the fields were reminders and looked so ugly in the otherwise enchanting surroundings. But the cost of removing such heavy concrete was too great. Meggie felt sad and for the hundredth time realized just how well off they had been in their little valley at Glen Afton and Pukemiro.

One day, when Arnika was just three years old, Kees came out with a decision that stunned Meggie. "No more children," he said quite firmly. "You must now go and study at the Universiteit in Amsterdam to study art. Moeder and Tonte Meip will look after the children each day after kindergarten."

Meggie could not believe her ears. Already her cup was running over. A wonderful kind husband with a loving family, two beautiful children and a nice home to live in. And now, being given a chance to develop her talent further. The old Chinese saying that Merv Bowman had once quoted her, 'everyone lives a hundred lives but only one to remember – this may be yours – don't waste it', flooded back into her mind and now she fully understood the meaning. Sometimes she pinched herself quite hard to make sure it wasn't all just a fantasy. The life of booze and endless talk of politics all seemed so far away now. As though it had only happened in a dream. There was seldom any news from New Zealand. Sarry wrote sporadically, as now she was married she had her children to attend to. There was an occasional letter from Emmie and her health was deteriorating. Meggie sent her photos of her babies.

The next news Meggie was to receive from New Zealand was that Emmie, her frail sister, had died.

CHAPTER TWENTY-THREE

ALKMAAR 1980

Sarry and Meggie's correspondence had become no more than a letter in the annual Christmas card. Over the years Sarry had kept Meggie informed about the changes at Glen Afton. Both Rose and Tom Griffith passed away in the same year that Meggie was receiving her art degrees. In the 1960's Sarry wrote of the coalmines closing down leaving Glen Afton and Pukemiro literally ghost towns. At the time she received this news Meggie was opening her first Gallery in Alkmaar. Jaap and Arnika Roobeck died in this decade. Her father, Dai Morgan, had been killed outright in a car crash in 1965 and Florrie had sold the farm and, swallowing her pride, had returned to the family in the King Country. The farm had been sold several times since then, Sarry wrote, and was no longer a dairy farm but dry stock. In all the letters written there was never any mention of Simon. Meggie never asked after him in her letters though she often thought of him. But her life was so full and so different now she rarely had time to ponder.

The years had gone by so quickly and their children Jack and Arnika were both married. It had been a great thrill for Meggie when Sarry's and Hans son, Derek, had visited them at Alkmaar while on his big O. E. Jack had followed in his father's footsteps and was an equal partner in the electrical shops while Arnika managed Meggie's Gallery in Amsterdam. Life could not be better.

There was a ripping in Meggie's heart on that cold mid-winter day when they brought her the news of Kees's death. Kees was always so careful with electrical gear and that he would touch a live wire seemed wrong. That Kees was dead was unbelievable. The snow was thick on the ground when they laid him to rest and she remembered again his strength the day they had buried her dear Granddad. God, she would give her soul to have him by her side right now. The children stayed with Meggie and they all grieved together. But then came the day that Meggie was, for the first time since she had arrived in Holland, alone in the house. They still lived at Breede Straat 21, having inherited the house when the old Roobeck's passed on. For weeks she felt as fragile as glass as she wandered the rooms alone. With each step she felt she would shatter and fall into glittering fragments on the floor. The only one thing she was grateful for was that Kees's death had been quick and painless.

Spring arrived and Meggie began to leave the house more.

"Spring is what we live through winter for," Kees had often said, as she had shivered, slipped and slid on what remained of the winter ice.

Meggie was totally lost. When she first gathered the courage to go out she only ventured as far as the dikes at Petten, the place where she and Kees had ridden their bikes over to almost every weekend, when she had first arrived in Alkmaar. The dikes were higher now, with walking paths. She would watch from the top of the dikes the ever-changing sea, as she made her way across the crisp grass and into the teeth of the cold north wind.

How can I live without someone who has given me so much, she would ask as she watched a mother-of-pearl haze building over the sea. I would never be where I am now in the art world if he hadn't encouraged me so much.

He had worked too hard and seen too much horror in his formative years, she would concede, as along the horizon the sky glowed with golden light and the sea lightened, shading from a fathomless ink-blue to luminous silver. Yet he had the ability to calm and heal me of my hurts and disappointments. He gave me so much but did I give him enough, she wondered, as she glanced at the western sky where the soft grey rainclouds were swiftly darkening into purple.

Late spring brought with it its usual blaze of colour. As she looked back from the top of the dike across the endless landscape of tulip fields spreading out like a dazzling carpet, hundreds of acres of land transformed into a sea of delicate yellow, salmon pink, brilliant red, blue-black and pure white blooms, and instead of rejoicing at the beauty, she cried. She cried again as she thought of the flower festivals and the floral floats that Kees would not see this year. They were financially well off now, but Meggie would give everything she owned just to touch him again.

It took two whole years before Meggie felt she could pick up the threads of life again. Evan had written ages ago to tell her that Granddad's house was in dire need of repair. She called the children. "I'm going back to New Zealand to see to Granddad's house," she told them.

"Will you sell it, moeder?" Jack asked.

"I don't know. Evan said it needs a lot of work done on it now. If I can busy myself doing it up that may help me to accept life without your father." She cried again. "I was so upset when Granddad died but I had Kees next to me then. This pain and longing is like nothing I have ever experienced and I hope I never have to again," she sobbed.

Jack and Arnika held their mother tightly. How can we lessen her grief, they both thought. Perhaps some time in New Zealand would help her to heal.

CHAPTER TWENTY-FOUR

GLEN AFTON 1984

Meggie had heard the Pukemiro School reunion being advertised over Radio Pacific. After sending for an enrolment form she decided it would be a mistake to go back and put the form to one side. She'd hummed and hawed for another two weeks then sent the papers off. Tom wanted to come with her but she knew that if she did go back it had to be alone. Besides, a weekend away from Tom's possessiveness would be a relief. Though her decision to go alone resulted in a row between them Meggie was adamant and so here she was returning to the place that had been both her heaven and her hell in those days so long ago …

Glancing around the landscape Meggie judged about a half-hour and she would be at Glen Afton. She took in the beauty of the countryside, green and rolling, so typically Waikato farming land. Soon, she knew, the scenery would change and become more rugged; its face scarred from old mine workings. And her mind flashed back and she remembered the days before Kees when she had loved Simon. Suddenly, she became aware that she was travelling much too fast and eased back on the accelerator as she negotiated the curves and bends that led on up and over the hill, and down into the little valley that had once been her home.

Hot tears blurred her vision and she was forced to halt her car on the shoulder of the hill, the very same place where Dai had stopped their little Austin Seven car all those years ago looked down at the little village and said, "Well, we made it, Missus."

The sweep of the hillsides was just the same, but the Glen had changed. Not one mine or railway building remained. Everywhere the hand of time had been at work and nothing had been spared it seemed. Even the railway line had been ripped up and a tar seal road ran right through where the Railway Station and Goods Shed had stood when she had lived at the Glen. The overhead footbridge, where as children they had raced breathless to stand while the hot steam from the engine passing beneath had lifted their skirts high, was no longer there. To her right the rattling screens were no more and the mine entrance had been sealed over with concrete. It had taken on the bizarre look of a giant's tooth holding a great grey filling. The few houses, that were still standing, dotted the landscape but only the cattle grazing around the hills gave indication that life did still exist in the valley of Glen Afton.

On the hill above where the potteries had stood, there was no evidence now of the house and farm buildings that she had lived in and worked around. Everything had gone without trace as though nothing had ever been there at all. The shock of change suspended Meggie in that narrow place between fantasy and reality. Had that violence, still tucked in the corners of her mind, really taken place at all? There was nothing here to support it! Just a large empty pastureland and dry stock grazing on the side of the hill. There should have been a house with an old Orion coal range in the kitchen and two ringed water tanks sitting on a wooden stand on the south side of the house. Outside the back door should have been the washhouse and coal shed. But they were not there. Only the stand of pines remained and as she gazed at that viridian splash on the hillside from the mists of time she could hear again her father's voice, thick with booze, "Get up yer lazy bitches and unload thish bloody coal." Meggie had never grieved at the death of her parents but she had missed her sister, Emmie. More than ever now as there was no one left to substantiate the reality of her memories.

She felt scared, not excited anticipation at the weekend ahead, but real deep down scared. It was so quiet that she felt as though she was trespassing. Where were all the colliery houses with coal smoke streaming from their chimneys? There was no noise. There should have been a loud musical rattle from the screens as they sieved coal endlessly into the waiting wagons below. There should have been the clatter of skips as they chased each other back and forth over the hill to the Mac mine. She strained her ears for a sound of a steam engine chuntering up a grade or two with its coal laden wagons, the sulphery smell from the smoke stack lingering on in the air long after the train had passed. But there was nothing now but silence.

Meggie had known deep down there had to be change but finding everything so drastically changed was followed by the realization that she didn't belong here anymore. So what in God's name was she doing sitting on top of a hill looking into a valley that to her was now completely alien. Tears pricked behind her eyes as she attempted to quell the fear that was fast rising in her. Perhaps it was no more than feeling she would be a stranger in her hometown, she told herself sensibly. But she knew in her heart it was more. She was going to have to face Simon again after all these long years. She supposed that he still lived at the Glen and would be at the Reunion.

She must make the choice right now. Could she cope with meeting him again or would she be better to turn around now and go back to Grey Lynn?

The afterglow of the sunset had faded from the sky as Meggie drove into the old rundown township of Pukemiro. A large moon that was rising above the brow of the hill lorded it over the quaint houses below. The walk to the school, built right on the hilltop, had seemed such a steep climb to her as a child but now as she looked with adult eyes it wasn't that steep at all.

The street was already lined with cars but she managed to find a gap some distance away from the hall and even from there the steady rumble of the celebrating crowd could be heard. Not that it would worry anyone living in the area as they would all be at this evenings function held to open the school reunion weekend.

There was already quite a chill in the air and Meggie paused to reflect on those cold winter days when the kids from the Glen had dawdled around the old metal road to school, stopping at every muddy puddle to break off and suck the dirty ice that formed on the surfaces. She shuddered now at the thought of eating the disgustingly dirty ice. How they hadn't contracted some terrible disease had been a miracle!

They had been the war years and she remembered the cloth bags that hung on the side of their desks and she smiled when she remembered that Simon had told her the cork was to stop them biting their tongues off. But really, as children they hadn't realized the danger there had been of being bombed by the Japanese. Only in adulthood, and seeing the devastation of war on the other side of the world, had she become completely aware of the strategic targets those coalmines had been in those war years.

Anxiety pricked at her as she walked up the footpath, still unsure that her decision to stay had been the right one. As she neared the hall the clicking of her high-heels seemed to tap out her tense thoughts – 'Will Si be there? Will Si be there?'

Entering the hall she stood for some moments in the foyer to get her bearings. The noise, reminiscent of a hive of very angry bees, was deafening. She wasn't sure she could go through with this weekend reunion and knew she could easily turn back right now. But from somewhere she gathered the courage she needed to push through the crowd to the bar. A stiff vodka helped to steady her nerves. She got herself another then pressed through the crowd again with hopes of seeing someone she might know.

The first person she recognized was, wouldn't you know, Hazel Hutchins, prancing around the hall making sure everyone knew she was there. She hasn't changed any, thought Meggie, at the same time suffering a sharp twinge of jealousy. She was convinced Hazel had been Simon's first … but she had no time to pursue the thought as suddenly she was being hugged and kissed by people she had not seen for forty years. Nor would she have recognized some of them if they hadn't made themselves known to her. Someone grabbed her roughly from behind and swung her around.

"It is you, yer old buggar," screeched Simon's sister, Cissy. "How the hell are you?" After embracing they attempted a conversation over the din. "Does Si know you're here? He's not coming, you know," Cissy bellowed.

"Not to anything?" Meggie shouted back, ignoring Cissy's first question.

Cissy shook her head. "Why don't you go around and see him?" she suggested. "He's at home on his own right now."

"Why should I?" Meggie retorted.

Cissy shook her head again, this time in exasperation. "You're both a pair of pig-headed bastards. You bloody deserve each other, you know that." she yelled back at Meggie. "Go and see him. He never got married, you know. He lives on his own in the old house now that everyone's gone."

Meggie again ignored Cissy's statement. "Is Sarry here? I can't see her anywhere."

Cissy gave up. "Yep. She's out in the marquee," she said, indicating the side door with a nod of her head. "Just follow the loud cackle and you'll find her."

Outside in the marquee the old gang surrounded Sarry. Gerry Dunstan, Mick Galloway, Brian Harmon, Riki Whetu and Bigfoot Raynor, all much older but recognizable. Brian looked just as his Dad had done when they were all kids. Bigfoot Raynor was taller than she remembered, must be easily 6ft plus, she thought. Mick Galloway's bald head reminded her of when she had first seen Bill Cowie's shiny bald pate. Rikki Whetu, though overweight, had retained his handsome face and curly jet-black hair. And the years had been good to Gerry Dunstan too. He stood straight and tall and looked most distinguished with his thick mass of steel gray hair. The years peeled back for her as she stood watching her childhood friends laughing and talking over old times.

Gerry was the first to spot her. He held her so tight for what seemed an age, and then holding her out at arm's length he shook his head. "Megs. I would have known you anywhere."

"Are you still flying, Gerry?" she asked, when he finally released her.

Gerry flew for British Airways now and lived in England permanently. But then what other career would a person who had a full set of Sgt. Dan – The Creamota man, Aircraft cards have?

"Yip. Retire next year," he answered in his clipped accent.

Sarry was still shrieking as she grabbed Meggie and danced her around the canvas flooring in the marquee. "Why didn't ya let me know you were coming? I thought ya were still in Holland. Where are ya staying? You can stay with us."

Meggie couldn't answer all the questions being thrown at her and no one seemed to want answers, anyway. Rikki stood back hesitant. Meggie knew he had remarried after Emmie had died and she guessed he felt uncomfortable about that. She reached out to him. "How are you, Rikki? It's years since I've seen you."

Rikki's black eyes glistened as they filled with tears. "Yeah. It's been a long time, Megs. A real long time."

He wiped his eyes with the back of his hand and turned away from the others. They were all silent for a moment as they remembered frail little Emmie Morgan.

After the greetings all round, the gang were soon heavily into reminiscences of the good old days.

"All that's missing now is Saint Si. Remember that day when ya first arrived, Megs, and you said he'd saved you. Ha! Ha! Ha!" cackled Sarry, and everyone laughed as they all talked at once.

It was midnight before Meggie drove back to the Waingaro Hotel, the very same hotel that her father had frequented so often forty years ago. The moon had risen high. Beyond it the light was brilliant, unearthly, surreal. It kindled in her a yearning and once more Simon was uppermost in her mind. She remembered other nights such as this when they had wanted each other so badly and she had denied him. In today's permissive society those reasons seemed pathetic.

CHAPTER TWENTY-FIVE

GLEN AFTON

At first Simon Griffith had felt enthusiastic about the School Reunion. Then, as the School Reunion Committee began receiving enrolments for the weekend one came from Meggie Morgan. Simon decided there and then not to attend the reunion.

By the time the weekend came around he was regretting his decision and even more so as the family began arriving at the big old rambling home of their childhood. Once again the house was filled with noise and overflowing with people. Simon loved the company of his family. He'd occupied the house alone since the old ones had died and often felt lonely.

"Come on, Si," Cissy had coaxed. "It'll be a great night."

He shook his head. "All the other bastards'll have a partner. I'll stick out like a sore bloody thumb."

"Si must be crook," Ronnie Holden commented to Cissy, on their way to the opening 'do' at the Pukemiro Hall. "I've never known him to turn down a good booze up before."

Simon, left to himself after the family had left, felt the house creak with emptiness. He opened a can of beer and settled down to watch the television. But he was restless and no way could he concentrate on the program. He kept wondering if she had arrived yet and knew in his heart that it was Meggie's presence in the district that was causing him to feel so ill at ease. One half of him was desperate to see her, the other half said no. And as the agitation grew within him he slammed his fist with force against the arm of the chair. The pain made his eyes smart. Shit, how he'd loved that girl. Her face floated before him and he imagined he could smell the sweetness of her young body. He remembered again the night of Olwyn's wedding when they had lain together and within the week she had left him.

A tingling began in his fingers and again in his mind they entwined her dark hair. His memory slid back to that first time, at first an innocent kiss, then changing in a flash to such a sensual passion that he'd lost control. He could taste those firm breasts moving under his mouth again and he developed a hard painful erection. He cursed as the dull ache of it spread around his groin. Christ, how he hadn't seduced her that day or at any time following was nothing short of a bloody miracle. And jeez, he wished the hell that he had done now.

The gnawing continued around his abdomen. "Bloody stay away from the reunion if she can still affect me this bad," he muttered, as his trembling hands poured out a neat whiskey.

The drink seemed to calm him and he poured another, and then sat back in the darkened room alone with his thoughts. Booze had been the thing that relieved his pain back then and he'd certainly drank his share. There was no denying that. He had to be fair and admit that he had given Meggie a hard time with his boozing. She'd had enough to put up with her own old man's drinking and the life she had once the silly old bastard had moved onto Arch Bell's farm up on the hill. They'd worked her like a bloody dog on that farm and that still got up his nose. They'd even taken her away from school to do heavy farm work. She was a clever little bugger, too, he thought. Always drawing great pictures and sketches of people. No wonder she left, or rather was sent away to look after her grandfather in Auckland. He could see everything clearly now but back then, when his blood ran hot, he could only see her as weak because she wouldn't stand up to her parents.

Simon grimaced as he thought how sexually liberal today's youth were. There was no agonizing over whether to have sex before marriage today. It was just part of the norm, their lives, their bodies; they'd do as they pleased seemed to be the general attitude. Simon wasn't sure that he agreed with that sort of freedom but they certainly were a world apart from the youth that he and Meggie had spent.

Most teenagers had not dared to disobey the dictates of their parents back then. But he had to be honest and admit that he would have disobeyed the morals of the day had Meggie allowed him to. It hadn't been her fault that she'd developed the body of a woman when she was still only a child. He remembered her succulent breasts with their nipples outlined and protruding as they fought to escape the bounds of the too tight hand-me-downs she had to wear. He bristled with resentment as he remembered Florrie Morgan. She had a lot on her plate with old Dai true, but he had taken a dislike to her for her unfairness. He wondered now if in middle age Meggie had grown to resemble her mother. If so perhaps he'd had a bloody lucky escape.

Simon poured another whiskey. The bottle was almost empty now. But so what! The liquor was having the desired effect on him and he sat back in the chair to reminisce about those early days again. Her image danced before him as she had been on the night she had been allowed to stay over with Cissy for a dance in the local hall. Cissy had dressed Meggie in her clothes and, jeez, did she look a million dollars. When they walked out into the sitting room he took one look and the blood had rushed to his head. He laughed out loud when he recalled thinking 'Sod the bloody dance, Meggie – you may be only thirteen but I need to take you to my bed right now.' He'd got himself pretty sozzled that night and had entertained thoughts of sneaking into the girls' room later, but Rose Griffith was one step ahead of him and locked the girls' bedroom door herself.

Still with pain he remembered her leaving the Glen as though it was just a recent happening. Her hurried departure had caused quite a stir and his work mates gave him a hard time.

"Got her up the duff, eh Si?" Wink, wink. Their smart-arse remarks had caused him a lot of grief and he tried to crack hardy in their company. But his mind had been in a state of turmoil and his body racked with the pain of loss. If he'd thought he knew pain from Meggie's rejections that had been a mere whisper, by comparison to the pain that had torn at his insides at her leaving the Glen. He'd thought about going after her but in truth he'd done nothing, not even answered her letters. A numbness had seemed to creep over him and for weeks all he could do was crawl out of bed, spend a long day underground, then crawl home and back to bed again. Nightly he had nursed his pain, bitter, but still longing for Meggie. His heart and abdomen had taken on the chill of the underground pit he worked in. And despite himself now, hot tears began to trickle from beneath his tightly closed eyelids as he remembered …

CHAPTER TWENTY-SIX

All houses in which men have lived and died

Are haunted houses; through their open doors

The harmless phantoms on their errands glide

With feet that make no sound upon the floors.

Longfellow.

The school reunion was a tremendous success. Old pupils and teachers had come from near and far to attend the 75th Jubilee weekend. Glorious sunshine and cloudless skies put the final touches to a great weekend. Merv and Olwyn Bowman, who now lived in Huntly, were there. Merv was delighted to see Meggie and monopolized a lot of her time. He'd heard she'd done well overseas and he had thought of her often over the years.

"You have your own Gallery in Auckland, I hear," he asked her.

"Yes. And I have one in Amsterdam and another in Alkmaar," she replied. "Here I try to concentrate on exhibiting for the unsung artists, always remembering my own beginning."

Merv was so proud of her. "Studying overseas must have been a wonderful experience."

"It was. But without Kees's encouragement I would never have done so well. He enrolled me at the University and kept pushing me on."

"He sounds like he was a wonderful man."

"Yes. He was. And I miss him very much."

Tears welled up in her eyes and Merv knew it was time to change the subject. They sank into a deep discussion about great Dutch painters. Olwyn, bored with the arty talk, left them to it.

Sunday morning came around all too soon and Meggie tried hard not to dwell on her disappointment at not having seen Simon. It had to be for the best, she rationalized, in view of her circumstances now. After checking out of the hotel she set off to attend the last event, an informal gathering at the Pukemiro Hall. There was already a large crowd there when she arrived. Everyone seemed reluctant to say that final goodbye after such a wonderful weekend.

Meggie was just about to leave herself and head back to Auckland when her eyes swept the room again and she saw him. He was at the far end of the hall talking to Bluey Aiken. Their eyes met. Meggie's heart made a thud as the room began spinning. Like something in slow motion he was moving towards her.

"Oh Megs," was all he said as he drew her to him.

His touch was so overwhelmingly familiar, even after all these years, that for a moment she thought she would faint. It seemed clear that there were still strong and unresolved feelings between them.

Simon broke the silence. "Ya haven't changed," he said, his eyes scanning her face.

Her smile was tremulous. "Oh no. The ravages of time must have got to me by now."

"Ya look just the same to me, honey."

The endearment slipped out so naturally, as though no time at all had passed since they had last been together. The volume of chatter rose in the hall and Simon frowned.

"How about coming around home where we can talk without all this noise?" he suggested, in a voice tinged with anxiety.

Meggie wanted to do that more than anything else in the world, but she tried not to appear too eager. "Well. For an hour. I will have to be making tracks soon."

"That'll be great." Simon's tone was elated.

Inside the old house nothing seemed changed at all. The lino in the entrance and hall was worn, while the same leafy patterned carpet in autumn colours, somewhat threadbare now, adorned the sitting room floor. Above the mantelpiece the Mickey Savage photo still hung and Meggie felt delight in seeing the old familiar face. No one hung the picture anymore and politics weren't discussed with the fervour of the bygone days. It seemed to her that the Unions today were filled with educated men whose stomachs had never known even as much as a twinge of a hunger pains. New Zealand had changed drastically in the years she had lived away in Holland.

The house seemed eerily quiet, as though all the ghosts from their past were assembling to listen in on their conversation. She had the feeling of being caught in a time warp and half-expected Rose Griffith to walk in from the hallway. Simon broke through her musings.

"Can I get you a drink?" he asked, as her eyes surveyed the room for the first time in forty years.

"Just tea thanks. I've got a long drive back to Auckland."

"Sensible girl, as always!" he retorted, with an edge to his voice. "Sit down and I'll put the jug on."

His comment stung and she flushed. She knew he was referring to her leaving the Glen and never returning. It was clear that Simon held bitter feelings towards her. In order not to give way to her emotions she deliberately stared at some tiny particles of dust spiraling in a shaft of afternoon sunlight. Her intense concentration made her unaware that Simon had returned to the sitting room. Then, sensing a presence, she turned and he was standing before her, his eyes shining with unconcealed tears.

"I'm sorry," he whispered. "What I said was out of order, I know. Ya never owed me nothin'."

Like quicksilver they were in each other's arms, their bodies straining to be together. His mouth savaged hers violently and she could hardly believe what was happening. She loved the pain and returned the kiss as eagerly as he gave it. Her nails scored at his skin and he shuddered wildly, their bodies writhing together with a primitive intensity. They forgot where they were, the time of day, or even what day it was. They forgot everything except that this was where they had always wanted to be. His teeth and mouth were stinging the skin on her breasts and drawing in her hardened nipples.

The squeal of a boiling kettle penetrated through their passion.

"Fuckin' jug!' Simon muttered thickly as he released her to attend to the interruption.

This gave Meggie time to take stock of herself. She couldn't believe what a mess she was in so short a time. Panic flooded through her. How could she return home in this state? The bodice of her dress was torn and the ragged gap revealed a patchwork of marks on her skin.

Simon returned and went straight to the liquor cabinet. He poured himself a large neat whiskey. "Drink?" he asked without looking at her.

"Yes please," she replied shakily.

Still without turning towards her he pleaded, "Meggie". Don't go. Stay with me tonight." His voice was broken and barely audible. "I lost ya once. My own stupidity, I know. But I can't go through that pain again." He gulped down the whiskey and poured himself another. "Nor can I lie awake night after night aching for ya like I did before"

He paused again to compose himself. "I want ya, Meggie. God alone knows how much. Just give me this one night. Please."

The scene was suspended in silence. Tears coursed down Meggie's face though she made no sound. Finally able to speak she whispered, "Si. Honey. Come here."

He crossed the room and knelt before her placing his face on her lap. She stroked and kissed his head and rocked him as she had done her babies. "I love you, Si. Deep down I probably never stopped loving you. Yes. I'll stay."

They remained as they were for a long time and the blue and gold autumn day was fading into twilight before they stirred.

"Si honey. I'll have to make a call to Auckland if I'm going to stay."

"Of course," he answered, and raised his head. His eyes rested on her stained skin.

"Christ, honey. Did I do that?" He was shocked. "Jeez, I'm sorry, honey. I wouldn't hurt ya for the world."

Her fingers silenced his lips. "Where is the phone?"

Nodding he pointed to the telephone and then left the room. For that Meggie was grateful.

Meggie dialled directly through. Tom Patterson answered. "Oh Tom," she quavered, her voice a fraction too high. "We're still partying down here. Everyone seems reluctant to go home."

"I was starting to get worried. Weekend a success then?" questioned Tom.

"Tremendous! Fantastic!" she oozed, and rambled on about the dance the night before. "I'm ringing from Sarry's place. It's been so good to see her again."

"Are you leaving now, then?" Tom's voice sounded anxious.

"No. That's actually why I'm ringing. Sarry wants me to stay for a few days. And I have been drinking so I wouldn't like to chance the drive tonight. Would you mind if I stayed, Tom?" Her voice was cajoling.

Tom's disappointment was barely disguised as he answered, "When do you think you might come back then?" he asked irritably.

Meggie thought quickly. She must stay long enough for the tell-tale marks to fade. "Probably the end of the week. I'll phone you."

Tom was immediately sorry he'd sounded so churlish. But he hated her being away and was constantly suspicious. He knew he was unreasonable and might drive her away if he didn't control the huge jealous streak in his nature.

"Okay," he spoke more softly, "I'll miss you of course. Have you got enough money?"

"Yes thanks," she answered. "And I've got my visa if I run short. Oh, Tom. Will you phone the Gallery? Mary can deal with anything that's urgent."

"Yes. I'll do that." Tom couldn't help sounding curt as he rang off.

Guilt and excitement surged through Meggie as she replaced the hand piece. It had been so goddamn easy. The lies had slithered off her tongue as effortlessly as a snake sliding through long grass.

In the bathroom Simon leaned on the wash bench and shook himself mentally. His heart was pumping in his ears. He took several deep breaths to calm him and lessen his racing heart. Get yourself together, he remonstrated. Isn't going to bed with Meggie what I've dreamed about all these goddamn long years. He remembered the pain of those years. No, he thought. I'm too bloody old to go through that again. He'd lost her once through doing nothing

317

and his instincts told him he'd never be offered another chance if he didn't take this opportunity. He filled the hand basin with cold water and splashed it around his face and the back of his neck and the cooling water balanced him. He straightened his clothes looking into the old peeling mirror attached to the wall.

"Jeez, what's wrong with ya, man," he said to his reflection. "Grab the bastard with both hands and make the most of it."

Returning to the sitting room he found that Meggie had finished with the phone. He was curious whom she had rung. Most likely her business but still, with a twinge of jealousy, he did wonder if she had a male friend in Auckland.

Meggie bathed completely immersed in the lovely deep old bath filled with water heated from the coal range. That it felt different from electrically heated water seemed illogical but it truly did. In the kitchen Simon prepared a meal for them. He still felt shocked, but elated. Never in his wildest dreams could he have envisaged that the reunion weekend, which he had planned not to attend, would result in Meggie staying with him. He whistled softly as he set out the china and glasses for wine. Christ, he thought, I haven't felt this good since … jeez … if I'm honest, since before Meggie left the Glen. In the time between he felt he had been just simply existing.

Meggie walked into the kitchen just as he was draining the last pot. He glanced up and she was wearing some flimsy see-through sort of stuff, and shit, she looked bloody gorgeous to him. They ate and drank and talked of the past. The wine blurred the edges of their old hurts and they were able talk about their childhood affair and their parting without according blame to each other.

Meggie told him about Kees. "He was a wonderful man. He was good for me. He gave me the confidence I lacked and encouraged me into getting my art degree. Kees brought me such joy and I loved him so well," she mused. "And it's hard to live without his strength beside me."

Simon felt the twinge of jealousy again and it hurt. "Would ya have come back here if he hadn't kark ... I mean, died?" he asked.

"Well, no. I don't think so. Kees didn't settle when he came out as an immigrant. He never complained but I think the land was too raw for him. Holland is so different from New Zealand. But I had been back several times to attend to Granddad's house. My cousin Evan rented it for quite a long time but after he built his own house and moved out it was hard to get tenants to look after it." She paused and took a sip of wine. "It was an absolute wreck when I got back this time and I've had to completely redo the inside."

"Yer mean you've been back here and yer never let any of us know?"

"Sarry always knew. We've always kept in touch."

"Yeah. She married a Dutch joker, too. Those bloody Dutchies took all our best sheilahs," he grumbled half joking.

They drank more wine and the subject came back again to their suppressed feelings of their teens.

"Remember the night of Olwyn's wedding," said Simon. "Jeez, I've existed on that night fer forty bloody years." He paused looking at her intensely. "Christ girl. Let's go put things right now."

Taking her by the hand he led her to the big bedroom that had once been his parent's room. Only when they were together in the bed did Simon's nagging doubt flash back into his mind.

"Meggie, honey," he murmured. "Ya know I've never been all the way with a woman, don't ya?"

But she appeared not to hear, and as her mouth found his, Meggie and Simon at last knew the joy of mutual surrender.

It wasn't the sunlight coming through the open window that had awakened her. It was the absolute silence. City living tended to make one think that a constant hum of traffic was the norm. Meggie stretched and felt good. She hadn't had much sleep and a lot to drink last night, but she still felt good. Her mind slipped back to the night she had just spent with Simon. She knew she should have been feeling guilty, but she didn't! She felt aglow. The night had been wonderful, magical, spellbinding. Simon's body, due to a lifetime of hewing coal she supposed, was still well set and sinewy. He was every bit as masculine as she remembered him.

Simon looked peaceful sleeping beside her and as her gaze lingered on his handsome features she realized the full measure of what she had walked away from so long ago. Regret stabbed at her newfound happiness. She knew that she shouldn't feel like this. If she had stayed here there would have been no Kees, no art degrees, no Galleries. Simon would never have made those things available to her. No, he would have just kept her barefoot and pregnant!

As though her watching disturbed him, Si turned over in the bed and opened his eyes. He smiled and the core of her being melted, leaving her weak with the love that she still felt for him. How in God's name had he escaped marriage with a smile like that? Leaning across the pillow he kissed her.

"Are ya really here, honey?" he asked. "Or have I karked it and gone ta heaven?"

She held his face in her hands. "I'm really here, Si. But was I dreaming or did you say last night that I was the first? You were kidding, weren't you?"

He shook his head. "No bullshit," he told her simply. "If it wasn't you then there would be no one. I only told ya because I was so goddamn scared that I wouldn't make it."

This was a real eye-opener for Meggie and she was shocked into silence. Simon had never been with anyone else. Had he been prepared to live out his whole life as celibate if she hadn't stayed this weekend? Simon misunderstood her quietness.

"Yer weren't disappointed with me, were ya, honey?"

With difficulty Meggie dragged herself back from the bombshell he had dropped. "Do I look like a disappointed woman?" she teased.

He kissed her on the tip of her nose. "Well, my lady. Ya do have plenty to answer for now," he joked. "Yer realize you've taken away my virginity, don't ya."

But her mind was still reeling from his disclosure. Simon slid his fingers under her chin and tilted her face to look at him.

"What's wrong, honey?" he asked.

"It's just what you told me, Si. About there not being anyone else in your life."

"Well, Megs. It's the truth."

"I believe you, Si. It's just stunned me that's all."

"Well, I'm stunned that we are together here in the old house." He smiled and kissed her gently. "Honey, let's get married. Like we should have years ago. As soon as we can arrange it, let's get married."

My God! She hadn't anticipated this. She turned her face away from him. Simon knew then there was something wrong.

"What's wrong, Meggie. Yer free, aren't ya? Yer old man karked it in Holland, didn't he? There's nothing to stop us getting married now, is there?"

Pain closed her throat. When she still didn't answer him he shook her. His eyes were dark with fear. "Answer me, damn you. What's ta stop us now?"

Stupefied she blurted, "Si. I got married again. I married Tom last year." Her eyes fell away from his and the words she had just uttered seemed to hang in the air. "I wanted to tell you but you didn't give me a chance."

But he wasn't listening. He had risen up in the bed and his breath was coming in short ragged bursts. "You bitch," he bellowed. "Ya fuckin' rotten bitch!"

Fury spread through her. "You bloody hypocrite," she yelled back. "How dare you."

"You were the one that left," he raged.

"And you kept in touch with me? Begged me to come back, didn't you. You couldn't even answer a letter." she sneered back at him sarcastically.

"Jeez, yer so effin' hot fer it you couldn't wait ta get back in the sack with someone."

Meggie was furious and determined to retaliate. "That bloody garbage about there being no one else. Don't kid me you didn't have Hazel after I'd gone. Or was it before? That's it isn't it, you were on with her before I even left, weren't you!" she screeched, as she flounced out of the bed.

Simon's mind flashed back to the memory of that awful night he had spent out on the Waingaro road with Hazel.

"I wouldn't have touched her with a ten foot barge-pole," he denied. "But it seems yer not so fussy."

The accusations continued to fly as Meggie gathered up her belongings and stormed out to her car. Simon ran after her. The fear of her leaving had calmed him down.

"Don't go, honey," he yelled. "Ya can't drive like that. Ya'll kill yerself. Come back and we'll talk it over."

"What's to talk about with a fuckin' bitch," she screamed back at him.

"I'm sorry. I'm sorry," he kept repeating, as he held her in a vice like grip to prevent her getting into the car.

Even through her anger Meggie knew he was right. If she drove this angry she'd be history. And how could she return to Tom displaying signs of her adultery.

In the kitchen, sipping hot sugared tea, Meggie told Simon about her re-marriage. "Tom is a carpenter and joiner. I employed him to do up Rona Avenue. He's done a wonderful job. We've decorated the house throughout in the old art deco style." She smiled when she thought about the house. "Tom stripped down and restored all of Granddad's old furniture and it fits in beautifully with the décor."

Simon felt the jealousy rise in him again. "Why didn't ya get in touch with me?" he asked.

"How was I to know you still wanted me? Nearly forty years have passed, Simon. You never even contacted me when Granddad died."

"I know. I know. Meggie ya know I'm no writer."

"No. I don't know that," she argued back. "And there have been telephones for some years now."

Simon didn't answer and silence reigned. Then she spoke again about Tom.

"Tom became a habit, I think. I was so shattered when Kees died so suddenly." She paused as she thought about Kees. "I came back with the intention of doing up the house and selling it. Tom took on restoring the old house as though it was his own ... he's a wonderful help with my exhibitions, too. And I was lonely, I guess. I'd had such a wonderful companion in Kees. And I was missing the kids back in Holland. Tom kept on proposing and eventually I gave in. There didn't seem to be anything else for my life," she finished sadly.

Minutes passed before Si spoke again. "Ya obviously don't love the joker. What about a divorce?"

"On what grounds," she answered. "Tom's done nothing wrong. He's a good man really. It's only that his possessiveness that gets me down."

"Of course," Simon nodded. His voice sounded flat. "I understand, honey. But we can't end it here. Not after last night!"

"I know. I know," she wept. "Why have things always gone so wrong for us?"

Simon pulled her close. "I don't know, honey. I don't effin' well know," he growled angrily.

"Don't you be using that language in my kitchen," Meggie laughed, imitating Rose Griffith.

Meggie stayed for the week and though guilt was often with her, the days following that they spent together were touched with magic. They loved and teased each other and sang all the old war songs that had been hits when they were young. They walked over the old Mac track and lay in the glen inhaling the special bush smells. The hurtful things that had been said in anger were never mentioned. As she prepared to leave at the end of the week, Simon held her at arm length, his eyes searching hers. "Jest promise that yer'll come to me whenever ya can. I'll always be here for ya, honey."

Then he kissed her with so much tenderness that she feared her heart might burst.

CHAPTER TWENTY-SEVEN

GREY LYNN

Tom Patterson fingered Meggie's gift, an expensive Parker pen. He was really suspicious and felt she had not been completely truthful with him when she'd phoned last week. Now she was back and there was something different about her. She looked more alive and radiant than he'd ever seen her and, she'd informed him immediately she had arrived that she was going back to stay with Sarry in Huntly at the end of the month. Once again she didn't want him to go with her. Something about the ex-pupils of the school keeping in touch once a month and he'd feel out of place. It didn't ring true, all this sudden enthusiasm about an old rundown coal-mining town that she hadn't been back to since she was a girl.

Tom's mind skimmed back to their wedding a year ago. In hindsight it had been a rather bleak affair. The Registry Office, one cold Friday morning with no reception. He'd wanted a big wedding to show off his bride but Meggie made it clear that she wanted no fuss. With a hollow feeling in the pit of his stomach he had to admit that he knew then that Meggie had not wanted to marry him. He'd badgered her into it. He loved her so possessively and had determined at their first meeting that he would marry her. He had thought she would feel different once they were married. But though she was always kind and considerate to him he sensed she still did not love him.

He was unsure how he should tackle her about going away again so soon. "But what the hell," he spoke aloud. "I can't just sit back and accept the situation. Allowing her to take off for God knows where whenever she feels like it."

Tom's possessiveness was well and truly to the fore now. He was a man who liked his own way and, one way or another, he usually got it. He had done over marrying her, hadn't he? But Tom wondered now, as he tapped the pen on the desktop, if that might be a victory he may have to wear in the future like a hump on his back.

Meggie found it easy to rearrange her schedule to be back with Simon in June. She phoned to tell him.

"Can't yer make it sooner?" he grumbled. "I've missed ya like hell."

"Don't pressure me, Si," she pleaded. "It's hard enough to deceive Tom as it is."

"I'm sorry, honey," he apologized. "Wanting you makes me selfish."

She too wanted to rush to him this very minute, longing to feel his hard strength against her again. Simon cut through her thoughts. "By the way. I've been shopping and I've got a surprise for ya."

"You've been shopping? She exclaimed. "My God it's a wonder the town didn't topple over!" she laughed. "Anyway, what is it?"

"Ya'll have ta wait and see, won't ya," he finished teasingly.

The waiting time seemed to drag ever so slowly. Meggie was fidgety and distant and Tom kept commenting on her behaviour, and that annoyed her immensely. He was really starting to get on her nerves.

The morning finally dawned and she phoned Si to tell him she was on her way. He was waiting for her at the end of the lane and they'd made love before she'd unpacked the car. Straight after, Simon gave her present; a solitaire diamond ring set on a high gold bridge and a matching diamond studded wedding band.

"With these rings I thee wed," he whispered, as he slid them onto her finger. "If I hadn't been such a weak bastard always drinkin' piss I'd have done this forty years ago. And ta hell with yer old lady."

Meggie's life fell into the pattern of staying with Simon once every month. She and Tom rowed about her going away and she started to hate returning to him. She knew she wasn't being fair to Tom but she had reached a point where she no longer cared. He slept in the spare room now and they moved about the Grey Lynn house as polite strangers would have done.

At Glen Afton, the affair had breathed new life into Simon. He re-decorated the old house, and made the master bedroom their room. The time they spent together now was like a dream, seductive and magical. They took long walks deep into the bush, the same bush where Merv Bowman had taught Meggie how to sketch the native flora, and they made love there with the cool dankness of ponga scenting the air. When summer came around they loved each other outside on the dewy grass, their bodies pale and ghostly in the silver moonlight, and they would lie close together and listen to the deep summer night breathe softly around them.

They always returned to their own special place in the bush clearing beyond the ridge where they lay on the sweet smelling grass and read pictures in the ever-changing cloud patterns, as they had done when they were children.

More than a year had passed since the School Reunion, that fateful weekend that had brought them together again to finally consummate their love for each other. A time in which Meggie had broken every marriage vow she had taken with Tom, but whatever the force that had reunited her with Simon, it was greater than any guilt that she felt. Tom no longer dictated her life and she came and went in his life with no qualms at all.

Simon lived for her visits. Just to look at her sent a warm caress across his skin. For him, she still possessed that magical something that had driven him wild in his youth. He wanted her with him all the time. "Christ, don'tcha reckon it's time ya left yer joker in Auckland? Ya don't love him. Come down here and live with me," Simon said around a meat sandwich.

"And what about the Gallery? And I can't sell Granddad's house." Meggie felt threatened. Trying to run two lives was becoming a strain. What Simon said did make sense. "What about you living with me in Grey Lynn?" she asked.

Simon shuddered. "No bloody way! I couldn't hack it in the city.' He took a long swig from his beer can. "I've lived in this same bloody house all me life. I'll kark it here, too."

So once again Meggie did nothing to sever her marriage to Tom. Perhaps in her mind she was afraid to tamper with anything so fragile as the relationship she had with Simon. When they were together they were so superbly attuned to each other it was as if they were one soul, one being. How could she interfere with such perfection?

Meggie sometimes allowed herself to wonder that if she and Simon had married all those years ago would they still have this incredible love for each other now. Or would the familiarity of marriage have destroyed it and it only survived now because it was an affair? Was it possible that had they been married for forty odd years would they still have known the joy of making love outside under a vast night sky so full of stars?

It was summer again, warm delightful summer and as Meggie drove back to Auckland she felt leaving Simon was becoming harder for her as each month passed. When she was with him there appeared to be no time, as past, present and future seemed to fuse into one. But once she returned to the outside world she became very aware that time was moving on.

She left Simon late that evening. He had come out into the twilight and kissed her long and hard through the car window. Twenty minutes later she was turning onto the main highway. For some reason she felt really uneasy about leaving him and considered returning to Glen Afton.

Maybe it was because of his needling her to leave Tom. And he was right. She could no longer live this dual role. Tom would have to be told that she wanted a separation. She steeled herself to tell him of her decision when she arrived home.

CHAPTER TWENTY-EIGHT

GLEN AFTON

Simon felt particularly lonely after Meggie left that evening. More than usual. These partings are getting to me, he thought. He'd had that pain back in his chest throughout the day but said nothing to Meggie, as he knew she would worry. He wandered into the kitchen and mixed himself some more indigestion powder.

"I must get to the quack," he muttered, as he drank the powdery liquid.

Cissy was always on his back to get to the doctor whenever she saw him and had even threatened to tell Meggie about the pain if he didn't make an appointment with the doctor. Simon had kidded her that it was the result of too much sex after being celibate for so long. He picked up his novel and settled into bed to read but couldn't concentrate on the book. He felt more aware than ever that Meggie was not beside him.

Jeez, if ever I needed her, I need her now, he thought.

The grandfather clock, in the hallway, ticked loudly in the silent house. At ten-thirty the first agonizing pain struck him. It had the impact of a bullet hitting his chest. It seemed to take hours for him to crawl to the phone and dial Cissy's number. He heard himself cry out loud, expelling his last breath as his lungs ceased to function, the deep blackness was enfolding him, numbing his mind and he slipped out of the world with Meggie's name on his lips. She had been his life, his only love. Simon was dead when the ambulance arrived at his house.

Once home at Grey Lynn sleep eluded Meggie that same night. Perhaps it was the late drive home, or the strain of living a double life. Tom was already in bed when she arrived home so there had been no opportunity to ask him for a separation. Now that she'd made up her mind she wanted to get it over as soon as possible. She would speak to him tomorrow without fail.

Still she couldn't sleep. She couldn't shake off the feeling that something monumental was about to happen. From her bedroom window she watched the last shadows of the night fade and a new day was born.

Next day at the Gallery the sense of dread continued to enfold her and she knew long before the telephone rang that something was very wrong.

"There's no easy way to tell you," Cissy said with her usual directness. "Simon had a heart attack last night. He died just after midnight, Meggie."

The information was clear enough but Meggie refused to believe it. Simon dead! Never. She'd only left him hours before and he was okay then. He may have had a slight heart attack but he'd recover. She knew he would. Anyway, she was sure that God would not be that cruel and take away, for a second time, a man she loved.

Cissy was quite alarmed at Meggie's reaction to her news. Meggie refused to attend the funeral as that would be an admission on her part that Simon was dead. And she knew he was not. She remembered seeing Kees in his coffin and had been physically sick so she stayed in her state of denial about Simon. Through the days she carried on as normal at the Gallery but at night she imagined that Simon came to her. That he filled her room with his unseen presence, a tender ghost beckoning her to go with him. Oh, that she could.

Tom Patterson felt no compassion at the news of Simon's death. He could see the man as no more than a traitor. Enticing Meggie to go to him when he'd failed to get a wife of his own. In his opinion there had to be something seriously wrong with a bloke who had never married.

And though Tom was both jealous, and angry, at the same time he was quite elated. It excited him to know he had won. He had followed his instincts to do nothing and it had paid off. He no longer need fear losing Meggie as his wife; something that had concerned him greatly of late. Give her a week or two and she'd come right. Main thing was the fellow was dead now so she'd soon forget him. He'd see her through this rough patch and things would get back to normal again. After all, he thought, Meggie should be grateful that he was prepared to forgive and forget. Not every bloke would be prepared to overlook her infidelity, of that he was sure. To Tom Meggie was a possession and he had never been able to cope with losing his possessions. What was his remained his, and that was the end of it. As well, her adultery gave him the lever he needed to take control of the marriage from now on.

The day marked in Meggie's diary to visit Simon again finally came around. She drove to Glen Afton but instead of Simon waiting for her the lane was empty. The old house was locked and deserted. Panic crept into her heart and set it pounding. She became desperate to get inside and lie on the bed and remember the pain of too much tenderness. Frantically she circled the house trying all the doors and windows but they were all firmly locked. She began to accept that Simon may really be dead.

Blindly she stumbled towards the hill and over the ridge to the bush clearing. Perspiration drenched her clothing and the sun burned deeply into her skin as she fell to her knees at their special place. She remained kneeling there in silence for an indeterminable time somehow imagining that if she remained quite still Simon would materialize before her. Eventually she had to give up and acknowledge that no such miracle was going to take place. Uncontrollable anger surged through her as she stood up shaking her fists at the sky. "You're a bastard, God," she screamed. "A fuckin' rotten bastard."

Her screams of pain reverberated on the surrounding hills sending back their shrill echo to her. "You didn't need him," she bellowed again, through a throat that was raw from screaming. "You didn't need him, but I did," she sobbed.

Sinking to her knees again she beat the ground with clenched fists. "You're no God," she accused him again. "You're just a bastard, bass … taaard … bas … taaa … arrrrr … d."

And she wept with such helplessness and despair as she finally accepted that Simon was dead. That he would never come to her again in flesh and bone, and the bright sunlight paled with her terrible sense of loss. She didn't want to go on living herself. So she cried into the cool grass and asked God take her, too. "You've taken them all now. Granddad and Kees and now Simon. Take me, too," she begged.

But deep within herself she knew He would not. Despite the abuse she had hurled at him He would make her go on living, however miserably, until He saw fit to take her.

Raising her hand to her lips she kissed the rings Simon had given her and as she did so she saw him. She saw again his dear face, young and handsome, as he had been in the beginning. The smell of crushed grass became strong and pungent around her and she was with him again. Playing, hiding, running in the wind. And as she listened it seemed to her that the wind was singing all the old and sad songs.

She heard again the whine of the Jap spotter plane as it swooped low over the valley and the boom of the handmade grenades. The air rushing past as they rode their toe toe horses over the ridge and down the hill. All so long ago, but like yesterday to her in these moments. Their world had been so very small then but there had been such magic in it. Lifting her tear stained face she called softly into the wind, "Si, honey. I've come to say goodbye to you."

She shivered as his fingers stroked the curve of her cheek and she felt his soft mouth brush hers. And she knew in that moment that it was not goodbye for them, that Simon wanted her to know that though death may have robbed her of his body, it could not steal his soul. That would stay with her forever wherever she may go. No grave could break the power of what had been theirs. She knew he would be waiting for her as constant in death as he had been in life. Meggie stayed long after she could no longer sense Simon's presence. And as she rocked to soothe herself on the sweet green grass she imagined then that Kees was with her. She fancied she could hear his broken accent telling her that it was time to sell Granddad's house. Time to let go of that security Granddad had given her for so long. Her reason for being here was over, he told her. It was time now to return to her family in Holland.

Feeling the heat of the afternoon sun burning into her back, Meggie stood up and walked slowly to the crest of the hill. There she stopped and looked back at the bush clearing for the last time, but it showed her nothing now, other than its emptiness.

Breathless we flung us on the windy hill,
Laughed in the sun and kissed the lovely grass.
You said, 'Through glory and ecstasy we pass;
Wind, sun, and earth remain, the birds sing still,
When we are old, are old ...' And when we die
All's over that was ours; and life burns on ...

Rupert Brooke.